CAUSE OF DEATH

Hall the coroner held up a finger. "You didn't let me finish. We've found traces of her blood on the blue cord left at the scene, so it's likely that the weapon used to stab her was used to cut the cord. This attack was very vicious. You're dealing with an unstable person. The wounds to her face are particularly troubling and there are two kinds of stab wounds."

"Two weapons?" asked Mornay.

Dr. Hall nodded. "There are seventeen separate lacerations from forehead to chin; it's too frenzied and the damage is too extensive for a random attack."

"Which would rule out an attack by an outsider," Mornay said.

Anne dropped her hand away from her mouth and stood up.

Damn! Mornay thought. Without uttering a word, he'd just told Anne that Ina Matthews had been stabbed, mutilated, and left in a desolate corner of the cemetery to slowly bleed to death.

Anne took a tentative step, and then fell in a faint onto the cold flagstones.

THE LAST VICTIM

IN GLEN ROSS

M.G. KINCAID

POCKET BOOKS

New York London Toronto Sydney Singapore

This book is a work of fiction. Names, characters, places and incidents are products of the author's imagination or are used fictitiously. Any resemblance to actual events or locales or persons, living or dead, is entirely coincidental.

An *Original* Publication of POCKET BOOKS

 POCKET BOOKS, a division of Simon & Schuster, Inc.
1230 Avenue of the Americas, New York, NY 10020

Copyright © 2003 by Moira Maus

ISBN: 0-7434-6756-6

First Pocket Books printing December 2003

10 9 8 7 6 5 4 3 2 1

POCKET and colophon are registered trademarks of Simon & Schuster, Inc.

Interior design by Davina Mock

Cover design and photo illustration by John Vairo Jr.
Front cover photo © Kirsty McLaren/Tony Stone Images

For information regarding special discounts for bulk purchases, please contact Simon & Schuster Special Sales at 1-800-456-6798 or business@simonandschuster.com

Manufactured in the United States of America

To John ~

Thank you for your faith, love, and encouragement. You knew I could do it long before I believed it was even possible.

To Loretta Hudson ~

Thank you for being my first editor and mentor; I value your frankness and cherish your friendship.

To Aunt Jo ~

You were delighted with the first piece of writing I had published—at age seven— I wish you were here so I could tell you what I'm writing next.

acknowledgments

Special thanks to Mike Taylor for cheerfully answering questions and arranging a wonderful tour of the headquarters for the Grampian Police Force. I had no intention of populating my novel with cops, but the information you provided was too good not to use. I hope you, and your colleagues on the force, will forgive the liberties I've taken with police procedure and the rearranging I've done with your facilities.

To my agent, Elaine Koster, your encouragement and support have helped me become a more confident writer; I'm grateful beyond words for everything you do. My editor, Micki Nuding, thank you for your insight, your enthusiasm, and for being so delightful to work with! My copyeditor, Judy Steer, and production editor, Linda Roberts, I'm in awe of the amazing job you do; thank you.

To the founders of the Santa Barbara Writers' Conference, Mary and Barnaby Conrad, thank you for creating such a marvelous environment to nurture writers.

Lastly, I want to thank my mother, Mary Bledsoe, for teaching me the importance of staying connected with family, and my father, Charlie Bledsoe, the best storyteller I know.

chapter one

Conversations in the Macduff police office ceased the moment Detective Inspector Walter Byrne barreled through the plate-glass doors. Detective Sergeant Seth Mornay slouched further down into his chair, but his legs were too long and the office too small for him to disappear from view.

The noxious smell of cigar smoke preceded Byrne past the four molded plastic chairs in the small reception area, past the duty office, and into the main room. The office had four detectives assigned to the Criminal Investigation Division (CID); Byrne was the second in command and Mornay's immediate superior. Byrne veered left around the conference table, his face its usual shade of prestroke red, coattails flapping, leaving cigar ashes floating behind him.

A collective sigh of relief went through the room as Byrne barged into the office of Detective Chief Inspector McNab, the senior CID officer.

Mornay had a perfect view of McNab's office—not that it was necessary, since Byrne's voice boomed loud enough to be heard at the chip shop three doors down busy Fife Street.

"What's with the bloody roster change?" Byrne shouted. "When I was a constable, you had to be on death's door to ask for the night off."

Byrne's husky smoker's voice contrasted completely with his appearance. If Byrne had worn a red woolen cap, he would've looked exactly like the garden gnome Mornay's best pal, Victoria, had put beneath her dying roses last spring in an attempt to revive them. As if a pug nose, mottled red cheeks, and piggy eyes were a magical ward against mildew and leaf rot. Byrne's gnomelike features lent no magic in closing cases; that was achieved by delegation, by harassment, by sheer luck half the time.

McNab answered Byrne's question in a calm tone. "Lawrence's son was put in hospital this morning. He has meningitis."

"I've motors being stolen all over the north of Scotland, and you're giving Lawrence the night off!"

"You've got four open cases involving stolen vehicles—hardly what I'd call an overload. But we can always hand some cases over to Peterhead if they're proving a bit of a bother."

"Bugger that!"

There were a few snickers when Byrne's curse exploded. His disdain for the CID officers working in the other offices was as legendary as his temper.

"Perhaps if you'd take Sergeant Mornay along—"

"I'd rather—"

McNab spoke again, cutting off whatever Byrne had been about to say. Mornay couldn't quite hear what McNab was saying, but Byrne's response was to change the subject.

"Fucking cutbacks. They bloody overwork everyone who's left, that's what they do." Byrne pulled out his cigar and tapped the long ash on McNab's floor. "I'll be in Strichen. Working," he said as if he were the only person in the building who knew the meaning of the word.

He stomped out of McNab's office and sent a black look Mornay's way. Then his gaze drifted to the empty chair next to Mornay: Claire's chair. Mornay shared his desk with Detective Constable Claire Gillespie, who was responsible for the homey touches: smooth beach stones she used as paperweights, a pot of trailing ivy, and a small round fishbowl for Willie, her pet goldfish. Mornay's contribution to their communal workspace was sticky coffee rings and piles of unfinished reports.

"Finally getting to the Gregory file?" Byrne flicked more ash on the floor. The Gregorys had a vintage Rolls-Royce stolen three weeks ago, the fourth stolen car in the Macduff area this month.

"Aye," Mornay answered slowly. He always kept his voice neutral around Byrne. Another year, Mornay kept reminding himself. Another year and the stubby wee bastard would retire.

Byrne flicked a nail against Willie's tank. The fish ignored him. "Leave it for Gillespie," he said. "At least I know she'll check the spelling when she's

through." Byrne grinned, exposing crooked, nico-
tine-stained teeth. "You've work to do in Strichen.
We've had another stolen motor." He left.

When Mornay tagged along with Byrne, he
always got the menial jobs, such as staking out the
search area for the forensic team, their time being
too valuable to waste. If there was anything filthy to
crawl through, climb over, or shift, he was Byrne's
man.

Constable Kashik Sahotra sidled up to Mornay's
desk as soon as Byrne cleared the area. Sahotra had
dark eyes and skin, a wide grin, and glow-in-the-
dark white teeth; he looked like a twelve-year-old
dressed in his father's woolens, playing cop.

"What's so funny?" Mornay's voice was gruff, but
Sahotra never seemed to notice his black moods.

"There's rain in Strichen. You'll ruin another suit."

"Keep laughing, you heathen bastard—Byrne will
get round to you sooner or later."

Sahotra's grin widened. He had a gift for escaping
Byrne's scrutiny, and everyone in the office, particularly Mornay, envied him this ability. He pulled a
ragged notebook out of his pocket. "Up for this
week's pool?" he asked. Besides his pedal patrol
duties—a job he got because he was the only officer
in Traffic who didn't get winded bicycling up and
down Macduff's hills—Sahotra ran the weekly bet-
ting pools.

"What is it?"

"The time Pratt's wife calls—the first time only."

"Pratt?" Mornay asked.

"Short." Sahotra cupped his hand and made a
curved motion in front of his flat abdomen, pan-

tomiming Pratt's well-rounded belly. "You're always calling him Clark, which is curious since we don't have anyone named Clark in our office. And you do the same with the PC Bensen."

"Right," Mornay said, vaguely recalling Constable Pratt's face. Pratt was so newly married he still had the sunburn from his honeymoon in Florida. "His wife calls often?"

"Is whiskey wet?"

Mornay pulled a crumpled ten-pound note out of his pocket. Sahotra whistled appreciatively. "What shift is he?" Mornay asked.

"Second."

"Put me down for 5:03, exactly."

Sahotra plucked the note out of Mornay's fingers before he could change his mind and strolled away to make another collection.

"Mind you use the digital clock," Mornay called after him.

9:05 A.M.
Glen Ross

Rector Evan Whelan stared at his cold eggs and congealed sausage. His coffee had gone cold as well. Anymore, Evan was too distracted to drink his coffee or tea while it was still warm and palatable. For Mary's sake, he took a small, quick gulp.

"Eat your toast so I won't feel I've wasted my time cooking another untouched meal." Mary Hodgeson smiled to soften her admonishment. Mary had worked for his parents for twenty-five years before coming to work at the rectory. "We both know no one will be in your study yet. And if they were, the wait wouldn't harm them. Time you started worrying about yourself and your health instead of listening to everyone else's problems."

Mary hovered at the sink. Tucked and pressed to perfection, she wore a gray woolen skirt and a silk sweater threaded with silver strands. Her hair was pulled into its usual severe bun at the nape of her neck.

Evan's cup clattered in its saucer when he put it down. He reached across his plate for a slice of Mary's homemade toasted bread and then the jam.

Mary nodded her approval. "I'll bring you fresh coffee as soon as it's finished."

At least she'd stopped lecturing him on how thin he'd grown; they spent a fortune on food, keeping up this pretense of him eating proper meals. Evan pushed away from the table, his chair scraping on the cold flagstone floor. Taking his toast, he slowly walked out of the kitchen and up the dark hall toward his study. He liked to be seated at his desk by nine. He tried to be punctual with his office hours; his older parishioners found the regularity comforting.

On clear days, sunlight would stream in through the windows at either end of the hall, softening the fortress-thick walls of the rectory. Double glazing kept the chill on the outside as well as the rain, but nothing could diminish the pervasive gray that set in during these dreary, overcast days. It was May, yet they'd only had a few fair spring days.

Evan left a trail of crumbs as he dutifully chewed his toast and then swallowed. During his childhood, the scent of Mary's baked bread used to fill him with a sense of completeness. He'd felt guilty when Mary first came to work for him; his mother had been so helpless, and so angry about Mary's departure. After so many years, he knew he couldn't carry out his duties without Mary's assistance.

But now the simple pleasures of his life had disappeared. It was one of his many regrets that he couldn't simply enjoy eating a warm piece of bread or have a laugh with a friend without a shadow clinging to the back of his thoughts, reminding him how quickly it would be over—the experience, the day, the life. . . .

The crust of bread crumbled in Evan's clenched fist. While he went through most days in a hazy awareness of time passing, there were moments, like now, when rage would sear through his body. It would consume him, leaving him feeling completely without substance. A nonperson stitched together with skin and sinew and muscles.

Evan had somehow managed to hold this rage in check since his wife had died, but he felt the seams of his control straining daily to pull apart.

He gulped a lungful of air and quickly opened the door to his study before Mary found him sweating in the hall. He closed the door behind him, his breath coming out raggedly, as if he'd just sprinted two hundred meters instead of walked a dozen paces. Slowly, a single heartbeat at a time, the rage dissipated. Sweat trickled down Evan's brow and down the center of his chest. His pulse returned to a more normal rate, and then his breathing. Though he unclenched his fists, the muscles running the length of his arms and down his back remained bunched in hard cords of tissue that refused to relax. If they didn't loosen soon, he'd have another of his headaches.

Mary's footsteps sounded briskly down the hall. Evan stepped away from the door and quickly crossed the room to stand behind his desk. He stared out the window, hoping his fair coloring wouldn't give him away.

Mary opened the door. "Here's some coffee and fresh scones." She balanced a tray that held a white porcelain urn of coffee, several heavy mugs, a basket of steaming scones, and small white porcelain containers of cream and sugar. "Are you going back to Sandrington Hall this morning?" she asked.

"I've promised to string lights."

Mary put the tray on the one empty corner of his desk and smoothed the front of her apron, not bothering to hide her disapproval of Evan helping anyone do anything at Sandrington Hall. "Humph! And that Crownlow girl is rambling around the cemetery again, not even wearing a proper coat. Perhaps you'd have a word with her on your way back to the Hall?"

Evan watched silvery pale curls of steam rise above the scones. Anne Crownlow was a wealthy student from Edinburgh University. She was working on a genealogy project and had made a generous donation to the rectory's building repair fund in exchange for the use of a room for a week, access to the rectory's marriage and baptism records, and the cemetery records. While he didn't think it was entirely proper to have her staying at the rectory, her donation would make it possible to make desperately needed repairs to their leaking roof. Mary was still angry he'd accepted the donation.

"Anne's a grown woman; she doesn't need a lecture on how to dress for a stroll in the country."

The slamming of the mudroom door echoed through the house. Then running footsteps pounded loudly down the hall. Evan and Mary turned toward the study door, waiting.

Anne Crownlow caught the door casing with both hands in an attempt to slow her momentum as she ran into the room. Her shoulder connected with one of the bookcases flanking the door, books spilled off the shelves, and Anne was knocked to her knees.

Mary's voice was shrill. "What's happened to your pullover?"

Anne's pullover was gone; she was wearing only a thin, stretchy camisole. Her jeans were soaking wet and streaked with mud. She was shivering violently.

As Evan helped her to her feet, Anne's fingers dug through his jacket and into his forearms with amazing strength. Her pale hair clung in damp ringlets to a face devoid of color—except for her lips, which were turning blue—and gooseflesh covered every inch of her exposed skin.

"There's a woman," she said between chattering teeth, her horror-struck eyes wide. "She's in the cemetery. The crows . . . those horrible crows. I had to cover her face. Oh, God . . ." Anne was nearly incoherent. "Her face . . ."

Evan removed his jacket and draped it around Anne's shoulders. "Mary, make the 999 call. I'll see about the crows."

Mary didn't move. "Maybe you should wait for the police," she said quietly.

He paused in the doorway and held her gaze.

Mary had been looking out for him for nearly thirty years, but sometimes she could be overprotective. "See to her, Mary, please. I'll wait by the body until the police arrive." Then he strode out of the room.

He needed to see whom Anne Crownlow had found. It was too wet for the casual tourist to be wandering among the gravestones—that rarely happened even in good weather. She might have found a bed-and-breakfast guest—Sandrington Hall was nearly half a kilometer up the road. It had been converted to a B and B about ten years earlier, and occasionally a guest would get lost walking from the Hall to Glen Ross. The mists that crept from the North Sea could get so heavy that some people lost all sense of direction.

Please let it be a stranger.

Evan strode rapidly toward the cemetery, which on sunny days was partially shaded by massive beech and oak trees that had been planted the same year the seventh Lord Sandrington put a new roof on the rectory his grandfather had built. Evan neglected to ask Anne in which part of the cemetery she'd found the body. But it turned out that directions were unnecessary; the sharp snapping of crow's wings was impossible to miss, as were their strident, high-pitched squawks.

Damp crept into Evan's shoes as he squelched across the grass toward the spot where the large black birds had gathered. *Where had they come from?*

The fine mist that surrounded him seemed to thicken the farther away from the rectory he walked.

Visibility was diminishing. Sounds echoed weirdly. Fat plops of water dripped off beech leaves onto the gravestones beneath the heavily drooped branches.

The crows' squabbling grew fiercer. They were taking quick hops off the ground to slash at one another with their sharply taloned claws or take short stabs at each other with their wide black beaks.

He quickened his pace. "YA!" he shouted, flinging out his arms. The crows retreated only a few paces away. He walked across the narrow grassy path and found her. She was behind a row of headstones from the early 1800s; they were smaller and less ornately carved than the Celtic crosses and obelisks of their predecessors.

Shock prevented Evan from uttering even the faintest of sounds. He recognized the body immediately. He fell to his knees, oblivious to the cold and damp. "*Ina.*" The tortured whisper was absorbed immediately by the mist.

The crows had been trying to rip away Anne Crownlow's yellow pullover, which covered Ina's face. The pullover was soaked in blood. Ina's denim jumper was also soaked with blood.

Evan looked away, his vision blurring with tears. "Oh, Christ, Ina," he whispered. "What happened?"

chapter two

The geographic area covered by the Grampian Police Force encompassed a landmass of just over three thousand acres and was split among five command areas. The population served by the force was close to half a million, half of whom resided in the area's largest city, Aberdeen. The North Aberdeenshire Command Area, including Mornay's patch, contained Macduff, a coastal town nearly two hours from Aberdeen. It was the only office, except for the Command Area Headquarters in Peterhead, which remained open around the clock.

A 999 call had come from the rectory of St. David's Episcopal Church, just south of Glen Ross, at 9:27 A.M. The town was a twenty-minute drive from Macduff—less if you sped, but Mornay had seen enough fatal crashes to respect the narrow, twisty roads that were a necessary evil in their mountainous landscape.

Glen Ross had a cobbled High Street and a large, square park lined with oaks at its center. The square was empty when Mornay drove past; the wet weather was keeping the majority of the population indoors. Around the square were eight silvered mahogany benches with puddles of water in front of them, the depressions left by the feet of countless pedestrians taking a rest.

Mornay's best pal, Victoria, a photographer, would've found the scene picturesque: the water dripping from the leaves, the muted colors, and the mist capping the whole soggy scene. Mornay found it depressing. He cast a longing look at the pub as he passed. The door was open and he caught a brief glimpse of a man in a black leather jacket hunched over the jukebox.

The drizzle was steady enough to warrant wipers when Mornay pulled up alongside Claire's car. She stepped out of her car, leaving the motor running, and walked to his.

"How'd you manage to get here first?" he asked.

Claire grinned. "The old-fashioned way. I drove the fastest. I've been here long enough to see where the body is and secure the site for the scene-of-crime team."

"Byrne's idea?" Mornay pointed to the way she'd angled her car to block the drive leading to the rectory and the cemetery, where the body had been discovered.

"He didn't want curious locals getting in the way," she replied. "I'm to let him know if McNab shows."

Byrne's open hostility to his former partner and present superior officer was something of a mystery to Mornay. Like taxes and hangovers, Byrne's jealousy was an immutable fact of life—something Chief Inspector McNab tried to ignore rather than pinch off before it grew to gargantuan proportions, as it was threatening to do.

"Is he coming, then?" Mornay asked. McNab rarely made it out of the office for anything except meetings in Peterhead or Aberdeen. The man was being suffocated in paperwork, a fact Byrne delighted in pointing out whenever the opportunity presented itself.

Claire shrugged. She'd been giving safety lectures at Macduff's only primary school and was in uniform: black rayon trousers, white collared shirt beneath a black woolen sweater that had shoulder patches and epaulets to show her rank. Over this she wore her black GORE-TEX rain jacket. Her large breasts, which he and every other male at the station ogled whenever they had the good fortune of looking down at her without her looking up at them, were well camouflaged beneath the layers.

Mornay enjoyed working with Claire. He was probably the only straight male in the command area who hadn't asked her out. He had no qualms about on-the-job relationships, but he'd decided early on that Claire was not a woman to pursue. They knew next to nothing about each other outside of work. And during working hours he admired her ability to coexist in the male-dominated police force without compromising her values or demeaning herself.

Mornay slouched down in his seat as far as he

could without knocking his knees on the steering column. He caught sight of his reflection in the side mirror. His nose was flattened at the bridge, and he had a dimple on the curve of his right cheek that looked as if a plug of bone had been removed—which was nearly the truth—leaving the skin to fill the void. Shadows had a habit of clinging to the hollows beneath his eyes and cheeks. His fierce primeval looks, courtesy of his eight years as a Royal Marine serving Her Royal Highness, were surprisingly attractive to women. The Beauty and the Beast complex, Victoria had once explained.

Today, the hollows beneath his eyes were darker than usual, and his eyelids were heavier.

"Are you feeling all right?" Claire asked, leaning into the window. "I've aspirin in my glove box."

"I've already had some. Where's the body?"

"In the back of the cemetery, just up on the right. The girl who found it is staying at the rectory through the end of the week. She's a student from Edinburgh."

"Has the doctor arrived yet?" asked Mornay. He stared across the bonnet of Claire's car, up the glistening road. He'd arrived ahead of the scene-of-crime team—not surprising since they had to travel all the way from Peterhead.

"He arrived just before you. Constable Dunn-holland is with him." Then she asked, "Think Peterhead will take over?"

"Not for a few days, at the least. If we look like we're going to bugger our first murder inquiry in eighteen months, then . . ." He shrugged.

"Speak for yourself," she said, grinning. "I don't bugger anything."

Rivulets of spitty rain slid down Mornay's neck as he walked to the far corner of the cemetery to join Constable Dunnholland and the doctor. The air held only the slightest hint of the sea, as they were nearly a kilometer inland. The cemetery was preternaturally quiet except for the crows. He wasn't one to get spooked very easily, but with the trees looming in the mist, dark and shadowy, like grotesquely shaped mourners, he was glad to reach the company of the other men. Mornay nodded to Dunnholland—called "Dunheap" behind his back—and introduced himself to the gangly man Dunnholland was trying to protect from the rain with an umbrella. The skin of the doctor's face was an ashen gray color and his shoulders were hunched forward in his dark green anorak. He appeared oblivious to the rain dribbling on his head and down his gaunt cheeks as well as to Dunnholland's attempts to keep the cold drizzle from reaching his skin. As soon as the introductions were over, Dr. Edwin Hartwick, the village's only doctor, returned his gaze to the branches of a nearby beech.

Mornay examined the body. The woman lay on her back in a snarled patch of ivy, her face covered with a knitted pullover. Her legs were straight. One arm was flung out and looked to be grasping the ivy; the other was pinned beneath her body, as if someone had kicked her over to make sure she was dead. Given the drizzle, Mornay couldn't believe the amount of blood still on the ivy leaves. The beech tree had acted like an umbrella. What blood hadn't seeped onto the surrounding ivy had been soaked up by the victim's clothing. There seemed to be a faint trail of bent grass leading to the woman, as if she'd been dragged off the main path—he couldn't tell how far—and put behind the row of headstones. A narrow ribbon of rumpled grass bisected the trail the dragged body had left. Someone had disturbed the path the body had made.

"Who is she?" Mornay asked.

"A Ms. Ina Matthews," Dunnholland said.

"We're sure about the ID?" Mornay's gaze flicked to the doctor.

"Positive," the doctor replied between clenched teeth. "She was thirty-eight and"—the doctor paused, slowly giving Mornay a closer examination—"far healthier than you've ever been in your life."

"You're probably right," Mornay said to defuse Hartwick's anger. "Any idea how long she's been here?"

"No more than four hours. She called me at six to enlist my help, moving tubs of flowers."

The front of Ina Matthews's faded denim jumper was dark with blood. There appeared to be defense wounds on her right hand and her right arm, but given the overall damage to the woman, they were minor. Mornay crouched and, using two fingers, pinched the pullover and lifted the material so he could see her face.

"Christ!" The word was ripped out of him before he could stifle his shock. Her face had been savagely slashed. "Did you see her face?"

"No," Dr. Hartwick said. He moved closer.

"Did the crows do this?" Mornay asked.

Dr. Hartwick's face twisted slightly as he examined the damage to Ina Matthews's face. "The lacerations seem too clean, but then, I'm not an expert."

Despite the brutal attack, Mornay could see that Ina Matthews had been an attractive woman. Her light brown hair was streaked with golden highlights from the sun, not a salon. There were laugh lines around what remained of her eyes, and blood had seeped into these fine creases. He let the pullover fall back into place as a wave of nausea hit him. He had to take several deep breaths before asking, "How many times was she stabbed?"

"Obviously enough to do the job." Dr. Hartwick stared at Mornay, daring him to make another pointless comment.

"Were you her doctor?"

"Yes."

"Do you have any idea what might have cut her face?"

"I would assume the same weapon that was used to stab her."

"And the pullover?"

The doctor shrugged.

Mornay turned to Dunnholland. "Is it the student's?" he asked.

"To keep the crows off," Dunnholland answered. "The rector's chased the last of them away."

Another eerie squawk filled the silence. Mornay looked behind him. Four black crows were sitting on headstones just a couple of rows away from the body. The crows were intensely focused on the scene, awaiting their next opportunity to get at the body. The sight would have given even the most ardent animal lover a queasy stomach. "Not far enough, it appears. Dunnholland, get rid of those bloody things."

Dunnholland rushed the birds, wildly swinging the umbrella around, nearly tripping on an exposed root. Abruptly, the doctor turned away from Mornay. "Since I'm obviously not needed here, I'll walk to Sarah's and let her know what's happened to Ina."

"Sarah who?"

"Jenkins. Sarah Jenkins. She was Ina's cousin. They shared a house."

Dunnholland, panting from the exertion of chasing crows, returned to Mornay's side. They watched Dr. Hartwick slog through the grass, listing slightly to the left, then to the right, as if the weight of the water on his trouser legs was causing him to meander off the path.

"Want me to go after him?" Dunnholland asked.

The doctor was angling toward the public path that led to Glen Ross. "Give him a lift. And I want you to stay with this woman's cousin, keep your eyes and ears open. Understand?"

Dunnholland nodded emphatically, sending ripples through the roll of flesh beneath his jaw. The young constable sucked in his stomach as if trying to toughen up for the task, though it had been assigned because it was easy. It had the added advantage of keeping the nervous young constable as far away from the crime scene as possible. Most suspicious death inquiries in their command area were the result of pub brawls or domestic violence, with arrests made within hours, sometimes minutes, of the crime. This was probably Dunnholland's first real inquiry and Mornay didn't want him mucking it up.

Mornay glanced down the road, searching for the scene-of-crime team, then checked his watch. It was too soon to look for their arrival. Dunnholland hadn't budged from his patch of crushed grass; probably he was awaiting further orders.

"Look at that." Dunnholland pointed to a narrow gravestone just off the path. A piece of blue synthetic twine had been tied firmly around the stone and cleanly cut near the knot. The twine wasn't faded or frayed from exposure to the elements, which meant it might be part of the crime scene. Dunnholland moved closer.

Mornay clamped a hand on his shoulder. "Leave it for the experts." Then he shouted to the doctor. "Dr. Hartwick!" The man turned, perilously close to walking into the part of the cemetery Mornay wanted to section off. "We'll give you a lift."

Mornay gave Dunnholland a push that sent the constable stumbling. "Hurry up, then."

Dunnholland lumbered off, one hand on his cap to keep it from bouncing off his head and the other clutching the still raised umbrella.

Two small white vans, each bearing a blazing orange stripe along its side, pulled off of the road next to the cemetery entrance. The scene-of-crime officers, in record time.

As the SOC team set up a tent over the body, there was still no sign of Byrne. Mornay rounded up two constables who usually worked in traffic and, with their help, traced out the path of crushed grass the victim made as she was dragged behind the headstones. They put up a barricade of tape around the entire area, then Mornay posted one of the constables by the entrance to the scene with directions to point out the blue twine to Forensics, and then he sent the other to take Claire's place on the road. He needed her with him during the interviews at the rectory.

A flash of color in the long grass caught his attention.

Mornay crouched down to have a closer look. Nestled in the dark green grass was a single pale pink rose petal. Bowl shaped, the petal was darker at the base than at the slightly fringed edge. There was no bruising or sign of wilt; the petal was fresh. He reached down to pick it up and studied the grass around his feet, searching for more petals. Then he glanced around the graves nearest him. There were no roses on any of them.

He stood, not sure what to make of his minuscule find, so for lack of a better idea, he pocketed the petal and promptly forgot about it.

The cemetery was surprisingly large. Time and years of exposure to the elements had sent many of the older headstones tumbling over. There was no telling how long the body would have lain undiscovered if not for the exploring university student. This section of the cemetery was older, more crowded, which probably meant it was less visited. Mornay flipped open his notebook and jotted a note to check whether the rectory kept a log of the daily visitors.

Claire met him at the rectory's front door.

"Where's Byrne?" he asked.

Claire shrugged. "He'll show soon."

He probably should wait for Byrne, but Mornay wasn't keen on waiting.

He knocked on the massive wooden door.

The door opened so quickly he had no doubt the housekeeper had been on the other side, waiting. Short, silvery, slightly plump in a pleasant, motherly sort of way, the housekeeper introduced herself as Mary Hodgeson and showed them into the first room to their right, the rector's study.

The rector of St. David's was sitting behind the largest and most cluttered desk Mornay had ever seen. He was absently tapping a pencil on a dusty stack of pamphlets as he stared out of the window behind his desk but stood when they entered the room.

Evan Whelan instantly recognized Mornay.

"You're a policeman?"

Mornay nodded and held out his hand. "Detective Sergeant Mornay. I'm sorry we have to meet so soon again under these circumstances." Mornay had visited the rectory just last month with Victoria. Whelan had found them wandering aimlessly around the cemetery, looking for the perfect combination of dappled light and moss-covered stone for Victoria to photograph. They started chatting and ended up being given a small tour. During the tour Victoria had discovered Whelan was a lover of poetry; the obscure, boring stuff she enjoyed reading. They'd chatted like old friends.

Whelan came around the desk to shake Mornay's proffered hand. "We get so few visitors . . ." Whelan's voice drifted as if he'd forgotten what he'd intended to say.

Tall and wiry thin, Whelan had ginger-colored hair and fair skin that betrayed every flush of emotion. Surrounded by his books and shadows, the gaunt man looked more substantial.

"How did Victoria's photos turn out?" Whelan asked. "She said when she had them developed she would stop by and show them to me. We don't get many people wanting to see the older stones."

"I'm sure she'll stop by soon," Mornay said. "This is Detective Constable Gillespie; we're both out of the Macduff office. I'd like to speak with . . ." He frowned, searching for a name he'd not been given. "I'm afraid I don't know her name—the woman who found the body?"

Mary Hodgeson spoke for Whelan, strengthening the protective mother impression. "Her name's Anne Crownlow. If you like, I'll bring her down."

"In a few minutes, please. Some tea would be grand, if you don't mind."

Mary Hodgeson waited for a nod from Whelan before she said, "Of course."

Claire took a position next to the door after the housekeeper exited. There she could discreetly take notes, which, as experience had proven, would be more comprehensive than his, but he still jotted notes down. They helped him organize his thoughts between questions.

Whelan pushed some papers away from the corner of his desk so he had room to prop himself against it. He caught Mornay's glance. "It's Victorian. Rather monstrous, isn't it? My brothers and sister gave it to me when I was ordained. They included a rather crude card correlating the size of a man's desk with the size . . ." He glanced to Claire, who stood impassively in the shadows next to the door. "You get the idea. I'm the youngest of five and still get teased."

Mornay nodded politely. His only brother had died when he was seven; Victoria was the closest he had to a sibling. He'd always wondered if his childhood would have been different—better—if his brother had lived.

Mornay wrote _Rector's background?_—underlining the words so they wouldn't get lost among his other notes.

"Did you make the 999 call?" Mornay asked.

Whelan shook his head. "Mary did."

"And she called as soon as Anne Crownlow reported the woman in the cemetery?"

"Yes. Anne told us she'd found someone, a woman. I couldn't wait for the . . . for you to arrive," he said. "I had to see who Anne had found."

"Did you remove the pullover to identify her?" Mornay asked.

"No, I recognized her denim jumper. Ina always wears them."

There was a nervous tension to Whelan that seemed out of place, excessive, so Mornay asked, "Do you have any idea why Ms. Matthews was in that part of the cemetery?"

"None," he replied, his gaze slipping away from Mornay's face to one of the shadowed corners of the room. "It's off the path, and she was too busy to go wandering, especially in such poor weather."

"Busy?"

"The Sandrington Flower Show starts tomorrow. It's to last through the weekend." Whelan's gaze drifted to the window behind his desk. "She and I were scheduled to help set up tables this morning at the Hall. I arrived just after six, but Ina never showed. I was supposed to call her when I returned to the rectory for breakfast."

"Was this a scheduled job? Something everyone knew about?"

"Yes. There've been quite a lot of people from town volunteering. We do it every year. I was unloading crates of kitchen supplies. I was going to return after breakfast to string lights if I hadn't rounded up Ina."

"Was it like her to not make an appearance?"

"No. Ina was very dependable."

Mornay, familiar with the area because of his last visit, knew about the public path—The Cut, as the locals called it—running from the square in Glen Ross to Sandrington Hall. The path was just over half a kilometer long and bisected the cemetery. It had been the original road to the rectory back when the Sandrington family owned most of the land in the area. Ina Matthews's body had been three rows over from the path. "Did you use the public path to walk to the hall this morning?" Mornay asked.

Whelan's answer was a moment in coming. Perhaps he was mentally reviewing the trip, trying to work out how he'd missed finding the body himself. But unless one had been looking directly at the headstones, Ina Matthews's body could have easily been overlooked.

"Yes, I did," he said. "I can't believe I walked past without seeing her." His long fingers, which had been limply knitted together in front of him, unraveled. He started twisting a button on his cuff.

Mornay glanced at Claire, wanting to see if she'd

noticed Whelan's nervousness. She gave him the slightest of shrugs. Mornay's gaze returned to Whelan. "What time did you return to the rectory this morning?"

"About quarter past eight."

"Was Mrs. Hodgeson at work?"

"Mary lives here. She's usually in the kitchen by seven."

Mornay flipped to a clean page. Whelan's energy was diminishing; he seemed to be growing thinner, more insubstantial with every question while his nervousness increased. "Do you keep a log of visitors to the cemetery or the rectory?"

"I'm afraid we're not that formal."

"How often does that part of the cemetery get visited?"

The fingers ceased twisting the button. "Every Sunday," Whelan said. His voice was hollow sounding. "My wife is buried there. I visit her grave after services."

chapter three

Anne Crownlow sat curled on the window seat behind Evan's desk. Her arms were wrapped around her knees, holding them tightly to her chest. Through the window Evan could see Sergeant Mornay and Constable Gillespie watching the scene-of-crime team work. It was just half past eleven and he was exhausted.

"Will they question us again?" she asked.

"I've no idea."

"Sergeant Mornay asked me odd questions."

Anne's voice didn't seem to have the strength to reach across the room, so Evan sat in his chair behind his desk, turning it slightly so he could face her.

Anne was watching him intently. Her eyes were dark moons that eclipsed the small, mundane features of her face. One didn't look into them; one submerged. If he hadn't given poetry up, he probably could've penned a verse or two about them, even though he found her intense scrutiny slightly uncomfortable. It made him feel like a curious zoological specimen instead of a man.

The slope of Anne's neck was pale and curiously vulnerable in its slender feminine perfection. Evan missed the intimacy of seeing the soft curves of a woman in unguarded moments. His wife, who had been exquisitely beautiful, had at heart been deeply insecure. Life as a rector's wife hadn't been as simple as she'd imagined. Perhaps if she'd been a plain woman, it could have been.

One of Evan's rare joys had been watching Julia in the filtered morning light, when she thought he was still sleeping. She would move around their bedroom in the half gloom of the drawn blinds with a surety and grace that had never failed to arouse him. It was excruciating, living with those memories. How willing she'd seemed in those private moments, when he'd call her name and she'd come to their bed, smiling. He'd thought they were happy.

Bloody fool, you.

"Do the police want you to remain in Glen Ross?"

"Yes," Anne said. "They said it'd be no more than a day or two. Would you prefer I get a room in the village?"

"We've got plenty of space. Have you called your family to let them know you'll be delayed?" he asked. Odd, she'd spent nearly a week with them and he knew next to nothing about her except where she lived and that she attended Edinburgh University. And that she was wealthy.

"There's only me." She looked away, plucking at nonexistent fluff on her trousers. "Do you think the police will want to question my professors or my flatmate?"

"Why? You were just the unlucky one to find the body."

The curved handle of the bottom desk drawer intruded on the edge of his vision. Yesterday Ina had sat in the window seat, just as Anne was doing now. Ina had pulled out the bottom drawer to use as a footrest. He'd turned his chair around so they could chat more easily. She'd been trying to cajole him into having a glass of whiskey before his vestry meeting, telling him he could brush his teeth, no one would be the wiser. Ina didn't know the material of his shirt beneath his arms was wringing wet because he'd been fighting the urge to take a drink all day.

They never did pour the whiskey. Mary had come into the room unexpectedly, wanting him to have a look at a problem—nonexistent, it turned out—with the vacuum sweeper.

He stared at the carpet, remembering vividly how Ina's long, slender legs had looked stretched across the narrow space. As attractive as Ina had been, he'd never had the same feeling with her as he'd had with Julia. Ina lacked the one characteristic he seemed to find most attractive in women: vulnerability.

Beneath her cropped cap of pale golden curls, Anne watched him. "Were you and Ina Matthews close friends?" she asked.

"Yes." Evan looked fully at the drawer Ina's feet

had rested on. It held his whiskey. "She was a very close friend." It pained him to say the words aloud. Evan sucked in a breath and pulled open the desk drawer. A black presentation case was nestled at the back of the drawer, below the half-empty bottle of Antiquary. Inside the black presentation case was a bottle of Mortlach; the rare malt whiskey was his birthday present from Ina. "We'll have to find a very good reason indeed to drink this," she'd said when he'd unwrapped his present and nearly dropped it from shock. The bottle must have cost several hundred pounds. They didn't open it. They celebrated his thirty-fifth birthday last month by toasting each other with the Antiquary, which was less expensive but no less effective for inducing a pleasantly numb state. Except for their silly toasts to each other, he and Ina had said very little. Ina was one of the few people with whom Evan could remain completely silent and not feel as if he were breaching some delicate point of etiquette.

Evan removed the bottle of Antiquary from the drawer and centered it on his blotter. Glints of light reflected from the bottle's beveled shoulders. If he filled his coffee cup and took a mouthful of the dark gold liquid, a faint, fruity hint of apples would tease his palate. And after the whiskey had warmed him, a smooth, lingering aftertaste would remain.

Evan's hands shook with the need to numb his senses with the whiskey. But if he got drunk, he was afraid he would wake up tomorrow morning and get drunk again. And again in the afternoon. And when good sense surfaced through the bleary cloud of whiskey dreams—as it always did, eventually—Ina would still be dead. Just like Julia.

Evan lifted his coffee mug off the stack of counseling sheets he'd copied months ago for a marriage class he'd planned to give but never managed to get beyond the planning stage. The pages were becoming dog-eared and the top set was stained with brown ringlets. The mug was clean enough inside, so he filled it halfway with whiskey.

"Here." He pushed the mug toward Anne Crownlow. Maybe then she wouldn't watch him so closely with those damned eyes. It felt as if she were peeling past skin and muscles and bone to see the piteous man cowering beneath the facade.

"I don't want it," she said.

The mug remained halfway between them.

"It won't make you feel better," Evan admitted. "But it just might give you something else to think about."

Anne uncurled her legs, placing her feet—clad in fuzzy yellow socks—carefully on the floor so she didn't knock against his knees. She took the whiskey, and without shifting her gaze from his, drank it down without coughing or grimacing. A narrow dribble of whiskey trailed down her chin and dripped onto her cardigan. She wiped at her chin with the back of her hand and passed him back the mug. He put the mug back on its makeshift coaster.

"Where did you meet Julia?" she asked.

Icy shock coursed through his body at the sound of his wife's name. "What? How do you know who my wife was?"

"Her headstone," she said quietly. "I saw her headstone."

He felt a flush creep along his cheeks. Of course she'd seen the headstone; she'd been slogging through the cemetery all week, cataloging headstones.

"Where did you meet her?" Anne repeated.

He swallowed, needing the whiskey more than ever. "Why do you want to know?"

Anne shrugged. "I don't know, really. If you're uncomfortable talking about her, we can change the subject."

With the blinds closed and the door shut and the single lamp lit in the room, the world was reduced to a warm spot of light between pools of shadow. Comforting scents cocooned them: the musky scent of leather, the clean, sweet smell of Anne's hair, the faint yeasty smell of Mary's bread, the lemon polish Mary used on the oak shelving.

"I went to London for a conference," he said after several quiet moments had ticked past. He was staring into a puddle of shadows in the corner of the room, remembering. "Almost five years ago. It was early March, very raw and damp. I was bored with the conference, so I begged off sick for an afternoon. I had some shopping to do for my mother, and I decided to brave Harrods. After an hour walking through the departments I finally ended up in front of the perfume counter. That's where I met Julia. We were married less than two weeks later."

Evan attributed Anne's sharp laugh of surprise to the whiskey.

"Is that really true?" she asked.

"Yes."

"You must have bought the most expensive perfume to make such a good impression so quickly."

"I don't remember."

Anne leaned back against the paneled side of the bookcase, stretching her legs along the window seat. She pulled her hands into the sleeves of her cardigan, catching the material closed in her fists, forming the sleeves into mittens.

Evan put his elbow on the armrest of his chair and cradled his head in the palm of his hand. A wave of his hair fell forward; he left it lying across his brow, too drowsily comfortable to move for the sake of seeing clearly. They watched each other, keeping their thoughts hidden beneath their skin like secret tunnels that led to warm secret places.

"Do you miss your wife?" Anne asked.

"Every moment of every day." He surprised himself by answering honestly, but he wasn't sorry he'd told her until he realized her body had stiffened. Tension shattered the warm comfortable feeling. Anne's lips started trembling, as if she were on the verge of tears.

He put a hand on her arm, his fingers slipping easily around her slender wrist, holding her still. "Anne, what's wrong?"

The door to the study opened.

"Evan, Inspector Byrne is here . . ." Mary Hodgeson's voice faded away.

Inspector Byrne stepped from behind Mary and walked into the study. His lips pulled back, revealing yellow incisors. "Looks like we've interrupted a private tryst, Mrs. Hodgeson."

"A private conversation is hardly a tryst, Inspector" was Mary Hodgeson's cold reply.

"Whatever it is, they were right cozy," Byrne said as if Evan and Anne had disappeared from the room altogether.

Evan wished it were possible to vanish from sight as he watched Byrne advance slowly into the room, hands shoved deeply into his pockets, raincoat still on, his abdomen straining against his braces. The pungent, overly sweet scent of Byrne's cigar tainted the confines of Evan's only remaining refuge.

Anne Crownlow drew herself to her full height, almost as if she were expecting a physical blow from Byrne. Evan had felt the same reaction the first few times he'd had to deal with Detective Inspector Byrne. Now he was simply wary.

Byrne was staring directly at Anne. "According to my sergeant's notes, you're at university."

"That's right," Anne said.

"My daughter's at university. She's never had to do research like this."

"Perhaps that's because of the course of study she's chosen to follow."

Evan admired Anne's cool reserve.

"Right, right." Byrne's tone was dismissive. "What time were you out this morning, Ms. Crownlow?"

"Half past seven."

"Must be a top student if you're this dedicated with all your courses. Mrs. Hodgeson says you forgot your coat this morning."

"Rain doesn't bother me."

"Funny, that—what bothers people, I mean. Now me, I can't stand to get wet, but others, like you, don't seem to mind a bit of discomfort."

Though he was speaking to Anne, Evan got the

distinct feeling the words were really meant for him.

"I don't know what you mean," Anne said.

Byrne's grin returned. "I don't believe that for a moment."

"That's not my problem, Inspector. Is that all you needed from me?"

"For the moment," he said, sweeping a hand toward the door as if to hasten her exit.

When she'd gone Evan said, "You were a bit harsh on her, Inspector, don't you think?"

"She's tougher than she looks," Byrne said. He poked his cigar in Evan's direction, oblivious to the ash raining down on the carpet. "You'd do well to remember that."

Mornay committed half a dozen traffic violations during his drive to Victoria's cottage, the least of which was speeding.

"Cover for me," he'd asked Claire, after receiving Victoria's nearly incoherent call as they were preparing to leave Glen Ross.

"Now?" Claire had asked. "What am I going to do about Byrne?"

He'd grinned. "You know how to handle him."

"I've been trying to avoid *handling* him, thank you very much." Claire plucked at her GORE-TEX rain jacket. "I'm squelching wet and you want to run off to where?"

"Victoria's."

She pushed damp strands of hair off of her forehead. "Your pal?" she asked. "Or is she that dancer you met in Aberdeen?"

"My pal. It shouldn't take long. Her cottage is on the way to the office."

"Right," she said. "And if you're not back at two for the briefing, *you* can handle Byrne."

Mornay turned onto the rutted muddy track that led to Victoria's two-bedroom crofter's cottage. He skidded into her half-moon drive, the muck and loose stone beneath his tires turning liquid. Momentum carried him farther than he'd intended, and he nearly hit the gnarled apple tree that had captivated Victoria on her first visit with the estate agent. Had he not been there to question the thieving little bastard about the leaking pipes and crumbling foundation, Victoria would have purchased the cottage for its original, grossly inflated asking price, simply on the picturesque merits of an ancient tree that had ceased to produce edible fruit.

The old front door was painted bright turquoise blue. Victoria wouldn't let him replace it, insisting it was too charming to exchange for a modern door or to mar with a dead bolt. She also refused to let him cut back the ancient climbing rose that completely surrounded the door. To walk inside the cottage, one had to pass a gauntlet of heavily thorned runners.

Mornay didn't knock. He pushed sharply on the door, which had a tendency to stick. He stooped low to avoid getting snagged by one of the thorny runners; the climbing rose had already gotten him twice this month.

The front parlor was minuscule, cluttered with books, cardboard packing boxes, bits of broken furniture, and layered with dust. The catchall room; it was drifted through rather than lived in. The same

could be said for Victoria's kitchen at the far end of
the room, partially hidden behind a bamboo-screen
divider with a painted oriental scene faded beyond
recognition. The kitchen's cabinets were painted the
same shade of blue as the front door. Mornay knew
that if he looked, he would find the rubbish bin
overflowing with take-away boxes. Victoria shared
his dislike of cooking, though for entirely different
reasons than his own. He was useless at preparing
anything more complicated than omelets. Victoria
was a fantastic cook; she was just too busy to be
bothered.

He heard a creaking floorboard down the small
hall that separated the kitchen from Victoria's darkroom. And then he heard Victoria's voice, cursing.

A great crashing of metal drowned out her voice.
From the tinny echoes bouncing down the hall, he
determined she'd knocked down one of her metal
storage shelves. Her bedroom was to his left.
Through the open door he saw her battered suitcase
lying open on the floor next to the foot of her bed. It
was half stuffed with balls of clothing. A roll of toi-
let paper lay partially unwound on the floor. It had
been flung into the case but had bounced out, leaving a white tail dangling down the edge of the
unmade bed. She'd just returned from a monthlong
photography assignment in the Orkneys. He had no
idea what her frantic call was about.

Victoria came out of her darkroom and braced
herself in the center of the hall, her fists punching
depressions into her thick hips. She wore black spandex leggings and an oversized T-shirt bearing watery
stains down the front. Had she slanted eyes, she

would have resembled a sumo wrestler. An extremely short, pissed-off sumo wrestler.

Mornay hazarded his question. "What's happened, Tori?"

"A hell of a lot while I was gone, apparently."

Victoria turned on her heel and thumped back into her darkroom. He followed. Dark curtains hung from the windows. Two walls were devoted to metal storage shelves, the kind made from thin, chrome-plated wire. Two worktables were pushed against the remaining walls, leaving enough space in the center of the room for another narrow table. This is where Victoria kept her camera bodies and arsenal of lenses, stored in their metal traveling cases. A lamp with a low-wattage light bulb was lit in the corner. Its shade was bashed, from countless falls off of its precarious perch of stacked plastic tubs. His attention zoomed in on the photographs hanging above the porcelain double sink. The photographs were of him lying in the nude on Victoria's bed. Victoria's younger sister, Pamela, was also in the photographs. Her nearly nude body was reflected in the mirror next to the bed. Though her face was partially obscured, Pamela was still easily recognized.

He couldn't turn and face Victoria.

"How could you? She's a habitual liar. She's a drug addict. *And* she's barely eighteen. You had to have at least remembered *that*."

Her words were like tiny ice daggers that drilled through his temples. He turned.

She thumped her forehead with the palm of her hand. "Right, silly me, you're only after the young ones anymore. The ones who don't have enough sense to see you for the lying shell of a man you are."

Mornay stared holes into the natty carpet on the floor. Victoria wasn't waiting for an apology; she wanted an explanation for Pamela and for the other things that remained unsaid between them. He shifted his gaze to her bare feet. She'd painted her toenails dark red this week. She had pretty, little feet, dainty, high arched—a thin woman's feet, she'd always said. She always left them bare at home and wore spandex so she could see them.

"Seth, I don't know you anymore," Victoria said in a voice that sent a shiver of unease through him. "I've respected the fact you've tried to put your military past behind you. I've forgiven you for barely writing or calling me during all those years. But your changes go deeper than what's physically happened to you." Her voice grew quieter. "How could you?"

He sighed, wishing he had a better answer for her. "It took remarkably little thought, Tori."

"How long are you going to live your life as if there were no consequences to face?"

He had no answer for her or for himself. He'd been on a downward spiral for months, since his return into civilian life.

"This thing with Pamela," he said. Victoria raised her eyes at his euphemism. "It only happened the one time. That's all. I came to work on your leaky faucets and she was here."

"And you what? Accidentally fell into my bed? Naked?"

"It won't happen again," he said.

"It doesn't need to happen again. Pamela accomplished her mission."

He frowned, wondering what she meant.

She let out a long, exhausted sigh, and he realized she was near tears. "Pamela's pregnant," she said. "And she's gotten that way on purpose. She found out I was going to send her to a private rehab center. That's why I took that horrible job in the Orkneys— so I could afford to send her away for two months of treatment."

Mornay stared at Victoria. "She can't be," he said at last, his voice hoarse. "I'm not that thick. I used protection."

"She is pregnant, Seth. Fiona took her to the clinic yesterday and she's been telling God and everyone that you're the father. Now Fiona doesn't want me sending her to the rehab center. It took six months to get her to agree to send Pamela in the first place." Even when she was a child, Victoria always called her mother by her first name.

"When did Pamela find out you were going to send her to the rehab center?"

Victoria started pulling the photographs down. "She found out last month. She wanted to know why I was going to the Orkneys, so Fiona told her right before I left."

"Did she know I was going to work on your faucets while you were gone?"

Victoria shook one of the damp photographs. "Obviously," she said.

Victoria threw the photographs in the bin, then pushed past him. Her heels thudded against the floor as she turned into her bedroom, the shirt flaring behind her like a pennant. The sound of coat hangers screeching on metal followed. Mornay slumped against the wall, eyes closed, replaying what he'd thought was an accidental encounter. Nothing struck him as unusual. Pamela had been just another woman in a long, long string of women—or so he'd managed to convince himself.

Mornay walked down the hall and filled the bedroom doorway. Victoria was struggling to push her case underneath her bed.

"It can't be mine," he said, less sure of himself.

Victoria glanced to him from across the room. "Do you just happen to keep prophylactics stashed on that death machine of yours?" she asked. "Your bloody motorcycle barely has room for a seat."

He didn't keep condoms handy, nor had he stopped to purchase any before his visit to Victoria's. He'd used the condoms Pamela brought.

Victoria stood, brushing the dust off her knees. "Pamela said she sabotaged the condoms. She was quite proud of that fact."

Mornay felt the muscles in his neck constrict, threatening to choke off his air. He willed Tori to raise that mass of unruly hair and look at him again.

"What now?" he asked.

"She's still an addict, and rehab is the only chance that poor baby has of surviving." She pinned him with her astute photographer's gaze, making him uncomfortably aware there were other gulfs between them that transcended the difference in their sexes.

Victoria pushed her hair out of her eyes. "I've got to call—she might still be able to go during her first trimester. I've got another job lined up that should cover any additional expenses. It's going to be *your* job to convince Fiona to send her."

"Let me pay for the treatment," he said. "You know I can afford it."

"I think you've done quite enough."

Tori watched him with a detached look, as if he were some odd photographic specimen. Mornay felt like an alien.

"Where's your job?"

"France. Six weeks shooting dead, boring grapes. I'll need to leave in a couple of days, which means you need to convince Fiona what's best for her youngest daughter."

Victoria looked out of the tiny window above her chest, which offered an unenchanting view of a dilapidated woodshed. Winds had pushed the shed, so it listed to one side. If not for another ancient climbing rose, the ruddy thing would have toppled over years ago. Mornay had tried to talk her into a larger window, insisting that a photographer, of all people, should want something of a view. "All I do is sleep here," she'd answered. "I don't need an expanse of double-glazed glass to help me do that."

Victoria pulled on an oversized sweatshirt and shoved her feet into a pair of clogs. "I've got shopping to do. Mind you lock the door when you leave," she said, and walked out of the bedroom. A moment later, the car's engine turned over, and she spun the tires as she drove away.

His would be a bloody short CID career if he didn't return in time for Byrne's briefing. He had just twenty minutes to make it to Macduff, but even so, Mornay was reluctant to leave. He stared into Victoria's empty bedroom. Her pale blue bedsheets were rumpled and trailing on the floor. She'd not bothered to close two of her chest drawers and the closet gaped open. Above her bed hung a picture that had won her five thousand pounds in prize money. It had barely paid for the repairs to the cottage's crumbling foundation and ancient plumbing. Hanging askew on the wall, the black-and-white photograph of the twisted apple tree in Victoria's front garden still puzzled Mornay: the odd angle, the misty foreground, and fuzzy lump of mountain in the background. He thought the picture was creepy. Victoria said it was symbolic.

Symbolic or not, Mornay preferred the view of the mountains on a clear day rather than a blurry view of a nearly dead tree.

He turned away from the empty room and went to the front door Victoria had left open in her haste to get away from him. He stared out across a small hedge on the other side of the muddy road. The mist had cleared enough for him to catch a glimpse of Victoria's rusted Fiat going up the hill. A mile farther and she would turn on the A947, if her car's worn-out cylinders survived the forces of gravity as it drove up and down the hills.

He hated the way the house felt with Victoria gone. He hated the way she'd looked at him.

The stale scent of empty take-away boxes brought him back to the moment and he checked his watch. He had fifteen minutes to make it back to Macduff.

chapter four

"Well," Byrne said loudly. "Look who's decided to grace us with his presence." Byrne made a show of checking his watch. "And only fifteen minutes late."

Mornay veered around the conference table and slid into a seat next to Claire.

"Tire back in good working order?" Byrne asked.

"Aye," Mornay said half under his breath. He sent a quick look in Claire's direction, but she was avoiding his gaze.

"Good," Byrne said. "Can't have the boy wonder of Macduff CID stranded with a flat, can we?"

Claire kicked Mornay in the shin to keep him from replying.

Byrne turned toward a white dry-erase board set up behind him. The board usually held a grid for

Sahotra's pools, and the shadows of the grid were still visible beneath Byrne's broad, loopy script.

"Right," Byrne said. "This is a list of principles." Byrne wrote *Sarah Jenkins* on the board, his script, already difficult to read, veering off at a sharp downward angle. "Ina Matthews was attacked between six or seven. Sarah Jenkins is Ina Matthews's only living relative. No one can corroborate her whereabouts during our crucial hour. She claims she was working in her kitchen."

Evan Whelan's name was the next to be scrawled on the board. "Says he was at Sandrington Hall from six to around eight. He arrived at the rectory at quarter past eight." Byrne turned and swept the table with a scathing glance, telling them without words that only a fool would believe that line. "We'll need to verify the accuracy of his statement." Byrne wrote "Lydia Sandrington." Then he added Gregor Sandrington's name. "Owner of Sandrington Hall and son. Not interviewed yet."

As Byrne started droning on about the housekeeper and Anne Crownlow, Mornay slouched down into his chair, banging his knee on one of the center table supports. "Flat tire?" he whispered to Claire.

"Had to tell him something, didn't I?" she whispered back. She kept her gaze fixed on Byrne. From this angle, Mornay could see the fine laugh lines around her pale green eyes. Claire rarely wore makeup. Her hair, just long enough to tuck behind her ears, was a dark honey color. There were a few silvery strands winking among the others; he wondered why he'd never noticed that she didn't color her hair to hide her gray. She'd changed from her uniform into one of the tailored pantsuits she favored. All of her suits were neutral colors and came with long double-breasted jackets loose enough to camouflage her curves. Because she was tall and trim, she looked attractive despite her efforts to neuter herself.

"Quit staring," she said out of the side of her mouth.

"The view's better this direction." He moved his shins out of kicking range. Byrne pointed to Evan Whelan's name, and from his tone, it was clear he didn't think highly of St. David's rector. "It's a miracle Byrne closes any case," he whispered. "He's already got everyone thinking it had to have been Whelan and we've only talked to him once."

"Sssh," Claire whispered back.

Byrne whacked the board with his pointer. "I'm not interrupting, am I?" he asked Mornay. "I could wait for you two to finish whatever urgent business you're conducting."

"I was just telling Constable Gillespie we'll need to question the bed-and-breakfast guests when we're back in Glen Ross."

"Good point," Byrne said after only the barest of hesitations. "We've got too many people wandering around. I know one of them saw something this morning. We've just got to pin them down." He gave the board another sound whack with his pointer to emphasize his statement, then eyed Mornay. "We'll work on the guest interviews later; first we'll need to interview the Sandringtons. I want to look each of them in the eye myself. Some of you might recall that business with Whelan's wife a couple of years ago. Before your time," Byrne said to Mornay before he could raise his hand and ask. "They're a closed-mouthed lot in Glen Ross; we'll have to pay attention to what they say and especially what they don't say. And for God's sake, no one tell them anything about the investigation." Byrne had his gaze fixed on Dunnholland when he said this. "As soon as one of them knows, the rest of them do. Tell them to talk to me if they have any questions or complaints."

"What happened with Whelan's wife?" Mornay asked.

"Overdosed on sleeping pills," Byrne said briskly. He told Claire, "While Sergeant Mornay and I are conducting the interviews at Sandrington Hall, you can look into this Ms. Crownlow's background. I want to make sure she's exactly what she says she is. I don't want any surprises."

"If you don't think she's a student, why do you think she's here?" Mornay asked when no one else spoke up, which wasn't unusual for Byrne's briefings.

"I think she's not telling us the real reason she's in Glen Ross. I think she's here because of the good rector."

Mornay smiled at that. "Whelan?"

Byrne shoved his fists into the pockets of his trousers, stretching his black suspenders another two inches. "Aye," he said slowly. "Once upon a time he was a guest lecturer at Edinburgh University. Maybe he ran across her during one of his lectures and asked her back for a visit."

"She's not the type, Inspector."

"What's that mean? The type? Everyone's the type given the right circumstances." Byrne's gaze swept across the room. "Gillespie, I want you at Sarah Jenkins's house after you see about Anne Crownlow. We'll meet you there. Now the good news. We're going to have six-hour shifts at the rectory's gates. Don't want to trip over any reporters, do we?" A collective groan swept around the room. Byrne ignored it. "Turriff will take the day shifts and we'll take the night shifts. Peterson, you're up first tonight. I want you on that gate by six, then Sahotra."

"I've pedal patrol tonight, sir," Sahotra said.

Byrne held up a hand. "All you need to do in Glen Ross is sit in a car and stay awake. We're all working double shifts here. Mornay, Gillespie, and I have mobiles. If anyone hears or sees anything, make sure and ring us, aye?" There was a smattering of unenthusiastic nods.

Chief Inspector McNab walked out of his office and motioned for everyone to keep their seats. Though he looked like a favorite uncle, with a subdued manner and quiet voice, he spoke with an authority molded by twenty-four years on the force. "Everyone wants answers, from the Chief Constable to the reporters sensationalizing a case that's not even"—McNab lifted a wrist to see his watch—"five hours old. I want to see a quick result, but we're going to be thorough on this inquiry. There'll be no doubts when we're finished." McNab's gaze turned in Byrne's direction. "I don't want *anything* interfering with our work."

Then he looked at Mornay. "Understood?"

Mornay nodded.

"Understood?" McNab repeated to his second in command.

Byrne's scowl deepened. "Aye, sir," Byrne said.

McNab's gaze returned to Mornay. "We need to have someone briskly walk the distance from Sandrington Hall to the rectory, as well as to Ina Matthews's house. No sense finding out who was where at what time if we don't take travel time into account."

"Yes, sir," Mornay said.

"Everyone clear on their duties?"

Nods all around.

"Good," McNab said. "Then we'll have no surprises."

"You'll have to keep your hands to yourself," Claire whispered to Mornay as they were dismissed.

"Tell it to the fireplug," he whispered back, nodding toward Byrne. "He's the one who always wants to fight."

"You're just an innocent victim? Is that it?"

He wanted to defend himself, but the truth was that Byrne had taken an instant dislike to him from day one, and his response had been to goad the man even further. Six months ago, Byrne, drunk at Max's—a pub four doors down from the police office—had taken a swing at him. Byrne only succeeded in losing his balance and, to his humiliation, had to be helped to his feet by the man he'd been trying to punch. Mornay should've stepped over the bastard.

"Why does he hate you?" Claire asked.

"Probably because I'm taller." He grinned. "No worries, Claire—I'll act professional."

"Now that's what really worries me."

The main kitchen in Sandrington Hall was massive, built in a time when one needed a small army of servants to run the place. The ceilings soared five meters high; the windows were almost of equal length. The original brickwork, smoky red, was still in place, but little else that was original remained. White plaster covered the walls, and white cabinetry topped with pebbly gray granite circled the room. Stainless-steel restaurant-grade appliances now filled the old hearths.

Down the center of the room ran a wide island. Lydia Sandrington stood next to it and glanced into her cup of tea, her second in the last hour. It had gone cold, like her first, barely tasted. Dark islands of unappetizing scum floated at the top of the pale liquid. Lydia upturned the cup, spilling the tea into the kitchen sink, then washed it down the drain.

Cardboard boxes of fresh vegetables lined much of the center island. Lydia had them situated in order; those nearest the sink were to be washed first. Boxes of plastic serving dishes, plastic tumblers, and plastic cutlery were stacked on the counter nearest the door so they could be carted out in the morning without interfering with the dozen or so women who would be working in the kitchen to replenish the refreshment table.

Lydia plucked another strawberry from the crate closest to her and ate it. She'd missed lunch directing where the boxes should be put, and she was tempted to bow out of dinner. She was in no mood to entertain the paying guests who were now in the west parlor, exchanging lies and drinking the third best whiskey she stocked, waiting for their police interviews.

Lydia glanced around the massive kitchen—a habit she practiced in quiet moments before chaos took over—and found the appliances glinting from every bricked corner obscene. She remembered very clearly a time when nothing but rotting plaster, cobwebs, and drafty shadows filled the room. It was a memory her son, Gregor, did not share. By the time he was old enough to notice such things, the kitchen had been renovated with the rest of Sandrington Hall.

She was widowed before Gregor was born. The entire history and future of a family that had survived through seven hundred years of human strife now rested on the shoulders of her reclusive son. Perhaps if she'd not shielded Gregor as a child, he would have turned out differently. Better.

It pained her to think of Gregor's childhood. He'd been such a handsome little boy, smiling and shouting "Mumma" whenever he wanted her attention. She'd almost allowed herself to hope her son would change, now that he shouldered many of the responsibilities of running the Hall, including giving the daily tours, which he led with nominal complaints. But he still drank heavily and had a tendency to sit and brood in the corner when drinks needed to be refilled or plates of pastries needed passing out. On bad days, he claimed he was no better than a trained monkey.

Lydia suspected life would be simpler if she didn't have to face daily the one part of it she'd failed at so miserably.

There was a scrape, a footstep, on the bright white tiled floor. Lydia turned. "Gregor."

He lifted the tumbler. The glass held a finger of a dark purplish liquid—brandy, perhaps—though he'd always preferred whiskey. He saluted her. "Mother."

"Where were you this morning?" she asked. "I've guests, the flower show, a boiler about to gasp its last, and you were nowhere to be found."

"You've got Evan to come running whenever you call; why would you miss me?"

"Ina's dead," she said, not bothering to break the terrible news in a gentle voice. She'd never approved of his friendship with the outspoken woman. "The police are coming to interview us."

Gregor's entire body went slack, his arms dropping to his sides, the tumbler slipping from his fingers. Burgundy liquid made a starburst pattern on the tile when the tumbler shattered. The fruity scent of grape juice wafted through the kitchen. "What happened to her?" he asked in a strangled, barely audible voice.

"Evan didn't say."

He turned his back to her, putting his hands on the counter. Had he really liked Ina so much that he needed to steady himself?

"Is there a possibility of a mistake?" he asked. "That it's not Ina?"

"Of course not. Dr. Hartwick was at the cemetery before the police. Ina's not the issue, Gregor. It's the police that I'm concerned about. We need to discuss what we're going to say to them when they arrive."

"Not the issue . . ." he echoed. Then he shook his head, as if trying to clear his thoughts. "Why do we need to worry about the police?" he asked. He was still shaking his head, his back toward her. "Are you afraid they'll find out what you really thought of Ina?" His voice sounded odd. He was genuinely upset; a reaction she hadn't anticipated. "That you despised her?"

"Don't be ridiculous, Gregor. I barely knew the woman. You can't despise someone you don't know. I didn't enjoy being in her company, and that's not a crime."

"Then there's nothing to be worried over, is there?"

The sound of Anne Crownlow's voice kept Evan from rounding the corner and entering the kitchen. Anne was on the telephone.

"I don't care if it isn't convenient, Roger," she said into the receiver, her voice hard and unyielding. "You're paid to do what you're told. So do it."

She's tougher than she looks. Inspector Byrne's words sprang up, unbidden. Unwanted.

There were a few moments of silence before Anne said, "Maybe another day or two. I can't imagine they'll require me to remain longer than that. No," she said, her voice decisive. "I've found out what I needed to know."

Evan shifted his weight, uncomfortable about eavesdropping but rooted to the spot, curious to find out more about this woman who'd been staying in his home.

"If that happens, then you'd better pack an overnighter and get up here fast to start the damage control."

Anne clunked the receiver down and cursed softly. Evan was frozen in indecision: bolt for the front stairs, which would leave him exposed for the length of the front hall, or remain here, hoping Anne would go into the kitchen?

He remained.

Anne went into the kitchen.

Heart pounding, Evan forced himself to wait a full minute before walking into the kitchen himself.

Anne was seated at one end of the table, nibbling on a biscuit she'd taken from the plate Mary had left in the center of the table.

"Hello," Evan said, feeling guilty for having eavesdropped on her conversation.

"Hello," she replied. The decisive edge had disappeared beneath softly spoken syllables.

"I was thinking about making myself a cup of tea. Would you . . ." his voice trailed off. He wasn't the accomplished actor Anne seemed to be; he could feel his pulse racing. He had an overwhelming need to fill the silence with words.

"I'd love a cup," she said.

Mary came in the back door just as he was pouring the boiling water from the electric kettle into their cups. She was dressed in a woolen skirt and thick sweater. "Well, they've made a right mess in the cemetery. I wonder if Lydia will cancel her flower show. Have you heard, Evan?"

"No, I haven't. But I doubt she would for anything short of an alien invasion. Every room in the area's booked."

Mary's glance took in Anne, who was sitting quietly, still nibbling on the biscuit. "You'll catch your death in that blouse."

"Thank you, Mary," Anne said, eyes downcast. "But I'm quite warm."

Evan passed out the mugs of tea.

"What will happen to Ina Matthews's roses?" Anne asked.

He wondered if she was trying to head off another lecture from Mary about underdressing for life in the Grampian highlands.

"Did you know Ina?" he asked.

"We met several times in the village and she invited me to her greenhouse once."

"You've seen her roses?"

Anne dipped her biscuit into her tea. "The other day. She has dozens and dozens. Did you know her cousin doesn't like roses? Do you think she'd throw them out after all the work Ina's put into them?"

"Surprises will never cease," Mary said, her tone unfriendly enough to startle him. "Who would have guessed you'd have an interest in gardening."

"I don't, really. I was just wondering what it would be like, spending most of your life working on just one thing with no one to appreciate what you've done."

Evan jumped to Ina's defense. "There was more to Ina than her roses and she was quite well regarded within the gardening community as well as here. She was not unappreciated."

Mary's cup clattered on the counter. "Can we

change the subject, please? Discussing anything to do with Ina seems a touch ghoulish to me." Mary took in a deep breath and slowly exhaled. "Evan, I've rearranged your schedule for the next two days. I've moved your appointments back into next week."

Evan smiled. "You do think of everything, Mary."

She lifted a hand and gently patted his cheek. "Always, my dear. Always. Remember I'll be visiting our Paul this evening."

Mary always referred to his parishioners like one would a member of the family. Paul Hume, an elderly widower, was a troublesome parishioner whom Evan could count on hearing from at least once a day to complain about one of the other parishioners. Paul's failing health had given Evan a blessed relief this past month. Mary visited Paul three times a week, as she did with all their ailing parishioners. Since most of his congregation was elderly, there always seemed to be two or three sick ones to tend. Mary carried out her visits cheerfully and compassionately, even if it was a parishioner she'd never particularly cared for.

Mornay kept his gaze strictly on the road during the drive to Glen Ross. He ignored Byrne and Byrne returned the favor.

Byrne had a sister in America. When he visited her, he spent his holiday watching cop shows on the television and cop movies in the theaters. *Columbo* and *Dirty Harry* were his favorites. In their honor he smoked noxious cigars and wore a beige mackintosh. If not for the Gun Amnesty Law, Byrne would probably be the only officer in the Grampian Police—perhaps in the whole of Scotland—to own a .44 Magnum, just like Dirty Harry's. Instead Byrne had a framed picture of one in his office. He did not have a photograph of his wife or daughter. Mornay would love to know what a psychologist would make of that fact.

Glen Ross's streets were clogged with traffic. "I didn't know flower shows were so popular," Mornay muttered as he carefully weaved around the parked cars.

He parked on a narrow strip of grass at the bottom of the rectory's drive, so the crime scene vans would have room to back out when they were ready to leave.

Byrne was out of the car and plodding to the cemetery before Mornay could set the parking brake.

Three men were working beneath the tent where Ina Matthews' body lay. They were finally preparing to move it; the steady rain and the thick grass had delayed the move by several hours. Two more men stood close at hand with a gurney. The slow progress was causing tempers to flare and Byrne didn't help matters, strolling around the taped perimeter barking out questions faster than answers could be flung back.

Mornay hunkered into his damp jacket, trying to keep the spitty rain from reaching his bare neck. He cursed himself for leaving his overcoat in Macduff. It was going to remain there for at least the next twenty-four hours, if he was reading the look in Byrne's eyes correctly.

"We might as well walk to Sandrington Hall and time ourselves," Byrne said.

The Hall was nearly half a kilometer away. Mornay looked up at the sky, which threatened even more rain. "You're having me on?"

Byrne cinched the belt on his mackintosh. "You'll no melt."

Mornay, still damp from his earlier excursion in the cemetery, recognized the futility of arguing with Byrne. The man was as decisive as the North Sea was cold. "Then at least let me find something to keep from drowning on the way."

Byrne pulled his bushy gray eyebrows together. "I saw some umbrellas in the rectory kitchen. Borrow one." Byrne waggled one of his short fingers back and forth. "As long as you mind to bring it back."

The Sandringtons were as artfully arranged as the furniture, Mornay thought, as he found an unobtrusive spot in which to stand. He stood next to a drafty window and had to work at concentrating on what was said rather than on the chilly breeze blowing across his shoulders.

It was just after four. He and Byrne were in the Sandrington family parlor and his stomach was grumbling because he'd missed lunch. The paying bed-and-breakfast guests were at the other end of the house, doing whatever it was that wealthy people on holiday did for entertainment while it rained.

Lydia Sandrington was porcelain perfect; pale skin, pale eyes, and silvery blond hair cut in a pageboy that fell in a soft line above the curve of her jaw. She sat with ramrod-straight posture on an ottoman in front of her son. Odd place, Mornay thought, considering her other, more comfortable choices.

Gregor Sandrington was a walking, talking Burberry ad. He sat, right leg crossed over left, in an imposing wing chair, smoking a cigar. He did not immediately look their way when they entered the room. Sandrington exhaled a pale cone cloud directly up to the ceiling, then leisurely raised his head from the back of the leather chair and studied Mornay, then turned his head slightly to look at Byrne. It was extraordinary how even in the lamp-lit gloom of the room, Sandrington's hair could glow all tawny. It was as if the man were carrying around his own little spotlight to shine on his perfect white teeth and tanned skin. The light didn't quite reach Sandrington's flat black eyes, which looked as if they would more easily spark against flint than show a glimmer of emotion. Then he returned his full attention to the cigar. But his tense body language belied his apparent disinterest in their arrival.

Another perfect cone of blue smoke floated toward the ceiling. Sandrington held up his cigar, studying its tightly wound surface in the lamplight. Ash trickled down, sprinkling pale splotches on his fawn-colored trousers. "Cigar, Inspector?" he asked in the unmistakable drawl of an overeducated member of the ruling class. A nod of his head indicated the humidor on a table near Byrne.

Byrne's lips tightened into a mocking smile, but he reached for the humidor. "Thank you." Still smiling, Byrne grabbed a fistful of cigars and shoved them in a pocket, saving one out to light.

Cigar in hand, Byrne took a turn around the room. Engrossed in studying the prints hanging near the fireplace, he didn't seem to notice how intently he was being watched. "The place seems busier since I was here about Julia Whelan's suicide."

"Really, Inspector," Lydia Sandrington said. "What a macabre way to measure time."

"But it works for me." Byrne fingered a fringed lamp shade. "Business good, Lord Sandrington?"

Though Byrne's question was directed to Gregor Sandrington, his mother answered. She'd been following Byrne's progress around the room as intently as her son wanted to appear to be ignoring him. Light and dark. Oil and water. The contrast between mother and son was that striking. Mornay wondered why Byrne even mentioned Julia Whelan. Was he trying to antagonize the Sandringtons? Both had flinched when Byrne mentioned her name.

"We're booked solid for the next eight months, Inspector, so yes, I'd say business is good."

Byrne scratched his head with nails frayed from chewing. Luxuriant tufts of wiry hair sprouted around his knuckles, an exact match to the tufts of wiry hair protruding from his ears, above his eyes, down the back of his neck, and, on occasion, from his nostrils.

He was doing his daft cop routine, something he'd picked up from Columbo.

"Really?" Byrne said. "That much business? What happens when the tourists leave?"

"Through the winter we book receptions and conferences. Some organizations are combining work with pleasure. They take advantage of our off-season rates."

Byrne nodded, as if he understood the finer points of bed-and-breakfast management.

"What's the regular rate for one of your rooms?"

The question bordered on the ridiculous. Byrne was a cop in a ratty, mud-stained mackintosh struggling with his daughter's university fees, but Lydia Sandrington answered as if he were a blue-blooded tourist.

"Our basic room is a hundred and twenty pounds a night. This includes two meals and use of the public parts of the house. Suites are slightly more."

Mornay almost smiled at the inflection she gave the word *slightly*. Try eighty pounds more. He'd checked into the rates one day out of curiosity.

Byrne plopped on a delicately carved wooden chair, his legs splayed in front of him. The chair creaked beneath his weight and bits of mud flaked off his shoes.

"How many people do you expect for your flower show tomorrow?"

Lydia took the mud on the carpet and the question in stride. She asked her son for his cigarette case. Gregor Sandrington pulled out a small, heavily engraved silver case that was probably worth a fortune, Mornay thought. With a lit cigarette in hand, Lydia focused on Byrne.

"We're hoping attendance will be well over a thousand," she said. "We've worked very hard putting the show together. Will the roadblocks be removed soon?"

Byrne worked on his cigar, taking three puffs before he exhaled noisily. He dropped the Columbo routine. "A woman was brutally killed today, Mrs. Sandrington. I'm not keen on a thousand or so people traipsing through the center of my investigation. This is hardly the Chelsea Flower Show."

"I'm sure Dr. Thomas's wife wouldn't be pleased to hear that the show might be canceled. Delilah Thomas has been a notable supporter of our event for years."

And Dr. Clive Thomas was the new chief constable of the Grampian Police. Lydia Sandrington had just issued an ultimatum: Cancel my show and I'll squeal to the chief constable's wife. It was all Mornay could do to keep from grinning.

Byrne ignored the threat. "What time did Evan Whelan arrive this morning?" he asked.

"Quarter to seven or maybe a shade later."

Byrne raised his brows at that since the time was significantly later than what Whelan had told Mornay. "You remember exactly?"

"I recall because I'd just pointed out the time to several other workers. And Evan arrived moments later. He left about an hour later, around eight thirty."

Byrne didn't point out the discrepancy between Lydia's and Whelan's statements. It wouldn't be the first time a witness was adamant about the information he was providing and be dead wrong. The trick was to sort out the lies.

"What was he doing?"

"Unloading supplies. There were six others from the village helping."

"And you?" Byrne said to Gregor Sandrington.

The man smiled and took another long pull from his cigar.

His mother answered Byrne's question: "Gregor was here, Inspector."

Byrne stood, letting his ash fall to the carpet. Why had he let Gregor Sandrington avoid answering the question? Mornay found the lapse surprising, considering what he'd said about the Sandringtons at the briefing. It was out of character for Byrne to back down from any confrontation.

"We'll need a list of the workers who were here this morning, as well as the names of all the guests. And they'll have to remain here until we interview them."

"When will that be, Inspector?"

"Maybe this evening. Maybe tomorrow morning."

Mornay wrote down the names Lydia Sandrington supplied. Then, because Byrne hadn't asked, he did. "When was the last time you saw Ina Matthews, Mrs. Sandrington?"

"Yesterday evening."

"Did she seem out of sorts in any way? Tired, depressed, anxious?"

Lydia Sandrington's features froze subtly, as if she disapproved of the question. Or maybe she disapproved of Ina Matthews. "Nothing about her appearance or her behavior struck me as unusual," she replied.

"Why did you see her yesterday evening?"

Lydia Sandrington hazarded a quick glance in her son's direction. He seemed oblivious to his surroundings. "She chairs our Events Committee," she said. "We had business regarding the flower show to discuss."

Despite her very controlled answer, he knew without a doubt that Lydia Sandrington was no fan of Ina Matthews.

chapter five

Byrne barreled beneath the borrowed umbrella, pushing most of Mornay's body into the rain. He lit another cigar. "Notice how they didn't bother to ask questions about how she died?" he said.

Mornay had noticed. Even the most unsympathetic of people will still wonder if there's a possibility of future incidents. Either the Sandringtons were too shocked by Ina's death, they didn't care, or they already knew. He was inclined to believe the latter.

"Bloody village solidarity. They probably already know she was stabbed." Byrne breathed out a geyser of cigar smoke that was promptly carried away by a gust of wind. The rain had grown finer while they were inside Sandrington Hall; now the sheerest of mists was swirled wildly by gusts of wind. There was more rain coming at them sideways, beneath the umbrella, than from above. "If we want to know what's really happening around here," Byrne continued, "we'll need to have a chat with Ollie."

"Who?"

"Oliver Tidmarsh, the senior gardener. Lives in a small cottage at the back of the grounds somewhere." Byrne peered out from beneath the umbrella's edge.

It took a dozen knocks to get Oliver Tidmarsh to open his door, and he opened it only the barest of cracks to see them. The small man's skin was the color of a used tea bag. It was so deeply seamed it was difficult to tell where one wrinkle ended and the next one began. His bright blue eyes stared warily at them as Byrne shoved his identification through the crack.

"Oliver," Byrne said. "Remember me? Saw you a couple of years ago when the rector's wife died. I brought you a bottle of whiskey."

Mornay watched the old man squint at Byrne's identification.

"I remember you," Oliver Tidmarsh said slowly, his voice not particularly friendly. "Weren't anyone talking to you then, was there? Don't imagine it's much different now." He opened the door wide enough to let them enter. "Who's this one?" he said when Mornay ducked beneath the lintel to enter the cramped one-room cottage.

"Detective Sergeant Mornay. He'll be taking notes."

Oliver Tidmarsh shrugged and took the only seat in the cottage, a bent-willow rocker placed next to the fireplace. The small man started slowly rocking.

Mornay, shivering, stood next to a broad beam that seemed to be the central post holding the roof up. The rafters were open, giving the room a drafty, cavelike feeling. The stale, smoke-filled air added to the cavelike atmosphere.

"Have you heard about Ina Matthews's death?" Byrne asked. He removed another of Sandrington's fine cigars from his pocket but didn't light it; instead he seemed content with examining its construction.

Oliver Tidmarsh nodded. "Who hasn't?"

"Did you know her?"

"Know everyone in the town and most everything they're up to." The old man leaned forward. "What do you want to hear about?"

"Ina Matthews."

Olive Tidmarsh sighed. He seemed disappointed they weren't asking him about a more interesting subject. "She was a good woman. Wasn't the sort that got offended when you had something to say."

"Say about what?" Mornay asked.

Tidmarsh trained his bright gaze in Mornay's direction. "Gardening," he said, his tone implying that gardening was the only subject worth discussing.

"What time were you up today, Oliver?" Byrne asked.

"Same as I am every day—half past four."

"Was anyone wandering the grounds this morning?"

"Damn near half the village went through here this morning. Crashing through hedges and mucking up my beds."

"How many is half? Three? Four? More?"

"Maybe three" was Tidmarsh's grudging reply. "The first one must've been out close to five. The birds were just starting up; they don't start unless it's sunrise or close to it."

Byrne pressed on. "Who was it?"

Mornay shifted his weight. If Oliver kept giving out his answers in dribs and drabs, they'd be here all night.

"Was the rector. He came off the path and tramped right through my new rose bed. Didn't so much as look down to see what he was tramping on. And that lassie staying at the rectory was following him." Oliver inclined his head forward and peered at them both in turn, lowering his voice. "Like she didn't want the man knowing she was there. Soon as she saw he was heading toward the Hall, she turned around. Wouldn't have noticed her at all except she popped out of my yew hedge instead of coming from the path like the rector had."

Oliver spent a few silent moments creaking in his rocking chair.

"Mr. Tidmarsh, who was the third person?"

"Saw Lydia's young master."

"Gregor Sandrington?" Mornay asked.

"Bit slow, this one," Tidmarsh said to Byrne. "How many young masters he think we have running around?" Tidmarsh pointed to the small dirty window above his sink. "Saw him out that window when I put the kettle on this morning. Clock was chiming six when he walked past like he was in a hurry to get to where he was going."

Mornay took the five paces necessary to cross the room. He stood in the corner that served as the kitchen and peered out the window. "Was he walking toward you or walking away from you?"

Mornay realized a clarification wouldn't be very useful, though. Sandrington Hall sat between Tidmarsh's cottage and the beginning of the public path. Someone passing Tidmarsh's window didn't necessarily have to use the path; they could have come from any direction.

"Mr. Tidmarsh, is there a view of the yew hedges from your kitchen window?"

Tidmarsh grinned. "You're not as dim as I thought. I was outside, switching off the sprinklers, when I saw Evan and that lassie. His Lordship passed the cottage after I returned."

"Where do you think he was going?"

"There's only the cliffs in the direction he was walking."

"What's at the cliffs?"

"Views," Tidmarsh answered. "Nothing but views." And then the old man started laughing.

Sarah Jenkins's kitchen was crowded with livid lime-green pails that'd once held plaster compound; the pails were now serving as containers to dozens and dozens of roses in nearly every imaginable hue.

"This scent is enough to choke you," Mornay said to Claire, lifting another four pails by their plastic handles to carry outside.

"They'll have it cleaned up in a tick," Mornay heard Byrne say to Sarah Jenkins. He was leading the woman to the front sitting room.

"Bastard," Mornay hissed under his breath. He reached for two more buckets and was promptly stabbed in the thumb with a thorn the size of a small paring knife.

Five trips later, the kitchen was empty of buckets and roses, though there was nothing they could do about the scent that still lingered thickly in the air. Mornay was thankful to finally shut out the soft sound of pattering rain. He edged up to the radiator, hoping its warmth would dry him and chase away his shivers. He examined his wounded thumb; the blood was already congealing. "Ever heard of Oliver Tidmarsh?" he asked Claire.

She shook her head.

"He's the gardener at Sandrington Hall. He's just told us he saw Evan Whelan, Anne Crownlow, and Gregor Sandrington wandering the grounds near dawn this morning."

"Interesting," she said, without really sounding interested. She filled the electric kettle with water, then plugged it in to boil.

"Suppose I shouldn't be surprised that not one of them mentioned their early morning strolls."

"Everyone lies," she said.

He sighed and turned to dry out his right side.

"Did you find out anything about Anne Crownlow?"

"Not yet; I'll have to try the registrar's office tomorrow. The entire office staff was at a conference today."

"What do you think about abortion?" he asked in the silence that enveloped them. The question came out suddenly, surprising him as much as it surprised Claire.

She looked up from the tea bag she was unwrapping from its foil wrapper. "I'm Catholic," she said. "I don't think about it."

She put the tea tin back into the cluttered cupboard and poured boiling water into the teapot, drowning the tea bags. Slivers of aromatic steam floated over to Mornay.

"What if an accident happens?"

Claire's shoulders stiffened and he immediately regretted his choice of words. Claire was fond of children.

"So," she said, her voice low, "has an *accident* happened between you and one of your girlfriends?" She poured his tea, remembering to put in the extra cream and extra sugar.

Mornay stared at some apricot-colored petals that had fallen to the floor; they reminded him of the petal he'd picked out of the grass earlier. He was too cold to fish it out of his pocket. Instead he held his mug of tea with both hands, trying to warm himself, though it was futile until he changed into dry clothes. "She's not a girlfriend," he said. "She's pregnant."

Claire loaded the tray she was to take into the sitting room. "If the baby's yours, then see that it's adopted. There are too many unwanted children in the world. If it isn't yours, tell her to find the father and have him worry about it." Her features softened when she turned his way. "Do you think the baby's yours?"

"Maybe," he said, still holding on to the hope that Pamela was lying, but even as he said the word he knew that Pamela wouldn't dare bluff Victoria. "Probably," he admitted.

"Well," Claire said softly. "I didn't think you could be so stupid."

"Just what my tender ego needs."

"But am I wrong?" she asked.

The ache that'd started in the center of his chest when he was talking to Victoria seemed to expand with every heartbeat. *Time to change the subject.* "You were around when Evan Whelan's wife killed herself, weren't you?"

She nodded. "I was Byrne's driver."

"Did he spend much time questioning the Sandringtons?"

"Only after he decided to pursue the suspicious-death inquiry. Why do you want to know?"

"Byrne was acting oddly around them. Polite. I've never seen the bastard put on a polite face, even for the chief constable."

"Maybe he's being cautious." Claire glanced to the door that led to the sitting room, assuring herself that no one was coming out. She lowered her voice even further. "Rumor had it Byrne wanted to have a sensational case under his belt so he could get promoted."

"Did Byrne have any evidence to support his suspicious-death inquiry?"

"He'd heard rumors in the town that Gregor Sandrington was having an affair with Julia Whelan. And he claimed the forensic evidence wasn't conclusive. You can imagine how Dr. Hall took the news, his staff being accused of having missed something."

"What about Whelan? Was he a suspect?"

"He had an alibi. He was out of town when she killed herself, so he wasn't even considered. And when

Byrne told him about his suspicions, the rector threatened to have his solicitors look into the matter to protect his wife's reputation. Then the Sandringtons broke out their firm of solicitors. I heard Byrne was warned off by the CID detective chief superintendent the next day."

"Little wonder. How many actual murders has our command area had in the last two years? Two? And Byrne's trying to tack on a third? Did anyone in her immediate family come forward, claim it wasn't suicide?"

"Not that I heard." Claire straightened the biscuit tin, aligning its edge with the lip of the tray. "I felt sorry for her husband. The poor man coming home to find his wife dead from tranquilizers, then to find out she was pregnant, as well."

"Did she know she was pregnant when she killed herself?"

"Aye, she knew. She'd had a doctor's appointment confirming the pregnancy the very same day she died."

Byrne bellowed from the parlor. "Gillespie! Where's the tea? Sergeant Mornay, I'd appreciate your presence in here, if you please."

Claire deposited the tea tray on a table in front of a stiffly cushioned couch, the only place for Mornay to sit. From his vantage point, Mornay watched Claire return to the kitchen and pull a broom from a niche beside the stove and begin to sweep the kitchen floor.

The sitting room was papered in pale green wallpaper. The furniture, too large for the room, was covered in rose-patterned chintz. He'd had enough of roses, Mornay thought, as he pulled the damp cloth of his shirt away from his chest. He shifted his legs carefully to keep from knocking the tea set on the table in front of him, and Byrne glared at him to stop fidgeting.

Mornay dropped his hand and tried to listen to the odd conversation Byrne was having with Sarah Jenkins.

". . . It was the cat, you see." Sarah Jenkins dabbed at the corners of her eyes with the hankie she had balled between her plump hands. "My husband, Gerry, bought it about a month before he died. I've never liked them myself, but Gerry adored cats. I think I would have tried to take it back if it hadn't been Gerry's. Daft thing would hover near the kitchen sink, waiting for me to leave the room so it could flip up the faucet lever with its paw. Once the water was on, it would swipe its paws through the stream, playing. Then, because its paws were wet, it would slip on the edge and fall into the sink. Out it'd come, a howling sponge of orange fur, slinging water everywhere—until it finally electrocuted itself on the lamp cord running beneath that ottoman you're sitting on." Sarah pointed to where Inspector Byrne sat.

Mornay had to give the man credit; he didn't scan the carpet for signs of charred cat.

"So Ms. Matthews moved in after your cat died?" Byrne asked.

Sarah Jenkins nodded. "Drove up every weekend afterward. I used to tease her that it was my large garden that brought her, she spent so much time in it. After a year or so of these trips, Ina suggested that if she retired at the end of the school term—something she'd been considering for months—she could move permanently to Glen Ross and live with me. She was so good at doing all the little things around the house that I simply couldn't do anymore. And she must have guessed I was desperate for the company."

Sarah stopped dabbing at her eyes and looked to the mantel and the vase of wilting flowers in its center. "Ina was canny when it came to people. . . ." Sarah looked away from the men, pushing the hankie against her mouth.

"Did she have any particular friends? Male friends?" Byrne asked.

"She was close with Evan—she'd been quite good friends with his wife before she died."

"Close romantically?"

Sarah shook her head. "Oh, no, they were just good friends. Chatted with each other—that sort of thing."

Byrne stood abruptly. "That's all we'll need for now. Sergeant Mornay will bring the tray."

"Inspector, no one's told me, precisely, what happened to Ina," Sarah Jenkins said as they walked into the kitchen. "I would like you to tell me what happened."

Mornay watched Byrne look down at his scuffed oxfords, then up again at the plump woman clutching the damp hankie to her green-stained bosom. "She was attacked, Mrs. Jenkins. On the path to Sandrington Hall. I'm afraid that's all I can say at this time." Byrne nodded toward Claire. "Constable

Gillespie will be around tomorrow, after our morning briefing. She'll give you whatever information might be available then."

"Attacked by whom? A man? A woman? A deranged child? An animal?"

"We're still gathering information."

"Will there be any more attacks? Half of our village will be using that path tomorrow. Lydia is adamant about not having her car park cluttered with local vehicles."

"The path's been blocked off and we've got officers posted near the cemetery. They'll be on duty around the clock. I think it's highly unlikely there will be another attack. And I doubt there will be a show tomorrow," Byrne added with a smug look in her direction.

Sarah's face lit with a smile. The smile vanished as quickly as it appeared, and once again exhaustion and grief dragged at her features, making her appear older than her fifty-plus years. "You don't know Lydia Sandrington very well then, Inspector."

Byrne reached for the umbrella Mornay had borrowed from the rectory, then paused, turning. "Was it raining this morning?"

"On and off." She was eyeing the umbrella.

"Did Ms. Matthews take any sort of rain gear with her when she left for Sandrington Hall?"

Sarah stared at Byrne as intently as if the man had suddenly sprouted a second nose. She pointed to the umbrella he held. "I thought you were returning Ina's umbrella."

Byrne lifted the umbrella. "*This* is your cousin's umbrella?"

They all stared at the umbrella with the aqua-blue canvas and carved ivory grip. Mornay had probably subconsciously chosen it because the canvas was Victoria's favorite color.

"Of course it is," Sarah said as if Inspector Byrne were trying to trick her into a lie.

"And she took *this* umbrella when she left for Sandrington Hall this morning?"

"Yes. She took that umbrella and an old gray mackintosh."

Byrne scowled at the umbrella, as if it were to blame for magically appearing in the rectory's mud-room. He turned his jowled scowl on Mornay next, as if he should have instinctively known who'd really owned the umbrella.

Mornay, in turn, scowled uselessly at the umbrella.

Mornay and Claire followed Lydia Sandrington down a long hall, the oak-paneled ceiling soaring over their heads. Dour portraits in massive gilt frames covered the walls. It was enough to make him claustrophobic; all those ponderous, overfed faces staring down at him. Claire seemed oblivious to her surroundings as she walked beside him, chin up, stride matching his. Their feet made quiet *shush, shush, shushing* sounds as they went down the plush, tomato-red carpet that ran the length of the hall.

He hoped their interviews with the Sandrington guests would yield something useful. Chief Inspector McNab's press conference had not supplied the information the reporters were hoping for—the name of the attacker—so they were supplying their own. During the evening news, pictures of a surly-looking lad had flashed across the screen. Tommy Torga, age sixteen, had escaped from the back of a police van in Inverness two days earlier. Though he was a minor, Tommy was being transferred to a higher security facility after attacking one of his detention center counselors with a broken piece of glass. He'd twice attacked teachers the same way. Tommy Torga was being offered to the public as a likely candidate for Ina Matthews's attacker, and the public had latched on to the theory with a vengeance. Calls of possible Tommy Torga sightings were starting to congest the phone lines.

Mornay had thin hope that the B-and-B guests would have seen something useful; the well-off had always struck him as too self-absorbed to be very observant. He'd made the mistake of sharing his opinion with Claire on the drive over.

"Is that an opinion formed during your misspent youth terrorizing the Banff citizens?"

"Now who's stereotyping whom?"

"You want to follow in Byrne's bigoted footsteps, be my guest. But don't expect me to follow you; I've a career to look after."

"Did I really sound like Byrne?" he asked. But they'd arrived at the Hall; Claire was already out of the car.

The first couple they interviewed was in their late sixties. The Hugheses lived in Aberdeen and were eager to be returning home. "I've never been so frightened in my life," Mrs. Hughes said for the third time. "Isn't that just so, Mr. H?" the short woman asked her husband. Mr. H nodded dutifully. Mrs. H crossed her thick ankles and peered at Mornay. He quickly asked a question before she could launch into a fourth account of her nervous tremors.

"Were you awake around six this morning?"

"Is that when it happened?" Curiosity shone brightly in her eyes.

"We're not sure when the attack occurred, Mrs. Hughes. However, at six it was light enough to see."

"Not through the mist," Mr. H said. "Bloody thick it was this morning."

Mrs. H stared at her husband. "We were up at half past seven, dear. How would you know the mist was thick at six?"

"Because it was still thick when we got up," Mr. H insisted. "Could hardly see past the front garden. Why should it have suddenly gotten thick at seven and not earlier?" Mr. H turned back to Mornay. "All the bloody hammering outside woke us."

Mrs. Hughes bounced back into the conversation. "I demanded a refund due to the noise. One expects a certain level of professionalism."

Mornay stood. "I'm sure you did." After reassuring them that they were free to leave once they provided Constable Dunnholland with their fingerprints downstairs in one of the kitchens, he led them out of the room as quickly as he could manage.

When they were through the door he said to Claire, "Want to bet they denied her a refund?"

"I gave up gambling."

"Since when?"

"Since you started winning all the office pools."

He lowered his voice to a whisper since the second couple was approaching. "We need to remember to ask Ollie how he saw everyone through the mist."

"Why do you always say *we* when we both know you mean me?"

He grinned down at her. "That's what you get for being efficient."

"Flattery will get you nowhere." She was struggling to maintain a stern expression.

"Don't I bloody know it," he shot back. The second couple's arrival prevented her reply. Their verbal sparring was a good sign; he'd hardly gotten three words out of her during their hastily eaten dinner at the pub.

The Tierneys were an unlikely couple. He was in his fifties, tall and athletic-looking. She was considerably younger, dumpy, her face badly scarred from acne. He wouldn't be surprised if Mrs. Tierney was often mistaken for her husband's daughter.

Mr. Tierney led his wife to a chair and put his hand on her shoulder, pushing her down into it. "It's about time you people came to do your duty," Mr. Tierney said.

"John." Mrs. Tierney's voice was soft. Too soft to register with John Tierney, who was warming to his subject: police incompetence.

Mornay laced his hands together on his lap and leaned back in his chair. "Have you something important to report, sir?"

"If I did, you certainly took long enough to find out about it."

"So you do?" Mornay's voice projected only a bland interest.

"Of course not."

Mornay held the man's gaze until a reddish flush crept into Tierney's cheeks. "Of all the . . ." Tierney's sputtering faded. "Who's your superior?" he demanded.

"Detective Inspector Walter Byrne."

"And his superior?"

"Detective Chief Inspector Andrew McNab."

"Mrs. Tierney," Claire asked, trying to get the interview back on track. "What time did you and your husband wake this morning?"

Mrs. Tierney blushed. "It was nearly nine when we got up. We missed breakfast." Another blush. Her face was now as red as the runner in the hall. Mr. Tierney was watching his wife's emotional display with thinly veiled annoyance.

Claire told the Tierneys they were free to check out as soon as they provided their fingerprints. Surprisingly, Tierney didn't protest this final indignity. He ushered his wife out of the room without a backward glance.

The last two guests, twin seventy-seven-year-old sisters from Virginia, provided the most interesting information.

"We're light sleepers, you see," Audrey Clark, the elder by three minutes, said.

"The van woke us up," Augusta Clark added.

"Van?"

Audrey sat perched on the edge of her seat, hands folded in her lap. She appeared to be the frailer sister and also seemed to do the majority of the talking. With each question, Augusta immediately looked to her sister to provide the answer. "The courtesy van. That nice young Mr. Sandrington was driving. Though he could hardly walk when he got out, could he, Augusta?"

"He was drunk as a lord," she said with a straight face.

Audrey turned to Mornay. "You'll have to forgive my sister's sense of humor. I know this isn't a laughing matter, but he really was quite drunk. He weaved his way to a door below our window, then came outside again barely ten minutes later. Did you know he prefers to be called Mr., not Lord?"

"No, I didn't. What did he do next?"

"He disappeared into the mist."

"What direction was he walking?" Claire asked.

"Toward the cemetery."

"Was there anyone else moving around the grounds?"

Audrey spoke. "We didn't see anyone else, but not long after Mr. Sandrington walked away, we heard someone speak."

"What did they say?"

The sisters exchanged a glance, then Audrey said, " 'Bugger.' "

"Male or female?" Mornay wanted to know.

"We've tried to decide that all day. We just aren't sure. We also couldn't tell how far away he or she was. I'm sorry we couldn't be more helpful."

After the twins left, he asked Claire, "Do we have time to talk to Sandrington before the autopsy?"

Claire checked her watch. "We're late as it is."

It was well after midnight when Mornay finally returned home after the autopsy. The drive to Aberdeen and back, made at a snail's pace because of the torrential rain, had taken over two hours each way.

The houses in his development were built in pairs, mirror images of each other, with the kitchens and sitting rooms sharing a common wall. Drives and minuscule front gardens were neatly divided by wrought-iron fences that came to knee level. Some of the owners had removed the original fences and replaced them with proper ones that could actually keep a dog larger than a miniature chihuahua inside the garden. Two left turns and a final right turn took him into his own drive. He parked next to Mrs. Stuck's blue Citroën.

He didn't turn on his lights inside the house; he navigated through the cardboard boxes cluttering his sitting room by instinct. His answering machine cast a greenish glow in the room. He pushed the Play button and Victoria's voice spoke.

"Seth, Pamela's gone missing. Have you seen her? Give me a ring as soon as you get this."

chapter six

It was going on seven when Mornay walked into the rectory's kitchen. Anne Crownlow sat in a chair next to the window, her arms wrapped around her knees, holding them against her chest. She was leaning against the window casing.

"Why aren't there more?" she asked. Her breath fogged the windowpane.

"What's that?" Mornay asked.

"Why aren't there more police officers? I didn't count those men in the white suits," she said, referring to the forensic team that had returned to their warm, dry offices in Aberdeen as soon as they'd found the missing half of the weapon used to kill Ina Matthews. Dr. Hall had removed its mate from Ina Matthews's right lung during the autopsy.

Anne waited for an answer. Her wide brown eyes

were as shadowy deep as the loch he and Victoria used to swim in when they were children; those summer days had seemed to last for weeks instead of mere hours. Mornay walked across the room until he was looking down at her.

"Counting the inspector and myself, there's six total," he said. "The whole of the evening shift from Macduff plus two constables from Turriff. We'll be working double shifts for the next few days."

She continued to watch him, that cool, distracted look still in her eyes. "That's not very many."

Privately, he agreed. There were just over fifty officers between the stations in Macduff and Turriff, from uniformed traffic constables to the five CID officers; Turriff's CID officer was on medical leave. There was just one chief inspector allotted to each office.

Mornay's eyes burned from too little sleep and from worry. He hadn't been able to reach Victoria or her mother. As far as he knew, Pamela was still missing. He leaned against the opposite side of the window casement, facing Anne, and studied her drawn face. "Did you sleep?"

She glanced up at him. "I can't even blink without seeing that poor woman's face," she said quietly. She returned to her scrutiny of the men outside.

They watched Byrne waddle through the halogen puddles cast from the telescoping lights that had been set up last night for the search of the rectory grounds. Claire was nowhere to be seen.

"Can you walk me through your movements yesterday?" Mornay thought he might as well ask now; Byrne would only make him do it later.

"Again?"

"Please." He gave her a lopsided half grin to put her at ease. "I know it's a bother, but we have to do it."

She considered him for a moment and then relaxed. "I woke up around seven, got dressed, and went out to do more research before breakfast. Then I found her."

"What door did you use?"

"I went through the kitchen."

"Was anyone else up?" Mornay asked.

"No."

"Did you use your watch or another clock to check the time?"

There was the barest of pauses before she said, "My watch."

"Do you remember what the mudroom looked like? The small details?"

"There's a bench running the length of the long wall and a row of wooden pegs above it. There were a few things hanging from the pegs—an anorak and a cane. There was something under the bench—maybe a crumpled box." It was clear she wasn't comfortable with his scrutiny. Her gaze kept darting back and forth from his face to the window. The watery pale light coming through the window made pockets of shadows around her eyes.

In a neutral, almost offhand voice, he asked, "Do you remember seeing any other rain gear?"

She shook her head.

"The cane—do you think it's possible it was an umbrella?"

Anne thought about it for a moment. "It's possible, now that I think about it. It was quite thick."

"Do you remember its color?"

"It had a dark handle, I think. I'm sorry; that's really all I can remember."

"Did you see anyone while you were out?"

"No," she whispered, keeping her gaze firmly toward the window. "It wasn't a very pleasant morning."

"Yet you were out."

Her gaze skittered in his direction. "Yes, but I had my project to finish. I only had another day or two to complete it, and some of the gravestones were quite difficult to make out."

"Tracing your family?"

"Yes."

"Did you have any luck?"

There was a long pause before she said, "I learned far more than I expected."

He considered asking her about the discrepancy in her times, but Byrne wouldn't want her tipped off just now, so instead he said, "How did you take notes?"

"What?"

"In the cemetery," he said. "How did you take notes? You didn't have a notebook of any kind when you returned to the rectory. And there wasn't one dropped in the cemetery after you discovered the body, or we would've found it during our search."

"I didn't take notes yesterday. It was too wet. I was scouting a different section of the cemetery."

It was a reasonable explanation if you bought into the ace student theory, which he didn't. He continued watching her, sensing there was something else she wanted to say.

"What a horrible way to die," she said, her voice barely audible. She was probably remembering how viciously the crows had been trying to protect their find. "She didn't suffer, did she? Can you tell something like that?"

Mornay shoved his hands in his pockets and turned to look out the window. *Aye, if you're a pathologist.* It was frightening the facts a pathologist could draw from the shade of a bruise.

Claire had managed better than he through the autopsy. He'd kept his attention on Ina Matthews's feet; high-arched and narrow like Victoria's, they were small for her height. Her toenails were painted a pale shade of pink.

Those small, intimate glimpses were difficult for Mornay to view. He wasn't prone to thoughts of mortality or bouts of conscience, but as he stood in the observation bay looking down at the porcelain table where Ina Matthews's body lay, he couldn't help but dwell on his life and the way he was so thoroughly ruining it. And how he was mucking up Victoria's by association.

Anne Crownlow's voice drifted through Mornay's thoughts. ". . . Her hand . . . and all that blood." Mornay watched Anne shiver. "I've never seen so much blood." Suddenly her eyes widened. "Dead people don't bleed. They can't."

Clever girl.

She searched his face for a glimpse of the truth. The search wasn't difficult; she'd caught him unawares. As unawares as Dr. Hall had caught him hours earlier, after he'd completed the first part of the autopsy. "When did you say she was found?" Dr.

Hall had had to ask him twice. Cedric Hall, chief of the Forensic Science Laboratory, was a small man in his mid-sixties. He had toffee-colored skin and a deep sonorous voice that still contained a hint of the accent he'd had growing up in Trinidad. He exuded an aura of authority that more than made up for any shortcomings in stature.

"Around nine fifteen," Mornay answered.

"These aren't fatal wounds. But they didn't clot like they should have. It's almost as if she were on anticoagulant medication. Though I'd find it very curious if that were the case. I'll have to look through her medical records." Dr. Hall pointed to her chest. "This is the most severe wound; it punctured right into the lung. When she managed to turn herself over, her lung started slowly to fill with blood, but it was still minute. Had someone called an ambulance, I believe she could have been saved. Perhaps losing a lung at worst. She appears to have been in marvelous health."

"How long did she lay bleeding?" Mornay asked.

"As long as three hours—I can't be any more specific than that. This is a significant blow." Hall touched a bruised area on Ina Matthews's right temple, his gesture surprisingly gentle. "She was probably unconscious."

Neither Mornay nor Claire asked Hall how an unconscious woman could manage to turn herself over and continue grasping the ivy so tightly that when she died the crushed leaves had to be pried from her fingers. Or how a physically fit woman could be caught unawares and brutally attacked, with such meager traces of the encounter left at the scene.

"Can you tell if she was tripped?"

"There's no physical evidence."

"Is it possible she was taken by surprise?" Mornay asked. "Someone hiding in the gloom jumps out, bashes her over the head with an as yet undiscovered object, and then proceeds to stab her?"

Hall held up a finger. "You didn't let me finish. While I don't have evidence on her person that she was tripped, we've found traces of her blood on the remnant of blue cord left at the scene. So it's very likely that the weapon used to stab her was used to cut the cord. This attack was very vicious. You're dealing with an unstable person. These wounds to her face are particularly troubling; it's almost as if the attacker were trying to cut her face away. And there are two kinds of stab wounds."

"Two weapons?"

Dr. Hall nodded.

"There are seventeen separate lacerations from forehead to chin: It's too frenzied and the damage too extensive for a random attack."

And Mornay knew that right now, just as in the examining room when Claire took his arm because she was afraid he was going to faint dead away, his emotions marched in plain view across his face.

Anne Crownlow dropped her hand away from her mouth and stood. Damn! Without uttering a word, he'd just told her that Ina Matthews had been left in a desolate corner of the cemetery to bleed to death.

Anne took a tentative step and then fell in a faint onto the cold flagstones.

* * *

Anne opened her eyes as Mornay dribbled another wave of water across her face. She sat up, spluttering, her hands slapping at him.

Mornay pushed her firmly back down against the pillow. "Settle down. It's only a few drops of water. Mary had me put you in your room."

"I take it I fainted?" she said, her voice calmer.

Mornay put the glass on the bedside table. The room was dark except for a narrow band of light sneaking between the closed curtains. "When was the last time you ate?" he asked.

Anne stared at him. "Do you always answer a question by asking another?"

"Do you?"

Anne crossed her arms and continued to stare defiantly at him. "You have one of the most unattractive faces I've ever seen. I feel I should be on my guard around you."

He leaned closer. "Are you hiding something you'd prefer I didn't find out about?"

She looked away from him, then back again. She lifted a hand and touched his scarred cheek. "How did you get this scar?"

"I got it from a bloke with bloody awful aim."

"Lucky for you."

"And not so lucky for him. Do you remember the last time you ate?"

"No."

"Then I'll bring some hot tea."

When he returned, Anne had opened the curtains in her room. The day was turning out brilliantly sunny. He plunked a spoon into one of the two cups on the tray and passed it to her. "I want

you to eat three of those biscuits and drink all of
your tea."

Anne sniffed her tea and wrinkled her nose. "I
prefer coffee."

"So do I, but I couldn't find the coffeepot. Drink
it down now."

Anne picked up one of the flat brown digestive biscuits and sniffed it. "Forcing me to eat these might be
considered police brutality," she said. He merely
waited for her to take a bite. She nibbled delicately on
the crumbling edge. Satisfied she was going to com-
ply, he pushed himself off the bed.

He walked around the edge of the bed and stood
in front of the chest. Light glinted from the polished
pewter frames she'd arranged, shrinelike, on top of a
lace doily. One was a shot of a smiling couple. Beside
the picture of the smiling couple stood a smaller picture of Anne at a funeral. She had stared directly at
the camera, eyes haunted.

"Are these your parents?" he asked.

"That picture was taken a couple of hours before
they were killed."

Anne looked into her teacup. "I don't want to forget what they look like," she said. "Sounds silly, but
sometimes I can't remember." She put her cup and
saucer on the tray.

Beside the bed was a straight-backed chair that
looked uncomfortable, despite the plump paisley
cushion. Mornay sat in it. "I assume the other picture is one taken during their funeral. Why do you
keep it?"

She stared at him for such a length of time, he

almost convinced himself she would fall asleep before she would answer.

"We had an argument the day they died. It had been one of those spectacular summer days that happen about once a year—so sunny and hot it almost hurt to breathe. I wanted Mum to take me swimming, but she was giving another of her garden fetes." Anne's fingers picked at a loose thread on the pillow sham she held. "Mum was always helping out some charity or another. She tried to make me feel better by telling me we could go swimming the next day. When that didn't work, she said she had a secret to tell me."

Mornay watched her curl her knees up to her chest, her voice lowered to a whisper; she kept her gaze on him. "I screamed so hard it made my throat sore. I told her I didn't want to hear her secret. I went to my room and they were killed less than five minutes later. A lorry blindsided their car right outside our front gates."

Through the open window, Mornay heard Byrne bellowing at Constable Dunnholland. Then he heard his own name being shouted. Dunnholland was being sent to look for him. Mornay stood and walked to the window. Through the trees, he could see the road leading to Sandrington Hall. Cars were driving past slowly so their occupants could see what was happening in the cemetery. Not much of a sight, Mornay thought—a few hundred yards of tape and a half dozen exhausted personnel. A tent had been erected over the site where Ina Matthews's body had been found. No one was allowed beneath the tent except for forensic personnel, even though not one of them had returned to the scene since the body had been removed late last evening.

Hands shoved into his pockets, Mornay turned back around. Anne Crownlow was still watching him, and he realized why she was keeping those pictures. She was punishing herself.

"Was your mother pregnant? Was that the secret?"

"I wasn't allowed to read their autopsy reports until I turned eighteen. My mother was four months pregnant when she died. They'd been trying to have a baby for years."

Byrne's shouting got louder. He was coming closer to the rectory.

"Try to get some rest," he told her on his way out of the room.

Byrne was in the kitchen, shouting on his mobile. "Bloody lot of good they'll do me there!" He punched buttons on the mobile until he hit the right one and ended the call.

"Tierney's gone," Byrne snapped. "Skipped off last night."

"What time?"

"He got lost on his way to the kitchen. Dunnholland didn't realize he'd missed one of the guests until this morning."

"Has someone been through his room yet for prints?"

"Gunning for my job, laddie?" Byrne asked softly. "Don't think I can run a proper inquiry? I don't know who you're in bed with, to get the promotions you've gotten over better men than you, but you can bloody well be sure you won't be seeing this rank anytime soon. Not while I'm living and breathing. I don't care if you've got enough medals to sink a fucking Volvo, they don't impress me. Got it?"

"My question was a reasonable one. If you feel threatened by my military background, that's your problem, not mine, so back off about it."

"There was a time when junior officers knew how to behave around their senior officers," Byrne told him.

"Really?" Mornay's sarcastic tone snapped out louder than he'd intended. "And some people in this world are actually appreciated for having half a fucking brain."

They held each other's gazes until Byrne scowled, cursed under his breath, and dug out another cigar.

"Who's going to question Mrs. Tierney?" Mornay asked.

"You are, when you go to collect prints in their room. Have a look." Byrne did an underhand toss, throwing Mornay a plastic bag.

He turned over the bag, examining the flat, oval piece of metal inside. The surface was a mottled brownish green, probably brass. One end of the oval had a broken-off tail of fluted metal three centimeters long. The jagged tail looked like it could be the mate to the jagged piece of brass stake that'd been found in Ina Matthews.

"This is all you found?"

"All? You wouldn't be saying that if you'd been on your hands and knees with the rest of us, sniffing under every blade of grass." Byrne's caustic comment snapped across the rectory kitchen.

"Who sent who to Aberdeen?"

"Bloody lot of good that did me. Fucking pathologists are about as easy to pin down as our fucking chief inspector. It's amazing McNab hasn't shown up, sporting a cravat like a prat for the cameras."

Byrne leaned against the counter and leisurely scratched his balls, stopping reluctantly when Mary Hodgeson bustled into the room a moment later. Byrne plucked the bag from Mornay's fingers and walked over to the housekeeper, who was standing in front of the sink.

"Have you ever seen this before?" Byrne asked, almost shoving the bag beneath the stream of steaming water she was running.

Mornay wondered if the hostility prickling from the old woman was from the shock of losing someone she knew or from the police intrusion into her kitchen.

"It's a garden marker," Mary Hodgeson said. "Looks like the ones Ina bought. Expensive."

Mary Hodgeson made *expensive* sound like a dirty word.

Byrne leaned on the counter, watching her wash the dishes. "You were up and about yesterday around six?" Byrne asked.

"That's what I told you yesterday." Mary Hodgeson wrenched the water from her dishcloth and turned to the wide worktable that dominated the center of the room. She began scrubbing its wooden top.

"I was just wondering if you'd noticed someone taking a morning stroll. Say, Ina Matthews or Anne Crownlow, perhaps the rector?"

"My answer is no different today than it was yesterday, Inspector Byrne. I saw no one. The mist was too thick."

Mrs. Hodgeson snapped the crumbs out of the cloth over the sink, and then plunged her hands into the steaming bubbles. Her hands came out lobster red with small bubbles clinging to her fingers.

The chill emanating from the broad flagstone floor wasn't nearly as frosty as the chill emanating from the small woman.

Byrne looked at Mornay and jerked his head toward the door. Outside, he lit another of Sandrington's expensive cigars. "Right bitch, she is," he said without a thought to his own aggressive demeanor.

"I spoke to Anne Crownlow," Mornay told him. "Ina Matthews's umbrella wasn't in the mudroom when she left for her morning walk yesterday."

"Is she sure?"

"I didn't ask her directly about it—I just asked her to describe the mudroom. She remembered that tarp folded beneath the bench, she described it as a crumpled box, and she remembered that the handle of the other umbrella was dark. So yes, I would tend to believe she's sure."

"All that after a second or two of walking through the room?"

"Maybe she's an exceptionally observant young woman."

"*Maybe* we'll find a treasure map that will lead to our next clue. We already know Ms. Crownlow has no problem tossing us lies; I'd rather we came up with a better witness to the contents of the mudroom. She could've planted the thing herself after she got back from her early morning stroll."

"Want me to ask Mrs. Hodgeson?"

At that moment Evan Whelan skirted one of the portable lights to reach the path leading to the rectory's entrance. He'd come from the direction of Glen Ross. Head down and shoulders hunched forward, he didn't notice them loitering on the lawn.

"Later," Byrne said. "Talk to the Tierney woman first. And take Claire; wouldn't want to scare the poor woman with your ugly mug." Byrne pinched the end off the expensive cigar and tucked the unsmoked length into his breast pocket. "I'm going to have a word with the good rector."

Jane Tierney sat in the same chair she had last night during her interview. Her hands were neatly folded in her lap, her gaze on the floor in front of her feet.

"We're going to find out eventually," Claire said. "It really is best that you tell us everything you can now."

Mornay was letting Claire do all the talking. She had a knack for putting people at ease. He remained in the background, trying to be as inconspicuous as possible.

"So I can be made a fool of in the papers?" Jane Tierney asked. "I can just imagine what they'll say." Tears glistened on her cheeks.

"Anyone who cares about you will be more concerned about you, not about what some misinformed reporters might say. That man took advantage of you because you're young."

Jane Tierney wiped at the tears. "And pathetic," she added.

"You're pathetic only if you let him get the better

of you," Claire insisted. She let the silence stretch out until Mornay's nerves were so taut he wanted to cough or make some other kind of noise to move them along.

"What do you want to know?" Jane Tierney asked. Claire's instincts were dead-on.

"What's John's real surname?"

"He said it was Buckland. John Buckland."

"How long have you known him?"

"About six months."

Claire was pacing near a bank of windows that overlooked a terraced courtyard. Spikes of lavender surrounded the courtyard. "Had he ever been in Glen Ross before?"

"He said he hadn't, but I did get the impression he had. He knew exactly where the public car park was in town, and it's not very well marked."

"Who made the reservation here?"

"I did. John said I needed to because I was using my credit card to pay for the room."

"Did he take everything he had in his holdall?"

There was a long pause. "No," Jane Tierney said finally. "He left a magazine. I'll get it."

Mornay joined Claire in pacing nervously. "Not bad," he complimented.

"You should see me in front of a live audience."

"Ouch!" He pantomimed being struck in the heart.

Jane Tierney returned with a gardening magazine simply called *Garden*. He and Claire exchanged looks. This wasn't the sort of reading material either of them imagined Buckland would choose.

"It falls open at this page." Jane opened the magazine and pointed out a crease pressed into the heavy, glossy paper.

Claire took the magazine, handling it with her fingertips.

"Look," Jane said, pointing out a small article about Ina Matthews. "It's about the woman who was attacked."

The article was a short interview. Ina Matthews's contact information, including her phone number, had been provided at the end of the article. John Buckland had circled the contact information.

"Did he meet her?" he asked.

"I don't know. He did take several long walks, alone."

"Is this all he left?" Claire asked.

"Yes."

"What about toiletries?" Mornay asked.

"Oh," Jane said, hand flying to her mouth. "I'd forgotten about those. He left everything under the sink."

"We should try and contact Inspector Byrne," Claire repeated.

"You try and reach him." Murnay slammed on the brakes. A man talking on a mobile stepped out from between two parked cars. "I should've run the fool over."

"You were driving too fast."

Mornay ground his teeth, biting back his reply. "Try Byrne one more time, and if he doesn't pick up it's not our problem. We need to get Tierney's shaving kit to Aberdeen."

"Why not let Sahotra take it?"

He turned and flashed a grin. "But then you wouldn't get a chance to meet a particular mate of mine."

"Who?"

"Patience, Claire. Patience."

chapter seven

Mornay flipped on his left turn signal and pulled off the main road onto a narrow, winding road that followed the left bank of a burbling mountain burn. His destination was near the end of the road, through a pair of stone pillars that marked the entrance to an old farm. Inside the pillars, beyond another short dry-stone wall, was a two-story cottage. The cottage had been built at the foot of the Hill of Lendrum, part of the spine of rugged mountains that made up the Grampian Highlands. A silvery mist clung to the tops of the Scots pines that forested part of the slope; the pines had been planted fifteen years earlier as part of a reforestation project. The pines brought the red deer, which brought no end of trouble to the local farmers. All this he'd discovered on his first visit. This was his fourth.

Claire sat up; she'd been dozing. "Where are we?"

"Just past Turriff. We'll only stop a minute," he said before she could protest the delay.

She spent the next few moments looking ahead. "So this is your latest discovery." She was trying not to sound impressed. "How'd you find it?"

"Advert in the Sunday paper."

"Going to set yourself up as a gentleman farmer when you retire?" she teased. "If I were to guess, I'd say the estate agent will want more for this place than a Detective Sergeant can afford."

"A bit."

"I don't suppose dreaming ever hurt anything," she murmured quietly as she took in the view.

He turned off his ignition and got out of the car. Claire followed. The air was fresh, damp, and just a bit chilly. The scent of pine was strong in the air. That was his favorite thing about this place—the clean smell.

"When was it built?"

"The original building was built in seventeen twelve. Part of the original foundation is still there. Everything else was built in the early eighteen hundreds."

"Why do you always pick the old ones?"

"Dunno," he replied, though he knew exactly why he was drawn to these old cottages. They were simple, solid, and permanent. They'd weathered wars and storms and troubles beyond his imagining and remained on. One of his commanders had lectured that permanence was an illusion for the weak, but he'd nurtured the fantasy of living somewhere exactly like this cottage for years—ever since his days in the desert chasing warlords who were as illusive as smoke. He shuddered, shaking off memories that were getting harder and harder to ignore.

"I just wanted a look, to see if it was still for sale. Time we were off." He'd never showed Victoria any of the farms he'd found; she would've urged him to take the next step. *Buy the farm. Settle down. Get on with your life.* But he couldn't get on with his life as long as those memories of the desert continued to haunt him.

On sunny days, the light reflecting off Aberdeen's famous granite buildings could blind you. The buildings of the Granite City were too bright in the sunlight and they were too dark and depressing when they were wet, he thought.

It was half past ten when they entered the Grampian Police headquarters. The reception area was empty this morning; the curved reception desk was being watched by a woman protected by bulletproof plate glass. They passed their badges through the slotted niche between glass and counter, signed in, and carried Tierney's toiletries directly to the forensics lab.

Mornay passed Tierney's kit to Claire before they entered the basement offices. "See if he can have them in the system today." It was a manageable request. "And while you're in there, ask Lothario for a copy—his copy—of Julia Whelan's lab work. I want everything, even the notes jotted on the backs of napkins." Lothario was his name for Dr. Hall's assistant, a fortysomething, bandy-legged man overly fond of plaid trousers. He also had a crush on Claire, a fact that had come in handy on more than one occasion.

"Why do you want to see an old file?"

"I was curious about Whelan, and when I dug it out I discovered half of our file is missing. You know how I hate to be kept in suspense."

"Fetch it yourself."

They'd reached the lab. "I'd have better luck prying milk out of an oyster than prying a file out of Lothario's sweaty mitts. And you know this place gives me the creepy crawlies." He glanced at the small plaque that read FORENSIC SCIENCE LABORATORY beside the large steel door and shuddered. "I barely made it outside this morning without being sick, and that was on an empty stomach."

"It's a closed case, Seth. Haven't we got enough to do on this one?"

"You'll just have to humor me. That thing that annoys you so much is happening again." She hated when he had a hunch about something, but his hunches almost always got them results. He winked.

She ignored his attempt at charm. "Why don't you trust Byrne?"

"Because he doesn't trust Andy McNab, who's probably the most thorough and conscientious police officer we've got on the force."

"They've got a long history."

"That doesn't negate the fact that McNab is good at what he does or that Byrne's unreasonably jealous of his success."

Claire spent less than fifteen minutes in the laboratory. She came out carrying a thick brown paper envelope. "He said he'll have everything done on the prints in a couple of hours, and we'll know shortly after if we get a hit on SCRO."

The Scottish Criminal Records Office maintained a database of all felons convicted in the country. While a hit on SCRO wouldn't help them find Tierney, at least they'd know *who* they were really chasing.

Mornay steered Claire toward the basement evidence room—a long, narrow, well-lit room filled with metal shelving that stored evidence from open cases. It was also a catchall room for things headquarters didn't know what to do with or didn't know where to route. The shelves were full and there appeared to be no order to the contents, but Mornay knew better. Police Sergeant Rory Williams knew exactly where to find anything anyone wanted.

Rory was at his desk, filling in a crossword. Blank boxes outnumbered the filled ones and, because Rory was using a pen, there were several overwritten letters. "That's why they invented erasers," Mornay said. "So illiterate bastards like yourself could eventually get their crosswords right."

Rory was in his early fifties; he'd reached the pinnacle of his career and was fading gracefully into his retirement years. His cheeks were gaunt and his belly was much leaner than the last time Mornay had seen him. Rory was an ace at darts and, for health reasons, had given up drinking anything stronger than milk last year. A wide grin split Rory's face when he saw who'd come to harass him. "Well, isn't this a treat. Byrne finally let you off your leash?"

"Bugger off," Mornay said, grinning back and

shaking Rory's hand. He introduced Claire and said, "I need a favor."

Rory, still grinning, looking appreciatively in Claire's direction, said, "Everyone does who comes down here. What magic trick do you want me to perform today?"

Mornay pulled out his notebook and read off a number to Rory. "It's from one of Byrne's cases, about two years back. I need to see the contents."

"It won't be stored here" was Rory's immediate reply.

"It was returned to the lab and never made it back to our office," Mornay told him.

Rory's eyes narrowed, as if he couldn't believe such a thing possible. "Was it lost in the fire?"

A fire had destroyed the original police office in Banff almost three years earlier. A temporary office had been established in a vacant building across the harbor, in Macduff. The move was not well received in Banff, but the force didn't want to go to the bother and expense of moving the office back.

"This happened after the fire," he told Rory.

"You have a look in Peterhead? This case happened before they opened the office in Macduff." As Rory spoke he typed in his password, and his screen filled with a chain-of-evidence list for Julia Whelan's inquiry. Rory glanced at him. "You're right. You're lucky it's still here. Another month, and it'd be archived and shipped off to Peterhead's basement."

"Can you print that out for me?"

"Why don't you just talk to Byrne?" Then Rory nodded. "Right, you're no wanting the wee fireplug to know." He grinned. "You *are* lucky; you wouldn't have been able to get to it in Peterhead without Byrne finding out."

He hit the Print icon and bustled off to begin his search. Claire looked supremely bored, but Mornay knew it was an act. She just didn't want to admit she was curious.

"Lydia Sandrington was tense today," she said.

"She was nervous as a Hibs fan in Glasgow."

Claire made a sound at the back of her throat.

Rather than argue football clubs and their merits, or lack of merits, he said, "Maybe Byrne knows something we don't. Or, maybe she's worried about keeping the crowds under control at her flower show."

"I was making a valid observation."

"Here we are, then." Rory returned with a paper sack. Inside, bagged in clear plastic, were the clothes Julia Whelan had worn the day she took her sleeping pills. "Since we're doing this quietlike, mind you bring these back by next Wednesday. That's my last shift before my holiday."

Out in the hall, Claire asked, "What will you do if you find something odd in the paperwork?" Mornay had tucked the bundle of evidence under his arm, along with the copies of Julia Whelan's files.

"I don't know."

"So this has nothing to do with the fact that Byrne hates you and would be more than happy to see the back of you? But not if you get rid of him first?"

"This is a separate issue from my problems with Byrne."

Claire laughed aloud. "Like hell it is. Finding out

he bollocked an old case might just get him an early retirement."

"Sergeant Mornay." Dr. Hall's deep voice rumbled behind them. "Since you're here, you can be the first to see the results of Ina Matthews's blood-work."

Mornay held his breath, literally, as he and Claire followed Dr. Hall through a short hallway and into his office. He'd been in cars with more elbowroom than Dr. Hall's office.

Not wanting to linger any longer than necessary, Mornay asked, "Have you ruled out the possibility that the wounds on Ina Matthews's face were caused by a broken bottle?"

"Tommy Torga style?"

"Exactly."

"Not yet. I did find several small fragments in the deepest lacerations, and in my opinion they're rust. But it's possible they're colored glass. We won't know until tomorrow. There were also traces of oil on her skin, particularly her right forearm, and a smudge of oil on her jumper."

"Baby oil?" Mornay asked.

"Petroleum oil—something not very refined, like automotive oil. Here." Dr. Hall passed him a photograph. "These are what I want you to see."

Mornay stared at the strange picture for a moment. "Is this Ina Matthews's blood?"

"Her red blood cells, to be exact. This is a textbook example of hemolysis."

"Is that hereditary?" Claire asked, taking the photograph from Mornay.

"It's a condition. Red blood cells normally live for

110 to 120 days. When they die, they're broken down and the spleen cleans out all the bits. Hemolysis is the premature breakdown of red blood cells, which leaves fewer cells than normal to transport oxygen. One of its symptoms is anemia. Ina Matthews had a lowered red blood cell count."

"A condition caused by what?" Mornay asked.

Dr. Hall gathered up the glossy photographs, handling them with something close to reverence. "In Ina Matthews's case, this condition was caused by ricin, which inhibits protein synthesis and can cause death within hours."

"She was being poisoned?" Mornay asked.

"Ricin is one of the most powerful cytotoxins in nature. One milligram of ricin can kill an adult. The symptoms usually begin within a few hours of ingestion. There's abdominal pain and vomiting. Within days, there's severe dehydration and a decrease in urine. If death doesn't occur in three to five days, the victim usually recovers. Ina Matthews was clearly recovering, which makes me wonder how she came in contact with it."

"Where does this toxin come from?"

"Castor beans."

"Ina was an avid gardener; she would know that castor beans are poisonous," Claire said.

Dr. Hall nodded. "Indeed she would. Which means someone else gave it to her."

"Poisoned?" Chief Inspector McNab repeated. He was holding one of the photographs Dr. Hall had released. They'd run into McNab on their way to Mornay's car. He'd offered to buy them lunch.

"For as long as a month," Mornay said. "Dr. Hall's pulling more tests so we'll have more information by this evening's briefing, but he's already spoken to her doctor and discovered she's been in twice during the last four weeks complaining of fatigue. Fatigue is one of the symptoms of anemia."

They were walking to a small café that specialized in Eastern food, just around the corner from headquarters. They'd arrived ahead of the lunch hour crowd and picked a table in front of the restaurant's only window.

"Her doctor didn't draw blood when she was in?"

"No. He thought she was overexerting herself, preparing for the flower show."

The waitress took their drink orders, coffees all around, and pointed out the menus printed on bookmark-sized slips of paper.

"Have you read this morning's *P and J*?" McNab asked.

Rather than admit he never read the *Press and Journal*, Mornay said, "No time."

"They're claiming Tommy Torga corresponded regularly with his aunt in Fyvie."

"Anyone see him there?"

The waitress arrived with their drinks and left with their lunch orders.

"A dozen are claiming they have. Peterhead is going to juggle those interviews, which will leave us to concentrate on Tierney." McNab held up a hand before either of them could protest. "Not a word. We need the manpower and this is the best way to ensure you two stay in the thick of it. Has Forensics given you any indication when they'll know if the garden stake was what used to inflict the damage to our victim's face?"

"The stake's not a practical weapon," Claire said. "It didn't look sharp enough to cut butter."

Mornay emptied the contents of three sugar packets into his coffee. "Hall isn't committing himself just yet. But why would our man take only one weapon and leave the other?"

Claire broke in correcting Mornay, "A woman could have just as easily committed this crime."

"The stabbing maybe, but Ina Matthews was a tall woman weighing nearly nine stone."

"You don't think a woman could have dragged a body three meters to hide it? An unconscious woman being dragged under the arms? A child could have probably moved her."

Mornay looked to McNab for help, and his boss shrugged. He was willing to let Claire think aloud.

"A woman didn't stab Ina Matthews," Mornay insisted. "She would've had to have been an amazon. There are no women like that in Glen Ross."

"What if the killer used the twine to trip her first, then gave the blow to the back of the head to stun her, and then attacked?"

"Then why take this mystery knife and leave the stake?"

"Easy," Claire said. "Heat of the moment, tall grass and thick fog. The attacker probably didn't want to take the time to look for the bit that was dropped."

"What happened to the mackintosh?" McNab wanted to know.

"Maybe the killer took it to cover bloodstains on

his or her clothes," Claire offered. "I don't know why else it would've been taken from Ina."

"Maybe that's why she was turned over," McNab added. "To get it off."

The arrival of their food saved Mornay from having to offer his own opinion.

Inspector McNab cut at his food with the edge of his fork and casually asked, "How are things going between you and Inspector Byrne?"

"Nearly civilized, sir."

"Keep it that way." McNab held up his fork. "I know he's the one that took the first swing last time."

"Both times, sir."

"Both times," McNab conceded. "He never used to be so hotheaded."

He's making up for it now. Mornay kept the thought to himself.

"Did you know he was best man at my wedding?" McNab continued.

Mornay glanced across the table to Claire. She lifted a shoulder, telling him she didn't know where McNab was going, either.

"So you were close. What happened?" Mornay asked. Claire lowered her head, concentrating on her curried potatoes.

"There was no single incident. I just always seemed to be promoted ahead of him." McNab held Mornay's gaze for several beats. "Inspector Byrne is very good at his job. He just doesn't get on with people, and his career has suffered for it. A good police officer needs to work well with a team. Do you get my meaning?"

"Yes, sir," Mornay said, glad he'd thought to put the evidence he'd "acquired" in the boot of his car before coming to the restaurant. Having McNab find it right about now wouldn't square well with his teamwork lecture.

"Have you brought any news?" Sarah Jenkins asked Mornay. Her voice was breathless, anxious. Her eyes were red rimmed. Sunlight from the window above the sink glistened across her narrow kitchen.

"We'll have more information later this afternoon."

She'd been cleaning; her bucket of rinse water was still on the floor and ammonia fumes filled the room. She followed his glance to the bucket. "I was trying to cut the scent of the roses. But you have to use so much ammonia, it's nearly impossible to breathe. Let's go into the garden. There's a bench; it might be more comfortable there."

Sarah sat on the garden bench while Mornay pulled out his notebook and studied the garden. Every leaf and flower and stem glimmered beneath the soft early-afternoon light. The lawn was a minimal swath of green that curved in a half-moon away from the bench. Three cobblestone paths radiated from this moon. At the back of the property was a glass-walled greenhouse that must have cost a fortune to maintain.

"Have you seen this before?" Mornay passed her a photograph of the stake fragment found that morning.

She held the photograph with two hands, rubbing the shiny surface back and forth with her thumbs. "Was this in the cemetery?" she asked.

Mornay chose to answer the question indirectly. "It was found during our search. Mary Hodgeson said it might have belonged to your cousin."

Sarah blew out a huff of breath. "Might have? Mary Hodgeson knows good and well this was one of Ina's markers. That woman told Ina not two months ago she was throwing away good money buying them."

"Markers? What did she use them for?"

Sarah stood and walked across the lawn to the closest flowerbed. She bent at the waist and pulled something from the ground: a brass stake, ten inches long, topped with a brass oval. Inside the oval was a flat piece of copper meant to be written on, the pressure of the writing denting the soft metal. Save for some inevitable oxidation, which gave the marker a rustic look, the marker was impervious to the elements.

The oval piece of marker found that morning in the cemetery was missing its bit of copper.

Mornay took the stake and ran his fingers down its length, brushing away the clumps of damp soil. It appeared identical to the stake Dr. Hall had pulled out of Ina Matthews.

"It's fluted, for strength," she explained. "There are stones in the soil. Ina kept all her plants marked in case someone else walked through and wanted to know their names. Not that anyone did; no one else was quite as keen on gardening."

"Do you have any of these markers that haven't been used?"

"Probably. Somewhere in the shed."

Ina Matthews kept her shed as pristine as some

women kept their kitchens. Empty flats used to hold young plants were stacked waist high next to the door. Pots of every size were neatly arranged beneath a narrow wooden potting bench. The markers were on a shelf above the bench.

Mornay took one of the new markers. "Any way to tell if one of these is missing from the garden?" he asked.

Sarah shook her head. "Ina would be the only one to know."

A door led from the shed into the greenhouse. Curious, Mornay wandered through. It was much warmer beneath the glass. The greenhouse was ten or so meters long and as cramped with potted plants and flats as the shed was with empty ones. What couldn't fit on the two tables running its length hung from the center beam or was shoved beneath the long tables creating the center aisle. There was another narrow aisle along the side walls, just wide enough to allow someone to walk down. From his battles with the old rose at Victoria's door, Mornay recognized the five-leafed clusters; the greenhouse was a rose nursery. It appeared to hold plants of every age.

On the end of the table to Mornay's left, the neatly arranged rows were pushed back to make room for several dozen small, bell-shaped vases with clear marbles at their bottoms. Each vase held a small clump of pale pink roses. The rose stems had been trimmed short and were pushed into the marbles to keep them upright.

Victoria would have loved it in here, Mornay thought—the roses, the sun, the thick earthy scent. "Pretty," he said, for lack of a better way to explain his thoughts when he looked up and found Sarah Jenkins watching him idly rubbing the petals of one of the pink roses.

"Never thought so myself," she said. "I've never been keen on roses—or any plants, for that matter. Not like Ina. Or the rest of her horticultural friends."

"Big, are they? On plants?"

"Positively batty." Sarah swept her hand out, indicating the room. "So batty that Ina created her own rose—as if we didn't have enough already. You're looking at nearly twenty years of work."

Stones crunched underneath his feet as he strolled down the center aisle. Twenty years of work. For Ina Matthews, that was more than half her life. His father, a boat builder for the last forty years, was the only other person he knew that could claim to look at twenty years of work in a single sweeping glance. In his father's case, all he needed to do was look across the boats moored in the Macduff harbor. Sometimes Mornay wondered if he'd be happier if he'd chosen professions that created something more tangible than statistics. The new job had him creating statistics on the Chief Constables Annual Report; the old one had him creating statistics that were a matter of national security. He thought about the reports he'd had printed out that morning.

"Out of curiosity, did you or your cousin ever speak with Inspector Byrne during his inquiry into Julia Whelan's suicide?"

"Why?"

"Gathering more background information. I just need to get a clearer picture of your cousin." Mornay smiled wryly. "Inspector Byrne can sometimes form opinions about people that aren't necessarily accurate."

Sarah returned his smile. "So I gathered the first time I met him, but he was kind yesterday." She leaned against a table. "Your Inspector Byrne and Ina didn't get on when he was here about Julia. And I must tell you, when I heard he was in charge of Ina's inquiry, I had my doubts. The last time they spoke, he threatened to arrest her for harassment if she didn't stop calling him."

"Why was she calling him?"

"Ina thought the inquiry into Julia's death was getting buggered. Her words, not mine. She called your inspector every day after poor Evan found Julia. A week or so after Julia died, Inspector Byrne finally stopped by and listened to what Ina had to say. Then he told her the inquiry had already been closed and there was nothing more he could do. I've never seen her so angry." Sarah starting fanning herself with a hand. "Called him incompetent and a few other things besides."

Mornay reached toward the end of the table and plucked a pink rose out of one of the vases. The flower was dainty and had a sweet scent. "Was your cousin carrying flowers with her yesterday? Roses?"

"Yes. Ina was taking some of those to show Lydia Sandrington. They were to be used as the centerpieces on the banquet tables at the flower show. They were the ones she was going to enter in the show."

Why hadn't they found roses near the body? Why had he only found a single petal?

"Why did she want to enter a contest?" he asked.

Sarah continued to stare at the vases, grief etched in every line on her face. "It was to be the first time she'd exhibited her new rose to the public." Sarah sighed. "She wanted to win Best of Show."

Chapter Eight

Evan didn't open the curtains in his room. He didn't want to let in the bright noonday sun. Instead he switched on the lamp and sat on his bed, staring at the fuzzy layer of dust coating the books on his bed stand.

It was childish to try to block the view of the police milling around on the lawn or to think the layers of dust on his favorite books would insulate him for any length of time. The sound of knuckles rapping loudly on his door startled him, though he'd been waiting for it, hadn't he? It was how he lived his life now—waiting for what would come next. He tried to prepare himself, but he always managed to be caught unawares.

Inspector Byrne strolled into Evan's bedroom,

sprinkling ashes like holy water and profanities like newly ordained priests granted absolution.

"What a fucking mausoleum." Byrne stood in the center of the room and turned in a slow circle. He plucked the dangling cigar from his mouth and pointed it at Evan. "You must barricade the door to keep Hodgeson out. Mind you, she'd have to use a bloody chisel on the dust in those corners."

Inspector Byrne still wore his mackintosh, though there was no hint of rain today. It was a useful place to shove his hands when his natural instincts were to put them around the neck of whomever he was questioning and squeeze out the truth. Byrne was a natural predator, and after twenty-odd years on the force, he could sense weakness like gardeners sensed a change in the weather.

"What are these?" Byrne toed one of the stacks of books Evan had sorted in various piles on the floor. "More potty poets?" He shoved the cigar between his teeth and peered at the book spines of the nearest pile. "Oscar Wilde? Wasn't he one of those queer bastards?"

Evan didn't answer.

Byrne squinted through the cigar smoke he was filling the room with and asked, "What was the nature of your relationship with Ina Matthews?"

"We were friends."

"Friends?" Byrne scrunched his scraggly brows at the word and shoved his hands further into his pocket. "Close friends?"

"We weren't lovers. That should save you half a dozen not-so-carefully-framed questions. Not that you've ever bothered with them in the past."

Byrne rounded Evan's bed and peered at a picture of his wife on the nightstand. "Oh, well—not so bad then, is it? Business as usual after the funeral, aye? And you've a guest to occupy your . . . attention."

Byrne's crude innuendos caused sweat to break out along Evan's lip. He curled his hands into the wrinkled duvet. Ina's body would be released soon. Sarah wanted a memorial service, wanted him to produce a pat summation of Ina's life to give comfort to those she'd left behind. Evan was barely able to unclench his jaws to speak. "My grief is not lessened by the absence of a physical relationship, Inspector. Ina was the dearest friend I've ever known."

"And you didn't sleep with her? Not once? Hard to believe that. Handsome woman, she was, if you could get around that bloody temper of hers. Me, I'd have had a go at her."

"I find your preoccupation over my celibacy revolting, Inspector Byrne. Your lack of compassion is insulting."

Byrne pulled the cigar out of his mouth, his hatred so close to the surface of his skin, Evan could smell it. "I couldn't give two shites what you think, laddie. You and your father and those lawyers of his in their fancy braces bollocked my inquiry the last time I was in this bloody village. You're not going to bollock this one." Ashes fell from the cigar clenched between Byrne's fingers as he pointed at Evan. "You were seen at the Hall yesterday around six, but, curiously, you didn't arrive to work in the kitchen there until nearly seven. You returned to the rectory in time to be told by Anne Crownlow that she'd found a body. At that point, Ina Matthews had been laying on the ground at least a couple of hours. Which means that you had ample opportunity to kill her, since we've got an entire hour unaccounted for. It's just a matter of time before I find the motive. And when I do, it won't matter how many lawyers your father dangles in front of the chief constable. They won't be able to help you this time."

Everything seemed to zoom away from Evan as he gripped the duvet even tighter. He could hear material ripping faintly as he thought about Ina's common sense and humor; they'd made his dreary days pass, if not pleasantly by, then at least mercifully quick. Evan's vision blurred black at the edges, his heartbeat punctuated each breath he labored to take, and beyond it all, the foul little man continued to cast insults.

Evan stared at Byrne as the extremes of emotion compressed into a space too small to contain them. Later, he couldn't remember how he managed to leap across the bed and knock Inspector Byrne into the narrow space between his desk and the wall. Though Byrne managed to throw in some of his own punches, Evan pummeled him until Sergeant Mornay ended the fight.

Evan, exhausted both mentally and physically at that point, collapsed at the foot of his bed as his room quickly filled with police officers. Someone put handcuffs on him, while Byrne waved away a redheaded woman's attempt to clean the blood off of his face.

As Mornay watched Whelan being handcuffed, he thought the rector looked like a man about to go over the edge. Whelan's skin was pale and damp from sweat. His eyes were vacant.

"I'm fine," Byrne growled when Claire tried to hand him a folded hankie to use for his bleeding nose. Claire continued to hover in front of Byrne, trying to be helpful. Mornay could have told her she was wasting her time, but being helpful was a compulsion she couldn't seem to control.

"Jesus fucking Christ, do I have to say it twice?" Byrne bellowed at her.

He turned his anger on Dunnholland when the hapless constable stood the rector up, steering him gently at the elbow. "Watch it, man! He's dangerous."

It was like a bull terrier being frightened of a sparrow. The rector was stooped over like a man twice his age, and Mornay remembered something he'd learned while training against terrorists. "He's not dangerous, Inspector—but even rabbits attack when they're cornered."

As Claire followed Dunnholland and the rector out of the room, Byrne scowled. "But rabbits don't tell lies to cover their tracks, now, do they? They leave their tracks where they made them. That bastard lied to us yesterday."

Mornay and Byrne walked into the hall. They heard a door slam downstairs.

"He wasn't the only one to lie," Mornay pointed out. "It seems everyone's been lying to us. Tidmarsh and Sarah Jenkins might be our only exceptions. But I wouldn't hold my breath."

Byrne made a noncommittal grunt.

"Are you going to charge Whelan?"

Byrne's mirthless laugh floated up as he started down the backstairs. The wooden treads, covered by a thin wool runner, creaked beneath their weight. "Bloody fucking right, I'm going to charge him. I'll start with aggravated assault, and maybe I'll end up with a confession to murder when I'm through with him, sometime early tomorrow morning. Did you see his face? He looked as guilty as anyone I've ever seen."

"How did he act when you questioned him during your inquiry into his wife's death?"

Byrne stopped dabbing at his nose with his handkerchief. "Who's been talking? McNab?"

Surprised at the sudden caution in Byrne's voice, Mornay paused on the bottom step, looking down at Byrne, who, bald spot exposed, seemed curiously vulnerable.

"Sarah Jenkins," Mornay said. "She told me how furious Ina was about the manner in which Julia Whelan's death was being investigated."

"Did she, now?" Byrne rubbed the back of his neck. He leaned against the wall and looked down the hall at the front door. "Sarah Jenkins is nothing but a silly old woman, but her cousin—what a temper she had! Called me a 'pontificating bastard.' "

"What did Whelan have to say?"

"He was like a man sleepwalking." Byrne slid his gaze to Mornay. "The woman killed herself. She was depressed. Had been for weeks. As soon as her husband left town for a conference, she popped a month's worth of tranquilizers. Open and shut."

"But you ordered additional forensic tests. Why would you do that if the case was so clearly an open-and-shut suicide?"

"Lydia Sandrington isn't the only person with her nose up the chief constable's arse. Whelan's father was old chums with our esteemed former chief constable. The good rector's father had high-priced solicitors circling Headquarters. After I discovered inconsistencies in the woman's past, I was told to pack it in or I'd be spending my remaining years on the force strapped to a North Sea oil rig, waiting for a suspicious gull to flap past." Byrne's features melded into the angry mask that he usually wore when making acid-etched comments about McNab.

There was the unmistakable sound of a creaking floorboard on the landing above them, but Byrne didn't seem to notice.

"What sort of inconsistencies?" Mornay asked, rather than listen to Byrne spout on about political intrigue on the force.

"Like, she had no past—not with the maiden name Julia Brenner, which was on her marriage license. She had no national insurance, no bank accounts, no credit cards, no police record—nothing. I even ran her prints through SCRO and found nothing, which only tells us she's never been arrested for a felony. She was a temporary hired by Harrods to work the perfume counter three days a week. She'd worked a total of six days before she met and married Evan Whelan."

"What did the rector say about this?"

Byrne gently probed around his right eye, feeling how extensive the swelling was; the eye was already half shut. "Sod all. Said he didn't know anything about her past. Didn't want to know."

Maybe he should've treaded more lightly, but curiosity drove Mornay to ask, "Did you bother to find out why Ina Matthews was calling? Sarah said she called several times every day for nearly a week, and then, when you came, the case was already closed."

If Mornay harbored any shred of respect for Byrne, it was washed away beneath a wave of contempt as the fat little man laughed heartily. "It was a suicide. Open and shut. Her calls had no bearing."

Mornay used his height and the added inches of the stair to loom over Byrne. "You had a close friend who had information about the case. How can that have no bearing?"

Byrne pressed his lips together into a narrow band of white flesh and held Mornay's gaze for another moment or two. Then he turned and, without a word, stomped down the hall.

Mornay watched him slam the front door, wondering what the hell had just happened. He'd been prepared to accept whatever Byrne told him, but after Byrne's strange behavior, he was even more curious about Julia Whelan's case.

Was that why he didn't tell Byrne about the roses? *Maybe you're afraid of what he won't say, rather than what he would.*

Another floorboard creaked upstairs.

Mornay caught Anne Crownlow by the arm just as she was darting back into her room. He scowled at her with unblinking dark eyes, then pulled her into her room, wondering exactly how much of the conversation she had heard.

"Why were you eavesdropping?"

She crossed her arms and stared at the center of his chest. She was pale, except where her pillow had pressed red wrinkles into her cheeks. "I didn't do it on purpose. But I could hardly keep walking after I stepped on the creaky floorboard, could I?"

Mornay didn't believe her for a moment. Not after what Tidmarsh had told them.

"The crashing and banging woke me," she explained. "After everything got quiet, I thought it would be safe to come out." Her expression clouded. "You don't think Julia Whelan killed herself, do you?"

The question came out quietly, almost hesitantly. It surprised him.

"Did you know her?" he asked.

Her head snapped up quickly and what little color there was in her lips disappeared. "Of course not," she said quickly. "But I've seen her gravestone and heard a few things in the village."

She'd just lied to him; he could tell from the way she'd dropped her gaze. She'd done the same thing yesterday when he'd asked her about the time she'd left for her walk. He shoved his hands in his pockets and pretended he didn't notice.

"What else, besides banging and crashing, did you hear?"

"I heard Inspector Byrne shouting. He was going on about a bollocked investigation. Then there was quiet and then he said something about motive. That's when the crashing started."

Mornay scratched at the stubble on his chin. Despite his own run-ins with Byrne, he was surprised by the inspector's bullying tactics. His mind whirred around in useless circles. He needed more caffeine.

Anne's scuffed, damp sneakers lay on their side near the bed. Mornay picked them up and tossed them to her. "Let's see if we can find some coffee."

Anne sat in the front seat, but had to lie down with Mornay's jacket covering her to get through the front gates. "So the reporters don't follow us," he explained.

After the gates were successfully maneuvered, she sat up. Mornay watched the traffic pass on the narrow road. What had been a wall of gray yesterday was now fields and trees and boulders dotting the rolling green hills. To the west, over his shoulder, the hills rose and faded into the purplish haze of the mountains.

Glen Ross looked picturesque in the sunshine, its buildings gathered around the tree-lined square. A large church sat like a grand patriarch at the far end of the square; its bell towers and stained glass gleamed in the sun. Flanking the church were several narrowly built homes. The post office, butcher, green grocer, and pub were huddled together at the oppo-site end of the square in squat, functional buildings. Cars lined both sides of the road. The pub, the only place to eat, was overflowing.

"I don't want to go in there," Anne said before Mornay could search for a parking spot. "Too many people."

"All right." Hunger and disappointment clawed at Mornay in equal proportions. At this point, he would willingly trade a week's worth of meals for a single cup of coffee. "Still want coffee?"

She nodded.

Nearly half an hour later, they parked in front of his house. He was conscious of the dust and unpacked boxes as he led Anne into his minuscule kitchen. An inspection of his cupboards revealed no coffee.

Anne opened his small icebox.

"What about these?" she asked. She brought out two cans of Tennent's Lager.

"It'll have to do." He took one of the cans. "Want a glass?"

"Don't bother," she said. She popped the tab and took a long pull from her lager. He did the same.

He watched her examine his kitchen. White pressed-wood cabinets ran the length of two walls, forming an L. A dusty coffeepot was shoved in the shadowed corner of the dingy yellow counter. At the sight of the crusty plates stacked in the sink, Anne wrinkled her nose.

"I survive on take-away," he explained.

"Understandable."

Then she turned and looked directly into his eyes. She seemed to be holding back a smile. How had she suddenly become so self-assured? She put her can down without taking another sip, continuing to hold his gaze.

A familiar rush of warmth flooded through his body, and he shifted his attention to the tops of his mud-splattered shoes. The last thing he needed was more trouble with a woman, particularly one involved with a case.

But why not?

The thought refused to go away.

"Do I get a tour?" she asked.

"There's not much to see."

The corner of her mouth quirked up as if she were holding back a sly smile. "Then we'll have plenty of time left, won't we?"

It was that smile that did it.

"The chief constable frowns on fraternization during lunch," he said with mock seriousness, already calculating how much time he could spare.

"Then forget you're a detective sergeant for a couple of hours."

He grinned. "We can only spare an hour."

The sly smile emerged fully, lifting both corners of her mouth. "Then why are we wasting time chatting?"

Their hour was gone by the time they'd both showered and returned to the kitchen to finish their lagers. He was dressed in a pair of Levis so well worn they were more white than blue, and Anne wore one of his old jerseys.

He smiled at her.

"What?" she asked.

The kitchen door banged open.

A slim, dark-haired young woman wearing heavy black clogs clomped into the kitchen. She wore a cropped, neon-pink cotton tank top, which showcased her tapered midriff and full breasts. A faded pair of denim shorts, their cuffs rolled to her crotch, showed off her long legs.

"Fucking cozy, this," the girl said. "Don't waste time, do you, Seth?"

Mornay put his lager down and combed his damp hair off his forehead. Pamela, Victoria's sister, wobbled across the floor until she towered in front of Anne. Pamela let her gaze slowly go up and down Anne's body, and her lip curled back. "You aren't his type."

Anne's movements only emphasized the fact that she had nothing on beneath the shirt. This didn't go unnoticed by Pamela, however high and drunk she was.

"I imagine you're quite the authority," Anne replied calmly. Then, with a lengthy glance at the cleavage threatening to topple out the front of Pamela's top, she said, "On at least one subject."

Pamela's lower lip pushed out a bit further. She wasn't so thick to realize she'd been insulted. "Seth don't like his women to just sit on it."

"Where've you been? Victoria's sick with worry," Mornay managed to interject.

"Fat cow's always worried about something."

Mornay crossed the room and took Pamela by the shoulders, looking into her eyes. "You've been drinking."

Pamela threw her head back and laughed. "That's not all I've been doing." She slithered her body against his, trying to rub his crotch with her hip.

Mornay roughly wheeled her around by the shoulders and kept her from toppling over when her feet couldn't keep up with the sudden change in direction. Then he pushed her through the door.

A glossy black Saab was parked at the curb behind Mornay's house. The Saab's driver wore dark glasses and slouched down into the seat when he saw Mornay.

"Who's this?" Mornay growled into Pamela's ear.

"I don't waste time, either."

Mornay was tempted to smack the sneer off of Pamela's petulant, overly made-up face. Was she too high to remember she was pregnant? Contempt, as much for himself as for her, welled up like bile in his throat. He pushed Pamela around the Saab, where he opened the passenger door and bent down to look at the driver. The whippet-thin man, his Adam's apple jerking spastically, looked as if he'd rather make a run for it than finish whatever business Pamela had talked him into doing here. They'd probably intended to go through his house and see if there was anything worth stealing.

Whippet man looked old enough to be Pamela's father, Mornay thought. But then, technically *he* was old enough to be her father.

"Didn't she tell you I'm a cop?"

No reply.

Mornay stabbed his finger at him. "I'll be seeing you later. Count on it."

Whippet man pressed further against his door with a squeak. Mornay pushed Pamela's head down and put her into the Saab, though she clawed at his chest with her nails and screeched into his face.

He slammed the door and walked around the Saab to read its reg number, memorizing it as Pamela's new man gunned the engine. He could hear Pamela

screaming above the engine noises. She'd turned her
attack on whippet man, swatting him with the flats of
her palms. Despite the barrage, he managed to shift
into first gear, sending the Saab lurching away from
the curb with a squeal of tires.

chapter nine

Back inside, Mornay found Anne in the lounge. Like the rest of his house, it was dismal and small. It had one chair and one lamp. His television sat on the box it'd come packed in, and he was using a carton of books as an end table.

Anne was studying a picture of him and Victoria taken over fifteen years ago. In the picture they held a string of small fish between them and were grinning like idiots. His chest wasn't quite as broad nor the hair on it quite as abundant as it was now. And his face was different; his nose wasn't flattened and pushed off to one side, and his cheekbones were symmetrical and less angular than they were now. There were no scars on his body. Victoria was thinner and looked relaxed. She was smiling.

The picture had been taken years before reality had

intruded on their dreams—which was why he kept it out. He liked to remind himself there was a time when he used to have hopes and aspirations beyond making it through to the end of the day without being haunted by faces and places he was desperate to forget.

"Sorry about that," he told Anne.

Anne turned. She studied the scars on his chest, comparing this man to the younger one in the picture. "You must have some interesting stories to tell. You've been shot."

"Souvenirs from my Royal Marine days." It was his standard response to any question regarding his scars, even to Victoria. Which was one of the reasons she was so angry with him.

To forestall any further questions about scars or former lovers, he put a hand at the small of her back and gently pushed her in the direction of his bedroom. "Time we were both dressed. You first. I've a call to make."

Mornay found his mobile in the pocket of his still damp wool jacket. He'd hung the jacket over the back of one of the dinette chairs in the hopes it would dry before he needed to wear it again; his other suits were at the cleaners.

He called the station and asked for Claire. When she came on the line, he said, "I need you to call one of your pals at Traffic and have them find this car." He recited the Saab's description and reg number. "It's just pulled away from my house. The driver and the passenger have been drinking."

She put him on hold. "You're at home?" she asked when she came back on. The question was more tentative than was Claire's usual style.

"Getting dry clothes."

There was a pause. "Dunnholland said he saw you leave with Anne Crownlow ages ago. Is she with you?"

Mornay debated lying but decided honesty would be the fastest way to close the conversation. "Yes."

There was another, lengthier pause. "I don't want to know."

"Then don't ask."

"Have you gone completely fucking mad?" she whispered urgently into the receiver.

Mornay didn't correct the accusation. In the two years they'd been working together, he'd heard Claire say *fuck* only twice before. She'd said it the first two times in reaction to being groped by Byrne in the storage room.

"We're not going to discuss it."

"Unfortunately for you, we're going to have to discuss Anne Crownlow. She's not at university and Crownlow isn't her real name."

"How'd you find that out?"

"The old-fashioned way—harassing people on the telephone. Except I think I've stepped in a nest of nasty-tempered lawyers. I haven't been able to find Byrne to tell him, so I'm telling you now."

"Lawyers?"

"Try to keep up. They're going straight to Aberdeen with their concerns that I'll—we'll—libel their client."

Christ, he could've used more sleep. He felt foggy and disconnected. "How did you find out she had lawyers?"

"I faxed her photograph to the registrar's office

at Edinburgh University. He told me who she was."

He didn't want to know but asked anyway. "Who is she?"

"Are you sitting down?"

"Get on with it, Claire," Mornay growled.

"It appears our Anne Crownlow is really Anne Knightsbridge. And the answer is yes, she belongs to *that* Knightsbridge family. Crownlow is her mother's maiden name. I've just spent the past fifteen minutes being threatened by her pack of solicitors."

"Claire, you really should take the act on the road. You're wasting your talent in Macduff."

"Let's hope I'm not wasting it working with you" was her quiet reply. "This isn't a joke, Seth."

Why would a woman with her wealth and family connections bother to seduce him? He didn't want to know the answer. "What brought her to Glen Ross?"

"Julia Whelan." She let him stew on that for a moment. "Anne was adopted at the age of two. When she turned twenty-one, she was told about the adoption and that she had a sister. The solicitors never knew what Anne's surname was; all they could tell her was that her sister was named Julia. That, and they had an old picture. They should be faxing me a copy of the picture any minute now. Anne's been spending a small fortune on private investigators searching for her sister."

"When did she turn twenty-one?"

"Nearly two months ago."

"And she thinks Julia Whelan was her sister? How does she know she's got the right person? People change their names."

"Apparently Julia Whelan had a birthmark. The solicitor I spoke with at first—the nice one—said it was one of the identifying marks they used to narrow their search."

"The birthmark was listed in a police report. How were they able to search police reports?"

"Money, money, money."

What had he gotten himself into now?

Claire continued rolling out the good news. "This solicitor said Anne was going to have her sister's body exhumed so they could perform DNA tests. But now they're considering having the force turn over that bag of goodies your friend Rory gave us, since there's hair samples inside. They can use those for the DNA tests."

"All this in two months?"

"It gets worse. Dunnholland has taken a statement from one of the other gardeners that works at Sandrington Hall. Seems the man overheard an argument that took place three days ago, in Ina Matthews's greenhouse. He heard Ina Matthews and Anne Knightsbridge arguing loudly."

"He's sure about who he heard?"

"Positive. I wouldn't be surprised if Byrne takes her in for formal questioning."

"He's not going to do that if he's not sure he can charge her."

"How hard would that be?" she asked. "Anne was in the cemetery at the right time and lied about it. She's young. She's strong. She was in town long enough to plan the perfect time to commit the crime."

"Ina Matthews had been getting poisoned for a

month, at least." Mornay closed his eyes and sank into one of the kitchen chairs. "There's no clear motive. What was her connection to Ina Matthews beyond an argument? We'll never get beyond the initial interview if we don't have an answer to that question."

"Maybe Forensics will find something that connects them when they go through Sarah Jenkins's house to look for poisoned food."

"Did the gardener hear what the argument was about?"

"He heard Evan Whelan's name mentioned several times."

Mornay looked up and found Anne Knightsbridge watching him from the doorway. God only knew how long she'd been standing there.

"Right," he said to Claire, all business. "I'll get back soon. I want a word with that gardener."

"Care to share?"

"Not right now. I'll have the mobile if you need to reach me." He flipped his mobile closed and absently stuffed it into one of the pockets in his jacket.

"You're not in trouble for taking a long lunch, are you?" Anne asked.

"There are all kinds of trouble, Anne. Tell me about the argument you had with Ina Matthews the day before she was killed. Then tell me why you pretended not to know who she was after you'd found her body."

There was no indication that Anne was surprised by his questions. She was far too intelligent not to realize the implications behind the questions, yet her control over her emotions was remarkable.

"Ina insulted me," Anne said. "She insinuated that I was taking advantage of a lonely widower."

"What tale did you spin for her? The one about the university student? Or were you more inventive?"

Again there was absolutely no change in her expression. It was a more telling reaction than she could ever realize.

"It was naive of you to assume we wouldn't discover who you really were, Ms. Knightsbridge."

"Aliases make life simpler for me."

He stood. "Be thankful you've a life left to complicate."

"You're not going to keep on with the Ms. Knightsbridge bit, are you, Seth?"

He crossed the kitchen, pausing in the doorway, looking down at her. "Would you prefer 'potential accused'?"

There was the slightest of flushes on her cheeks. "So you're going to arrest me?"

"Not at the moment." He held her gaze.

"You're a bastard," she hissed.

"Knowing my mother's reputation," he said over his shoulder as he walked to his bedroom, "that's a distinct possibility."

Gregor Sandrington watched flower show attendees milling on Sandrington Hall's wide green lawns like overfed ants as he sipped champagne. He sat in his mother's study—for the privacy, not the view. The record-breaking attendance was more of an irritant than a fact to be proud of; most of the show's attendees had paid the five-pound admission to ogle at the police hovering at the far end of the field rather than ogle at the flowers. The high attendance was doubly surprising considering the Tommy Torga coverage provided by the papers and the television. They were making the pathetic young brute sound like a serial killer.

The yew hedge that surrounded the cemetery successfully blocked any titillating glimpses of the crime scene the morbidly curious might have been hoping for.

Gregor's mother paced behind him, too nervous to sit down and too distracted to be much help with anything. She usually became calmer, more decisive, when events around her turned chaotic. It was strange to see her so rattled. But Gregor was beyond caring about her mental state.

"How can you be *sure* it's Ina's mackintosh?" she asked for the fourth time.

The numb irritation that had flared at the beginning of the conversation was burning its way into fury. It had never occurred to him that his mother wouldn't accept what he'd told her. "It was her father's mackintosh," he said. "It was a gift given to him by her mother. It looked bloody awful on, but Ina wouldn't part with it. She could be childishly sentimental. I can't believe you never noticed her wearing it, as many times as she was over here."

"I hardly paid attention to the woman, Gregor."

He laughed, the sound brittle. "You notice everything about any female coming within half a mile of me or this house."

She walked to the window, choosing to stare at his reflection rather than look him in the eye. His gaze followed hers.

The reflection off the windowpane was nearly as good as that in a mirror. There were none of the telltale signs of alcoholism stamped on his features, he thought dispassionately. His skin was clear of broken blood vessels. The tan probably helped hide some of the signs. There was a weathered, outdoor look to his cheeks. He looked healthy, if you didn't peer too deeply into his eyes. They were dark, like his father's, but they were missing the mischievous sparkle that was present in all the photographs he'd ever seen of his father; the charming drunk whom everyone loved even after he'd broken his own neck in a fall down the stairs. He was exactly like his father, only worse.

"Why shouldn't I take an interest in your women friends?"

He could hardly muster the energy to argue. "You almost sound like you care."

"I don't understand why you're upset that this woman was killed. You always seemed to be waging war when you were together in the same room."

Gregor stared into the distance, beyond the crowds and the fields to the dark line of trees. On the other side of the trees was the River Deveron. His tone was sardonic, his features emotionless when he said, "You could say we had a love-hate relationship."

"My God, you weren't lovers, were you?"

Gregor tilted his head and studied her for a fraction of a second before bursting into a sharp bark of laughter. The sound was mirthless and short. He ignored her tactless question.

His mother's face reddened. "So that's where you were yesterday morning? In the cemetery, with her, instead of here helping me?"

Gregor tilted his head back and held her gaze. "But you weren't here. I asked Sharon. She said she went looking for you at quarter past six and couldn't find you anywhere. Byrne is going to find that bit of information very interesting when Sharon tells him."

"I was in the cellars," his mother said. "The silly girl never thinks to check for me there."

"You're lying. What were you doing? Following me?"

She left the question unanswered. It layered between them, another brick being added to a wall that was being built in increments of disappointment and frustration. "Why couldn't you marry a nice girl?"

"Nice girls marry men like Evan Whelan. And then they die of boredom."

"What did you plan to do? Return Ina's mackintosh?"

"Why else would I have brought it home?"

"But you didn't come home. Not immediately. Where else did you go?"

So she *had* followed him. Did she do it out of concern or the need to control every part of his life?

Her voice was plaintive, desperate. "I need to know if we're to keep this from Byrne. We need to be clear about what we say or don't say to that man."

And there it was, Gregor thought. His mother had made the decision that concerned his future with less deliberation than she'd used choosing the fabric for the curtains in the front hall.

"I went to the cliffs."

"To meet someone? Yesterday was hardly the most opportune day to chase after scenic views."

"I like the view, even on rainy days."

"Didn't you think it odd that Ina would have dropped her raincoat with all the rain we had yesterday?" she asked. "Why didn't you simply walk to the village and look for her?"

"Because I thought I must have passed her in the mist."

"Did you call her name?"

"Of course I did. There was no answer—just crows squawking in the distance." He refilled his champagne flute. Bathed in a nimbus of sunlight, the champagne bubbles sparkled like diamonds in his slender glass.

"You should have told me yesterday about the mackintosh—especially after you found out what happened to Ina."

"My mind wasn't on damage control," he replied vaguely. How could she be so callous about Ina's death? Was she really that self-absorbed?

"Byrne is capable of anything, after those wretched accusations he made about you and Julia Whelan." Gregor didn't look up. His mother's voice was trembling. "He'll find out you weren't here all morning and he'll be back, Gregor. He'll—"

"Let him come back. In fact, let's ring him and

tell him the news before he has to go digging for it. Yes, I've got your attention now, don't I?" He leaned forward in his chair, his face flushed red with fury. "Ask me again why I went to the cemetery. Then ask why I go to the cliffs. I used to think you never asked because you were frightened by what I might tell you. I thought you were afraid it might link us in a way that you were determined to avoid, so that when I left you, as you thought was inevitable, it wouldn't be as much of a loss. After all, how could you miss someone you never really knew?

"But now I realize I'm just another prop in your carefully crafted world. And it's not my leaving that frightens you, it's my absence. If I were gone, the world would realize Lydia Sandrington wasn't the perfect hostess, the perfect wife, the perfect mother—"

Lydia slapped him so hard his champagne splashed into his lap.

"Where's the mackintosh?" She'd moved across to her desk, focusing on its neatly arranged surface.

"Why?"

"Damage control," she said. "I don't care if Byrne finds it, but I do care if he finds it here, on our property."

Gregor studied his mother's profile. It was pointless trying to fight her. Ina had been right; he'd been letting his mother rule him too long to fight back now. But he'd frightened her; she was squeezing her hands together to keep him from seeing how they trembled.

"It's in my room."

Gregor watched her walk from the room, head

held high, without glancing his way. When she closed the door, he stretched to reach the champagne bottle on the windowsill. He refilled his glass but didn't take a sip. The champagne had gone flat from the heat.

chapter ten

Mornay parked beneath the shade of a willow on the last curved stretch of road leading to San- drington Hall. He rolled down his window. There were ten perfectly spaced willows along a stream that meandered next to the road. Limp, ribbony branches cast swaying shadows across the cars parked along the asphalt in front of the Hall's imposing brick and wrought-iron gate. No flower show attendees were permitted to drive beyond the gate; they had to walk.

A breeze blew the scent of lavender through his car. God bless potty gardeners, Mornay thought. Listening to the breeze rippling through the branches overhead, and the stream burbling along on its way to join the River Deveron, it wasn't difficult to understand why some people felt compelled to spend their lives scrabbling around dirt.

Mornay drummed his hands on the steering wheel and tried to map out a plan for ambushing some answers out of Gregor Sandrington without Byrne's dampening presence. His mind wandered with the sound of the breeze, floating and pushing onward through the myriad unrelated facts that were spreading farther and farther apart the more he tried to focus on them and make some sense of what they meant. He needed some rest. He'd had a quarter hour's nap, at best, this afternoon with Anne in his bed. He closed his eyes. If his luck continued its present nose dive, Anne would probably press some sort of charge against him. The news would be the highlight of Byrne's year.

He wondered where Byrne had disappeared to as two women in sensible shoes and identical frizzy gray perms walked briskly past his car. They glanced curiously at him and continued on, heads close together, bodies stooped from the weight of their ponderous breasts. Anne wouldn't have that problem in forty years. Would she retain the slim figure and poise of her youth? Then his thoughts drifted to Pamela. Would she even *survive* her youth?

An incessant beeping intruded on Mornay's mental wanderings. He tried to place the sound and then realized it was his beeper. He plucked it off his waistband so he could read the message: MEET ME AT THE OFFICE. BYRNE.

Odd that Byrne hadn't used the mobile.

Mornay thought about the flat, angry look Byrne had worn on the stairs when he'd mentioned Julia Whelan. And now the man wanted him to dash to Macduff like an obedient puppy? He would've, for the sake of his career, except for the hostility that'd radiated from Byrne. The man appeared to be deliberately skewing the facts of his previous case and was making no apologies or explanations for his behavior, expecting Mornay to accept what was said, or not said, without argument. Mornay wondered what he'd find out when he started asking questions.

Mornay flung the beeper onto the passenger floorboard. Blind obedience was hard for him to manage anymore.

Gregor Sandrington spotted the tall detective sergeant walking purposefully through the crowds below. The sergeant had been with Byrne yesterday: silent but not dim-witted, if the sharp expression in his dark eyes was anything to judge him by.

Lydia rushed into the parlor a couple of minutes later, her hair wisping out around her face in silvery tendrils. She'd also spotted Mornay.

She took a quick, anxious breath when she saw Gregor's face, then let it out slowly. She smoothed the flyaway strands of hair and set her face in a placid mask of composure. "You're going to tell him about the mackintosh? Well, it's too late—I've already put it in the rubbish pile and told Oliver to burn everything immediately."

Gregor rushed out of his chair. "Of all the stupid . . ."

Fists clenched into tight balls, he stood in front of his mother. He blinked and kept his eyes focused on her as his adrenaline rush of anger slowly abated. He held fast in front of the woman who had spent her life trying to control every facet of his.

Then, when he was calm again, he turned and strode out of the room.

Gregor Sandrington met Mornay at the fountain near the refreshment tent. Up to that point, Mornay had passed fairly anonymously through the crowds. But Sandrington was not a man to go unnoticed; women gawked, gaped, and generally stopped what they were doing to nudge their companions to look up and pay attention. He seemed a different man today. There was an animation to his features that he'd lacked yesterday.

"Don't mind an audience, do you?" Mornay said quietly when Gregor pointed down a path that edged around the side of the Hall, away from the flower show tents.

When they were far enough away from the curious crowds to speak openly, Sandrington said, "I found Ina's mackintosh yesterday. Near the gate that separates the cemetery from our estate."

Mornay stopped walking. "Why didn't you mention this fairly important piece of information yesterday? In fact, I'd go so far as to say it's a damned crucial piece of information."

Gregor Sandrington stood very still in the center of the path, almost posing as he pushed his hands into his trouser pockets. His hair spilled in a boyish shock across his forehead as he looked toward a trio of quaintly decorated maintenance sheds. They looked like a miniature alpine village, with the mountains behind as the perfect backdrop. "I honestly forgot about it after I heard . . ." A haggard breath shuddered out of him.

Something in the sound of Sandrington's voice

restrained Mornay's urge to threaten Sandrington with a night or two in the lockup for obstruction. Instead he asked, "And your mother's claim that you were with her all morning?"

"Utter rubbish," Sandrington said. "Do you want the mackintosh or not? Mother pitched it earlier, but we might just find it before it's destroyed."

"Why were you in the cemetery so early in the morning?" Mornay asked when they resumed walking toward the sheds.

"I was going to use the path to reach Ina's cottage. I wanted to speak to her about . . . about a point we were disputing before she was caught up in the flower show preparations. She'd intended to come to Sandrington Hall to discuss something with my mother, but when she didn't arrive, I assumed she'd changed her mind. When I found her mackintosh I thought I must have passed Ina in the mist, so I changed *my* mind. I struck off for the cliffs."

"Why the cliffs?"

"Privacy." Sandrington's quick glance dared Mornay to refute his statement.

By rights, Mornay should have been angry for being misled and lied to; instead he was curious. Why did Sandrington suddenly feel compelled to tell the truth? If that's what this was.

Sandrington and Mornay circled the farthest of the sheds and came upon Oliver Tidmarsh minding a rubbish fire. The old man was poking at the flames with a garden hoe, prodding them to grow in crackling spurts to almost a meter in height. The smoke billowing above the flames was nearly black and was immediately washed away by a restless breeze.

Sandrington startled Tidmarsh by crashing through the flames and embers, scattering them around with his feet.

Mornay and Tidmarsh jumped to stop him, but Sandrington continued kicking at the contents of the fire. His trousers were starting to steam. As Mornay shouted for Tidmarsh to get some water, he tried to haul Sandrington away from the embers.

"There it is!" Sandrington kicked at a smoldering bundle until it rolled free of the charred debris to lay on the grass.

The mackintosh was the first to get drenched by the hose Oliver Tidmarsh had dragged from behind the shed.

Sandrington's trousers were next.

It was only natural that Sandrington's appearance would alarm his mother. What seemed unnatural, Mornay thought, was Sandrington's response to his mother's concern. He refused to let her near him. And then there was his complete lack of regard for what he'd just admitted in the garden about Ina Matthews's mackintosh. He simply opened a bottle of champagne and ignored his mother and Mornay.

They were in a part of the house Mornay hadn't seen the night before, an ornate parlor decorated in muted ivories, peaches, and pale greens. Lydia Sandrington left the room after her son rebuffed her attempts to look for burns. Her face was splotchy from repressed tears or, perhaps, anger.

Mornay dropped the mackintosh, stored now in a white plastic bag, onto an ornately carved chair. He hoped drenching the garment hadn't ruined what the fire had left untouched. Luckily the mac had been thrown on the fire inside out, so except for some soot and a little charring at the hem, it was intact.

Mornay wandered to the window and turned his attention to Sandrington. The man looked comical, charred from the knees down, sipping champagne. He sat staring out of the window and appeared to be enjoying a private joke.

"I'm not sure I understand what's so amusing," Mornay said, thinking that a trip to the office would be worth the trouble just to wipe the smile off his face.

"I'm not amused. I'm enjoying the irony of this moment." He glanced at Mornay. "I'm toasting myself as there's no one left to do it for me."

"Would Ina Matthews have offered you a toast?"

As Sandrington took a sip of champagne, his hand trembled slightly, causing the pale liquid to slosh back and forth in the narrow glass. It was a small sign, the merest glimpse of a human frailty. Sandrington was doing his best to put on a good show.

"Ina prided herself in being a friend to the oppressed."

There was an emotional undertone to Sandrington's voice, like an echo of unspoken words. Mornay proceeded cautiously. "Was she Julia Whelan's friend as well?"

Sandrington turned his head slowly. "Ask your inspector."

It was obvious that Byrne hadn't garnered many fans during his last trip to Glen Ross, which might explain why Sandrington had withheld the information about the mackintosh yesterday.

Mornay decided to be blunt. "I want the truth," he said. "I believe you and Julia Whelan might have been friends, but I highly doubt you were anything more. I wouldn't be surprised if all three of you were friends."

Sandrington's expression didn't change, but he held up his glass to Mornay in a mock toast. "Our *friendship*," he said ironically, "started after what Ina used to call 'the fall.' It was entirely innocent on Julia's part; she was desperate for acceptance."

"The fall?"

Sandrington leaned back into his chair, managing to look completely comfortable in the skimpily padded seat. He put his feet on the windowsill, crossing his charred ankles. "It happened about three months after Evan brought Julia home, during one of Mary's afternoon teas."

"Was there any antagonism between Mary Hodgeson and Julia Whelan?"

"Not especially. Julia was simply trying to win Mary's favor. Ina said she had a Rebecca complex. But back to your original question: Julia was clever enough to realize these teas were merely occasions for the women of St. David's to closely scrutinize her, and she took them very seriously. She was so concerned with making a good impression, she never told Mary she loathed tea and preferred coffee. Instead she started diluting her tea with whiskey— she claimed it was the only thing on earth that could make tea palatable enough to drink. Mary caught her at it." Sandrington noted Mornay's look. "Silly, isn't it? But Mary was quite embarrassed. It seemed that particular afternoon friends of Evan's father were visiting and Mary wanted Evan's new wife to make a good impression. Having Julia get caught pouring single malt in her Earl Grey didn't achieve quite the impression Mary had planned. Julia said afterward she felt like an unwelcome visitor in her own home. So Ina took her in, so to speak."

"What did Whelan think about his housekeeper's cold shoulder?"

"I doubt he even noticed. He spent most of his free time holed up in his study, scribbling out reams of deadly dull poetry. Julia was virtually excluded from any of the rectory's day-to-day running, so she spent time visiting Ina in her greenhouse or, occasionally, she came to see me."

"How long after this falling-out did you meet Mrs. Whelan?"

"About a week, I suppose. I'd escaped the Hall for the afternoon and talked Ina into buying me lunch at the pub. We returned to her greenhouse, slightly inebriated, to find Julia wandering the aisles, miserable. The rest, as they say, is history."

Mornay closed his notebook and returned it to his pocket. He looked down on Sandrington, who returned the direct gaze. "Were you Ina Matthews's lover?"

Sandrington smiled, but there was no humor in his eyes. "Why do you think Ina's death has anything to do with whom she was sleeping?"

"Were you?" Mornay persisted.

The humorless smile flattened into a grim line that echoed the flat, dark expression in the man's eyes. "Ina was a woman of many passions," Sandrington said. "Men weren't one of them."

Mornay managed to keep his surprise from showing. Either Ina Matthews was ultradiscreet and placed great trust in Sandrington or this was something convenient to misdirect the police's investigation. And he was getting sick of misdirection, inadvertent or otherwise, from witnesses and his colleagues on the force.

"Did Julia Whelan tell you she was pregnant?"

Sandrington swallowed and looked into the glass he held with a white-knuckled grip. "Yes. I was at Ina's when she stopped to share the news. We were to keep it a secret until she could tell Evan."

"When was this?"

"The morning of the day she died. She'd just come from the doctor."

"How did she think her husband would react to the news?"

Sandrington's gaze shifted to the window, then he quickly stood.

Mornay turned to look. Behind the cemetery, thick black smoke billowed, forming an ominous cloud above the tree line. The smoke could only be coming from a building.

Ina Matthews's greenhouse had been set on fire.

Mornay was one of the first to arrive on the scene. He found Sarah Jenkins at the back of her cottage, unconscious. She'd been hit over the head from behind. Fortunately for her, whoever had wielded the broken chair leg had miscalculated the stoutness of the old piece of wood. The leg had broken on impact, merely stunning Sarah instead of crushing her skull.

Sprinklers, which wound above the greenhouse roses in a serpentine maze of narrow black hoses, were set on an automatic timer and had kept the fire at bay since they'd come on shortly after it was set. The fire succeeded only in charring the edges of one of the tables and ruining a quarter of the plants on it. The shed, less damp than the greenhouse, was almost completely destroyed.

Claire arrived shortly after Mornay. She avoided his gaze by paying particular attention to the water puddles she had to navigate through. "Sarah's still too groggy to be coherent," she told him, her manner formal. "We'll have to question her after she's been through A and E."

"Let's hope Accident and Emergency are having a light day. I want to talk to her as soon as she's fully awake." Mornay crunched around the edges of the soggy, warm embers, avoiding the firemen. "Did Forensics say when they'd get here?"

"They were already on their way to search the house for poisons."

"They'll be earning overtime today."

Water was puddled in the grass around the ruined building; even the esteemed Dr. Hall wouldn't have been able to find any footprints in that sooty muck. Not that any would have been left that didn't belong to a fireman. He felt confident that he wouldn't ruin evidence by walking to the edges of the burned-out shed.

"Look at this," Claire said.

She was kneeling in front of the watering system. Two copper pipes fed out of the top of a square silver tank. The system had two gauges; each monitored the

water pressure to a copper tube. Timers were attached
to the gauges. Deep dents had been knocked into the
copper pipe and the aluminum cover on the timers.
More scars were gouged into the surface of the black
box. The glass on the gauges was shattered.

"Who'd want to hang around beating this?"
Mornay asked.

"Someone with a bloody awful temper," Claire
replied. Sahotra joined them, yawning, the skin
beneath his eyes puffy from lack of sleep. Claire
pointed to the ground, near Sahotra. "Looks like
that might've been the spade they used. The blade's
dented on its edges."

Mornay nodded.

"There's a service lane on that side of the cottage,"
Sahotra said pointing behind the shed, "Anyone
could've walked up it, got into the yard, and been
away"—he snapped his fingers—"that quick. They
could be back at the pub in under a minute."

"Marvelous." Mornay turned, hands on his hips.
What to do first? A police constable was standing
near the front gate. "Clark," he shouted. "Come
here. Quick." The young constable started running
as if he'd been hit with an electric prod. Eager to
please. Mornay liked to see that.

"His name's Bensen, sir," Sahotra whispered.

"As long as one of us remembers. Take him and
start a door-to-door. I want you to hit every house
and every business. Claire"—he handed her his
mobile—"call the office, see if we have any special
constables available. We'll need to post them all
around the property to keep the reporters out."

He paced out the distance to the service road, a

muddy pair of ruts between high hedges. Sahotra was right—anyone could've come down the road unseen. He blocked off the exit onto High Street and then taped off the road thirty paces past the end of Sarah Jenkins's property.

Claire handed back his mobile. She used a hand to shield her eyes from the sun's reflection off the greenhouse's panels. "I'll get a third-degree sunburn if I hang around here much longer," she grumbled.

"Where's Byrne? Has anyone seen him since this afternoon?"

"He called after we returned to the office and told us to release Whelan."

"Does he know about Anne Knightsbridge?" Mornay asked.

"Not yet," answered Claire. Then: "I do have good news."

He rolled his hand, trying to hurry her along.

"Sarah Jenkins is asking for you."

Sarah seemed grateful for the company. She was in a smallish ward—only eight beds. No curtains for privacy. Mornay sat in a chair next to Sarah's bed, his elbows on his knees. He looked at his hands, twisted together, knuckles white from the strain of sitting in the chair and fighting the urge to flee. He loathed hospitals, with their antiseptic smells and the sense-deadening surroundings—another souvenir of his years in the military.

"I didn't think you'd come," she said. Her voice was hoarse, her skin bluish. The curls on the left side of her head were covered with gauze; the plaster securing the gauze had pulled the left side of her mouth up at a sharp angle. It made him nauseated to see her so uncomfortable.

He reached out and took her hand. "Can I get you anything?"

"Water would be lovely. I'm parched."

"Did you see who hit you?" he asked after she'd drunk her fill. He placed her cup within her reach.

"No, I'm sorry. I didn't even hear him."

"Do you think it was a man and not a woman?"

Sarah blinked. "How silly of me. I've no idea who it could have been. I suppose a woman could have hit me as easily as a man."

"The chair leg. Where did that come from?"

"Chair leg?"

"It's what the attacker used to knock you out."

"What did it look like?"

"Turned, brown chipped paint, splintered where it'd been broken away from the seat."

"I don't think I've seen anything like that."

He watched a ward sister hurry into the ward, ignoring them, grab a clipboard, and rush back out.

"You've got more questions?" she asked.

"I feel like I'm pouncing on you, asking them here."

Sarah made her best attempt to smile, a difficult gesture to pull off given the amount of plaster on her skin. "You're doing your job and I want to find out who killed Ina. I'll answer questions for as long as it takes."

"If only everyone were as helpful. Do you know if your cousin had a relationship with Gregor Sandrington?"

"Sexual?"

"Yes."

She surprised him by laughing. "He does have quite the reputation, but I doubt Ina had any romantic interest in him. She was more interested in ruffling his aristocratic cool."

"They spent a fair amount of time together?"

"Now that I think about it, I suppose they did, though she spent as much time with Evan as she did with Gregor."

"Sandrington said he and Ina argued quite a bit."

"They did, but not in a bitter sort of way. Gregor wouldn't have kept coming back if there were any animosity between them. Ina certainly wouldn't have wanted him around if there were."

"He said that Ina was a friend to the oppressed." Mornay's gaze drifted up to Sarah, then back down to his hands. "What do you think he meant?"

"When did he say this?"

Mornay sat up straighter. "Today. Why?"

"It just seems too introspective for Gregor. Ina was good about seeing through things. She did it with me, after my Gerry passed. I fumbled through my days, trying to act normal—if there is such a thing as normal. I don't know what would have happened to me if Ina hadn't moved in. I just didn't care about anything anymore. Gregor is the same, to a certain extent. He helps his mother with their guests and does a splendid job of it, from what I've heard, but there's nothing that he lives passionately for. Sex with strange women doesn't equate to passion, so his existence is horribly empty. Ina's words, not mine. We had a long chat about this very subject a month or so ago. She pitied him, I think."

There was no way she could know how closely her words applied to his life. "Any reason she was talking about it?" he asked.

"Actually, we were talking about Evan and somehow the conversation meandered to Gregor."

"Why Evan?" Mornay asked.

"Evan's birthday is coming up, and Ina was wondering if he was going to start getting on with his life. Then she pointed out how similar he was to Gregor; that's when we discussed him. I'm sure it sounds like we were gossiping, but Ina was genuinely fond of both men. She wanted to see them happy."

"Is Evan happy?"

"Not really. To look at him you might not know, but to see what he'd been and what he is today—he's a completely different man. His wife's death utterly shattered him."

"And Gregor Sandrington?"

"I only know Gregor slightly, and what I do know of him, I don't particularly like."

"He said something this morning that you might find odd—disturbing, even. He said Ina had many passions and men weren't one of them."

"Did he, now?" Sarah blew out an angry huff of breath. "He must have made an advance and had it rejected, and then fell back on the chauvinistic explanation that if Ina didn't want him, she must be queer."

"Why would she turn him down? How many attractive bachelors are there in town?"

Sarah smoothed some wrinkles from her cotton sheet. "I suppose she didn't feel Gregor was on the same level, intellectually."

It occurred to him that if Ina had developed a closer relationship with either Gregor Sandrington or Evan Whelan, she probably would've moved out of Sarah Jenkins's house, leaving her alone. He wondered if the thought had ever occurred to Sarah. He liked this woman, but who else would know exactly when Ina Matthews left the cottage to walk to the Hall? It would've been simple for Sarah to follow her.

It was time to change the direction of his questions. "Did you know Julia Whelan?"

"Yes, quite well."

"What would have been so oppressing about *her* life?"

Sarah stopped folding and refolding the cuff of sheet laying across her lap. She studied him for a moment, maybe trying to assess where this particular crook in the conversation might lead. "Mary Hodgeson was the beginning and end of all of Julia's troubles. Evan should have pensioned her off as soon as he got married, but Mary had been with the family so long, he just couldn't do it."

"Was that your cousin's opinion as well?"

Sarah shook her head. "Mine alone. Ina was fond of Mary, despite the woman's constant interference in everything that surrounded Evan's life. She admired Mary's loyalty." Sarah furrowed her brow. "What has Julia's suicide to do with Ina's death?"

"I don't know" was Mornay's honest answer. "It just struck me as odd that except for a poor relationship with her housekeeper, there doesn't seem to be anything about her life distressing enough to commit suicide over. It was obvious your cousin had the same opinion. Do you know if Ina ever discussed Julia's death with the rector?"

She shook her head. "Evan has taken Julia's passing so hard, I don't think Ina would have wanted to upset him further."

"Did Julia ever discuss anything personal with Ina? Like her parents, or her childhood, or perhaps what she did before her job at Harrods, where she met the rector?"

"Not really," Sarah said after a moment. "I think once she mentioned she was from Cornwall. She was educated privately, I believe. I had the impression her parents had passed some time ago and she wasn't comfortable discussing that part of her life. She was so happy to have found Evan, and Evan seemed so happy, it just didn't seem worth talking about."

"Do you think she was happy with her life right before the end?" Mornay had unconsciously adopted Sarah Jenkins's oblique way of referring to death.

"Since Julia wasn't as open with me, I can only share Ina's impression. She said Julia was worried about becoming a burden to Evan, because she'd not adjusted as well to her new position as she'd hoped. But I think the lack of adjustment was more Mary's opinion than Julia's, and Julia simply adopted it. The only thing Mary truly approved of was Julia's cooking; she'd become something of a gourmet cook after she married Evan, while Mary was still very meat and potatoes." Sarah smiled.

"What?"

"I was just thinking about Mary and her cooking, which is very . . . unimaginative, to put it kindly. But her meat pies—you've never had such delicious meat pies. Ina loved them." Tears slid down Sarah's cheek. "Sorry, I don't know why something that silly should make me cry. What did you want to ask?"

"Was Julia content with her life and her marriage?"

Sarah smiled at him. "Are you trying to ask me nicely do I think Julia would have had an affair with Gregor Sandrington?"

Mornay's face felt like it was cracking when he smiled stiffly back. "Yes."

"No, I don't believe Julia had an affair despite the rumors that flew around after she died. From things Ina's told me, you'd probably get the same answer out of Gregor. He had a high opinion of Julia, probably because she was one of the few females who expected more out of him than the occasional witty anecdote."

"Do you think he was in love with Julia and would prefer I didn't discover this? Perhaps that would explain why he was trying to misdirect me today by questioning your cousin's sexual preferences."

As she considered the question, Mornay watched a nurse wheel a patient out of the ward. He was an elderly man who didn't look particularly frail and who appeared to be enjoying the close proximity with his nurse. He was trying to nuzzle his balding, liver-spotted head against her breasts, which forced the nurse to back away and push the wheelchair at arm's length.

"Gregor Sandrington was not in love with Julia."

"But you said you didn't know him well."

Sarah smiled and closed her eyes briefly, as if suffering from a spasm of pain. "I'm fine," she said when he stood to call a nurse. "Really, I am."

"How do you know Gregor Sandrington didn't love Julia?"

"You'll just have to trust me."

"You're not going to tell me?"

"No," Sarah replied gently.

Despite his surroundings, Mornay could feel a lassitude settling over his body like a heavy blanket. The time he'd been sitting had lulled his body into the false promise of rest. "Sarah, did a man named John Tierney or John Buckland ever contact Ina? Or stop by for a visit? He's tall, early fifties, trim."

"Who is he?"

"We're not sure. Just one of the leads we need to follow."

"I've never heard of him. Sorry."

"Just thought I'd take a shot. I . . ." He faltered as he looked down into her pale face, which looked as if it had aged ten years since yesterday. Acting on an impulse, he took her hand and squeezed it encouragingly. "When will you be released?"

"I'm being kept overnight for observation. My heart, you see."

"And tomorrow, do you have someone you could stay with after you're released?"

"Should I be worried?"

He shrugged. "Probably not, but I'd feel better if you had someone with you. Someone you trust." She paled even more and Mornay cursed himself for being so melodramatic. "Look, there's probably nothing to be worried about. I've just had a feeling and I was hoping you would humor me."

"I'll ring Mary and have her pick me up. She'll stay with me. I'll be fine."

chapter eleven

Outside the hospital, Mornay gulped air heavily scented with diesel fumes. The scents and sounds within the antiseptic walls had resurrected memories he preferred remain buried. But his memories never stayed neatly put away; they popped up continually, invading his new life. He raised his head and squinted against the bright afternoon sun, the ugly, flat facade of the Royal Infirmary behind him.

The sky's endless arc of rich blue rose above the visitors' car park, taunting Mornay with its glimpse of infinite freedom. He turned his attention to the ground below his feet and trudged to his car.

Slouched in his seat, window rolled down, he pulled out his mobile and called the office. "Claire, any word on the Saab's registration?"

"It's registered to Lenny Lester. Forty-four. Lives on Gannett Circle."

"Never heard of him." As if it mattered.

"There's no need to hurry back—our briefing's been pushed back till tomorrow morning. Eight sharp. Forensics needed more time to go through all the samples they'd collected from the Jenkins house. Sarah's freezer was packed."

"Anyone find out where Sandrington was Wednesday night?"

"Still working on it."

"Tommy Torga?"

"He's been sighted by every septuagenarian from John O'Groats to the borders. We still haven't been able to locate any of his family in Fyvie. Neighbors say they went on holiday last week. Torga's uncle hasn't showed up for work in a week—hasn't called either. His foreman says he was one of his most dependable drivers, despite his police record."

"Persistent offender?"

"Funny what runs in some families," she said.

"Has Lothario had any luck finding Tierney's prints on his gear?"

"Tierney slash Buckland's real name is John Dunbar and he has a history of violence against women. We also have seven aliases on file that he's used. His last attack was ten years ago—he sexually assaulted a woman in Glasgow. He did a runner before the police made it to his flat."

"Where does Jane Tierney fit in?"

"These days, women pay Dunbar for the privilege of his company."

"Gigolo? Jane confirmed this?"

"She was paying him a thousand a week. It was his idea to use her name."

He whistled. "For that much, he could've pretended to like her. How late are you working?"

"I was just heading out the door."

"Want to hear what I learned about Julia Whelan?"

"Want to hear what I think you should be doing with your time instead of sifting through old news?"

"I'll pass. Cheers—"

"Seth?"

"What?"

"You'll be on time tomorrow?"

"I'll even bring you a coffee."

Car horns blared when he squeezed his Corsa into the sluggish flow of traffic. It was going to take ages to work through Aberdeen's traffic to reach Macduff, which would give him ample time to mull over what he'd learned today when five minutes would have sufficed.

It was just past six when he arrived at Fiona's house. She lived in a two-story brick front at the end of a cul-de-sac. Fiona's four neighbors were older; their gardens were well manicured and their dogs were small.

Victoria opened the door, her face puffy from crying. "You haven't found her yet?" Her voice was dull and scratchy-sounding.

"Still working on it."

She turned and walked down the hall. He followed. In the kitchen, he pulled out a chair across the table from her. Victoria crossed her arms and looked away.

"How long do you intend to ignore me?"

Her gaze sliced his way. "How long will it take for you to go away?"

He grinned. The muscles down his neck and along his shoulders relaxed, he hadn't realized they were bunched up until that moment. It felt good to smile. It felt good to be sitting with Victoria, despite her anger.

After a long, tense moment, she grinned back, shaking her head. "Bastard. You know I deserve a better friend than you."

"You deserve better everything."

Her lips pressed together, the smile vanished.

"Pamela stopped by my house this afternoon."

"What'd she want?"

"She was with a man, Lenny Lester. Drives a black Saab. Forties, balding, eight or nine stone wringing wet."

"That sounds like Fiona's new man. He's a rat-faced cokehead."

"I think she was looking for something to lift."

"She's obviously never been to your house."

"Lenny nearly crapped himself when he saw me."

"Why'd you let them go?"

"I wasn't wearing my trainers. But I did call in the Saab's registration number. Every traffic constable on the force is on the lookout."

"What if they leave the area?"

"I've got a pal in Edinburgh owes me a couple of favors. He's got eyes in every dive and dark alleyway and close in the city."

"This pal—is he one of your old mates?"

"He's a cop."

The news didn't seem to set her at ease.

"Finding her is one thing," he said quietly. "But you know it'll mean sod all—Fiona's let Pamela get her own way for too long."

"I know, I know." Victoria ran her hands through her curls, fluffing them out another inch.

"You do know if it wasn't me, it was only a matter of time before one of these other blokes she's with got her pregnant."

"That's not the point, Seth." She tapped her forehead. "You're supposed to have a brain behind all that thick bone. You've got free will. You've got the ability to reason. You could've said no."

"How long are you going to stay angry with me?"

"Do you really care?"

"Yes," he said.

"I don't know. I really don't know."

Saturday, 7:49 A.M.
Macduff

"Shift your ass, Clark," Mornay said. He passed Claire her coffee and reached for the box of pastries in the center of the conference table.

"That's Bensen," Claire whispered after he'd settled into the chair next to hers. "First name Timothy. Been on the force a little over a year. Builds model airplanes. One of these days you should make an effort to remember his name."

"I don't care what his name is, as long as he does what he's told."

"Did you know he thinks the sun sets and rises on what you say and do?"

"As it should be."

She made the funny sound at the back of her throat she always did when she was going to start an argument.

"What?"

"You don't deserve to be someone's hero."

"So it's my fault he's got the IQ of a pretzel?"

She made the sound again and looked away.

A pair of detectives from Peterhead sat across the table—Detective Sergeant Mercer and Detective Constable Gillian. Mercer was in his mid-forties; he was balding and had a prominent wart on his chin. And he liked to be right. Gillian lifted weights and walked with a pigeon-toed gait; his chief asset was that he liked to agree with Mercer. Neither liked to get their hands dirty.

Dr. Hall's assistant—Claire's number one fan— was sitting at the head of the table talking on his mobile. Two portable easels, covered with photographs and notes, stood beside the white presentation board.

"Good to see everyone's made it on time," Chief Inspector McNab said as he approached the table. Byrne followed McNab and struck his usual pose— hands in pockets, belly extended, deep frown lines bracketing his mouth. No cigar this morning.

"Arthur, if you're ready?"

Mornay had never once called Arthur by his given name. It would always be Lothario, because the man's obvious admiration of Claire seemed to make her uncomfortable and there was damn little that ruffled Claire's calm exterior.

Lothario stood, clearing his throat. "Dr. Hall

would've been here this morning, but he's still working on samples we collected from the greenhouse fire
yesterday, running tests."

"What tests?" Byrne asked.

"We're testing for accelerants and processing
fibers we found."

"And Ina Matthews," Byrne demanded. "Have
you learned anything else about the weapon that was
used on her?"

"We've found two small particles of rust in one of
Ina Matthews's lacerations."

"No glass anywhere?" Byrne asked.

"None."

"Does that clear Tommy Torga?" Mornay asked
McNab. "A broken bottle is his weapon of choice."

"Maybe he learned a few tricks in prison,"
Mercer said.

McNab settled the issue. "We can't rule out
Tommy Torga simply because he's an unlikely suspect. We can't afford not to be thorough." McNab
returned his gaze to Hall's assistant. "What sort of
weapon are we looking for?"

"Something with an edge that isn't regularly
sharpened and that's been in the weather."

"Garden trowel?" Claire suggested. This elicited
chuckles from Gillian and Mercer. McNab squelched
them with a glance.

"It could be anything," Lothario continued.

"Now, about these castor bean plants—what do
they look like?" McNab asked.

"They're grown as an annual." Hall's assistant
walked to one of the boards and pointed out a color
photo of a plant with wide, star-shaped leaves. "This

is a good example of what the plant looks like. And
by the way, it's the wrong time of year for the beans."

"So someone harvested them ahead of time?"
Mornay asked.

"Or purchased them."

"Are you still positive on the time frame?" Claire
asked. "Was Ina Matthews being poisoned for just a
month?"

Lothario coughed, self-conscious. "It's possible
she was being poisoned for a longer period of time if
she was being given low doses."

"Who would hate her that much?" Claire asked.

"Another jealous gardener?" Mercer suggested.
The remark got a few snickers around the table.

"Or a jealous mother," Byrne offered. "I'll bet my
right arm there's an entire section of the Sandrington
garden filled with those bloody plants."

"Mercer and Gillian," McNab said. "You two
search Glen Ross, see if anyone has these plants.
Then you're to work on Tommy Torga. See where
some of the sightings lead us." And so it went,
McNab speaking to everyone in turn, handing out
assignments. "Right now, Inspector Byrne and I have
a press conference to attend. I expect to be kept
informed."

Mornay spent the morning making phone calls. He
was to find out where Gregor Sandrington had spent
his Wednesday evening. In between calls he read
through Julia Whelan's lab reports. After lunch,
instead of heading for Sandrington Hall, he presented
himself at the back door of St. David's rectory. Mrs.
Hodgeson's face settled into forbidding creases, and

she glanced around the stoop to see if he was alone.

"Just me. I'll only be a few minutes."

Mornay's hesitant tone was the right one to use. It made it appear as if she weren't being forced to another interview, that she had a choice.

She welcomed him into the kitchen by saying, "Mind, wipe your feet."

The kitchen was almost uncomfortably warm. Mornay loosened his tie, reinforcing the weary impression he was trying to make.

"Tea?"

From her tone, Mornay presumed she made the offer as a means to get the conversation going rather than as a demonstration of generosity in the face of another unwanted police intrusion into her kitchen.

"Please."

The creases in Mary Hodgeson's face deepened. Though she'd been preparing tea for someone else, she'd expected him to decline. A tray was laid on the wide butcher-block worktop. The heavy, sweet scent of baking scones reminded Mornay of how unsatisfactory his lunch—fish fingers and cold chips—had been.

Sensing he wasn't going to recant his acceptance, Mary Hodgeson slapped down a cup and saucer for him at the end of the worktop.

Mornay took an exaggerated breath, as if he couldn't get enough of the scent of her baking. "Evan is lucky to have you looking after him."

Instead of preening at the compliment, Mary Hodgeson eyed him warily.

"I was here a month ago with a photographer friend," Mornay expounded with an enthusiasm he didn't feel. "Evan took us on a tour. Had us drooling after he'd told us what he was having for tea. He'd invited us, you see, but Victoria, my friend, had another appointment. Evan said you always over-cook for him. He said he suspects you still think he's got the same appetite he had when he was seven-teen."

Mary Hodgeson stopped banging around stone-ware. "I wish he had. Eats like a mouse anymore. Not interested in food, he says."

"So you've been with his family for quite some time?"

"Since he was ten." Mary leaned against the counter, as close to a relaxed pose as Mornay had yet seen. She was almost smiling.

Got it in one. Evan Whelan was like a son to her.

Mornay twirled his empty teacup on its saucer. "I was curious. Evan mentioned he'd gone to Cambridge. Before he changed the subject, Victoria managed to discover he'd specialized in Classic Literature."

Mary Hodgeson was nodding her head. "They wanted Evan to stay on, said he had a promising academic career ahead of him."

"Why didn't he?"

Mary pushed away from the counter, pulled on a mitt and fetched the tray of freshly baked scones. The scones were dispatched to a linen-lined basket to cool. She filled the electric kettle and plugged it in. Her hesitation in answering the question was not lost on Mornay, though she tried to hide it by busy-ing herself with the tea preparations.

"He wanted to be a modern Robert Burns," Mary

said with what sounded uncannily like maternal bewilderment. Mornay wondered if the man's parents were as disappointed as Mary Hodgeson that he'd decided to throw in an academic career for the quiet oblivion of a poet's life.

"His godfather is the bishop of this diocese. Evan spent his school holidays with him," Mary said. "A natural choice, I suppose, Evan becoming ordained. Gave him plenty of time to write."

"Did it in reality?"

"Aye, but nothing ever came of it—not like he'd planned. I always hoped he'd change his mind . . ."

Mary Hodgeson's uncharacteristic chattiness either petered out or there was going to be a *but*. Waiting, Mornay watched steam curl above the scones and disappear into the sweetly scented air.

"Then he met Julia?" Mornay ventured when she continued to hold her silence.

"Then he met Julia," the woman said wearily, as if that explained all the troubles of the world.

The kettle sent a shrill whistle through the room. "I'd like to speak to Evan, if he's around," Mornay said.

She poured the hot water into the teapot; cold disapproval now radiated from her body. Mornay was unprepared for its withering effect. He wondered if this was anything like what Julia Whelan had endured, day after day.

"Thought you'd have had ample opportunity to do your speaking at the police office yesterday," she said.

Mornay rubbed the nick he'd given himself shaving. "I wasn't at the office, Mrs. Hodgeson. It'll only take a minute. I know he's as anxious to see us gone as we are to solve this case." She relented, but not without showing her general opinion of the police force with the set of her shoulders and her frown.

"Drink your tea. I'll take Evan his tray and tell him you're here."

"This was a good idea," Evan told Sergeant Mornay. "I needed some fresh air." They took the walk at the back of the rectory, away from the cemetery. A faint salty scent mingled with the scent of the damp ground and the decaying leaves that had blown around the trunks of the alders, where he'd been unable to rake them clear. Mary had been at him to clean the patch up, but Evan hadn't seen the sense of it. The leaves would only gather here again in another year's time. "But what about the parish?" she'd asked him. "What will everyone think? You wouldn't want the bishop dropping by to see the place in such a state." Mary had spoken as if she feared the very walls would crumble around them.

But his godfather, Bishop Richard Hartly, rarely visited anymore. There was nothing between them to discuss save the trivial business of running a dying parish.

"I wanted to talk to you about your wife," Sergeant Mornay said.

Evan stopped walking. "Why?"

"What happened during the days leading up to her death might help me understand what's happening with our current inquiry."

"I can't imagine how—they're wholly separate incidents."

"Perhaps," the tall man said.

Evan swallowed, vividly remembering the last day he'd spoken with his wife. She'd pleaded with him to take time off from his writing and his conferences and take her to London for a weekend. Three days was all she'd asked for, but he'd felt the illusory pressures of his impending conference—where he was to deliver a lecture—and he'd gotten angry. He remembered how he'd crashed around their bedroom, packing, while Julia stood at the window with her arms crossed, clearly regretting bringing up the subject. But Evan wouldn't let it go. He'd accused her of being selfish. He'd ranted on and on till he'd finished his packing, and then he'd left without saying goodbye.

"We had an argument the day I left for my conference in Edinburgh. All I could think about was myself—how rushed I was, how unprepared I felt."

"Did you speak with your wife while you were at the conference?"

The question catapulted Evan back in time.

During the drive to Edinburgh, he'd maintained his air of righteous anger at his wife. As soon as he saw St. Mary's twin spires, the tower of pride he'd scaled began to crumble beneath him. But he didn't call. His anger lasted two and a half days. On the last day of the conference, Evan made his plans. First, he claimed a headache after lunch and went immediately to his hotel to pack his golf kit and enough clothing to get him through the night. Then he headed home. He was proud of the fact he'd made the two-hundred-kilometer trip home in well under four hours. The day had been flawless, the traffic light, and his mood improved with each familiar landmark he passed.

He arrived in Glen Ross around half past three and was whistling when he skidded to a stop in his graveled spot. He'd walked through the mudroom, fully expecting to be met with a greeting and the scent of Mary's baking bread.

The rectory was empty.

He checked it from top to bottom, slowly at first, half smiling, thinking that at any moment he would startle Julia or Mary. As it became apparent there was no one around to greet him with pleasure or surprise, Evan stopped smiling and started searching for a note.

There wasn't one taped to the fridge or to the window above the sink; Julia's favorite places to leave them. Evan walked out of the mudroom and squinted into the bright afternoon sun, searching the flowerbeds at the back of the rectory.

Evan didn't see Julia in her gardening smock, her pale golden hair clipped back at the nape of her neck as she knelt in front of a bed.

Because the afternoon was so unseasonably warm and fine, Evan chose to walk to Ina's, where he hoped to find Julia perched on a table in the greenhouse discussing the planting list she'd put together after poring over seed catalogs.

But neither Ina nor Sarah was home.

So Evan had returned to the rectory, wondering where everyone had gone. As he walked, something prompted him to turn right and follow the path to Sandrington Hall instead of turning left and continuing into the rectory's garden. Then, for whatever reason, instead of following the path to its logical end, Evan turned right again and followed the narrow, winding path to the cliffs. These were nothing more than small hills that had been half quarried away several centuries earlier. The overlook from the cliffs offered a pastoral vista of the River Deveron.

By the time Evan wound his way to the overlook, the sun was starting to set. It was almost six and he was drained of the enthusiasm that had helped bolster him through the trip.

He sat on a grassy hillock that faced east and hooked his arms around his knees. He'd always preferred the muted aftermath of colors that followed the sunset. An indigo haze had risen above the tree line, the color so dark and fathomless it could have seeped directly from the depths of the North Sea.

He remembered how drowsy he'd gotten as he watched the shifting colors. A slight breeze picked up and the sound of laughter floated to where he sat. He looked around, wondering if guests from Sandrington Hall had been lulled to the cliffs by the mild weather. But as his gaze wandered across the rolling hillocks, he didn't spot any intrepid tourists. Evan stood and stepped forward, glancing to his left and right, then over the edge of the cliff. Once he started looking for it, the narrow path was easily seen. Not ten meters from where he'd sat, it led down at a diagonal to a small plateau carved into the hill about twenty meters below.

A couple was lolling comfortably on the grass. Evan's immediate response was to pull away from the edge of the cliff before he intruded on their privacy. Then the woman shook her head in a gesture that was as familiar as his own face. Julia.

Even now, as he reviewed those distant events, Evan felt a weakness come over him. The sight of Julia laughing so intimately with Gregor Sandrington had nearly brought him to his knees. He didn't confront them there, because he didn't think he'd be able to navigate the narrow path. He returned to the rectory in a daze and waited for Julia beneath the silver beech.

Perhaps that was why he'd chosen to bury her there, in the older, more run-down section of the cemetery where the ivy had taken over. That was where he'd started the chain of events that culminated with the death of his wife.

He'd stepped from behind the beech when he heard Julia walking down the path.

"Evan?" There was a lilt to Julia's voice when she was happy. He remembered how it'd pained him to hear it, knowing his sudden appearance couldn't account for that musical lilt. Her expression sobered when she looked into his eyes. "What's happened?"

"How long?" he asked. They were the last words he'd spoken to her. He'd returned immediately to Edinburgh, intending to stay for several days. But he'd lost his nerve early the next morning. He decided to return to the rectory and listen to Julia, rather than interrupt her with his assumptions. But he was too late. He arrived at half past six to find Julia dead in their bed.

"Evan?" Sergeant Mornay was staring at him, puzzled, but Evan was still in the past; he could hardly focus on the man. "Did you call your wife while you were at the conference?" the sergeant asked again.

"I didn't call," he finally managed to say.

"Did she call you, perhaps try and leave a message?"

"No, she didn't call, either."

"Is there anything puzzling you'd like to share— even the smallest thing?" Sergeant Mornay prodded, stepping in front of Evan to block his way down the path. Evan turned his back to him and walked in the other direction, but he couldn't get away from Mornay.

"This isn't how it works," Mornay said. "I ask questions. You answer them."

"Why aren't you out searching for that Torga boy? We've got a psychopath on the loose, and you're asking me about my dead wife? I don't understand the logic in that." Evan's voice shook, as did his hands and his will. He wanted to tell the man about driving from Edinburgh and finding Julia with Gregor Sandrington. And about what happened after. But he'd promised Mary he'd never tell anyone.

"What are you afraid of?" Mornay's voice was quiet and calming.

"Everything," Evan answered, and turned in the direction of the rectory.

chapter twelve

Anne stood on her tiptoes outside of the rector's room.

Should she or should she not?

There was a creaking on the backstairs, and the same sick feeling she'd gotten yesterday, when Seth had thundered up the stairs and caught her eavesdropping, flooded over her. She didn't want to be caught fleeing again, so she remained in front of the rector's door.

Mrs. Hodgeson's head appeared through the stair balusters. She didn't smile when she saw Anne standing in front of the door. Mrs. Hodgeson was carrying a wooden tray. Beside the teapot was a basket covered with a towel. It held something that smelled yeasty and sweet.

"You'll not be bothering Evan—he's had a tiring day."

"I just wanted . . ." Anne faltered beneath the older woman's fierce glare, and she started backing down the hall, away from the housekeeper. "I could do with a nap, I guess." Anne slipped into her room while the older woman watched.

How was she ever going to ask the man about Julia if she couldn't even get into the bloody room? By rights, she should've packed her things, gone home, and sent one of her private investigators to fetch the information for her. But the information was too important to hear secondhand. And Anne wanted to see the man's eyes when she told him who she was. She needed to see if there was any spark of recognition. Any guilt.

Anne walked to her window. Constable Gillespie came into view, hurrying up the walk with a bouncy stride. The constable clutched some folders to her chest and didn't lift her head once to admire the tangled profusion of flowers she passed. The rosy colored spires of foxgloves mingled amidst delicate towers of indigo delphiniums. The stately plants were drooping beneath the weight of their flowers and no doubt feeling the effects of the rain two days before. Beneath the foxgloves and delphiniums was a grouping of vigorous bushy plants with tiny yellow daisylike flowers.

Chamomile.

Anne almost smiled as the name effortlessly drifted through the flotsam cluttering her thoughts. This had been Julia's garden. The thought brought tears to her eyes. It was the closest she would ever get to Julia.

Anne tiptoed again to Evan Whelan's door, straining her ears for the sound of a footstep on the stairs.

The muted sounds of dishes clattering together were all she heard.

Anne knocked twice, then, before she could talk herself out of it, she turned the knob and slipped into the room.

Like his study, the walls of Evan Whelan's bedroom were covered in floor-to-ceiling bookshelves. And they were packed. With the curtains drawn and no lamps lit, eerily shaped shadows lurked in the corners. More books littered the floor in stacks. It was a maze of sharp edges for the unwary intruder. A desk at the far end of the claustrophobic room seemed to serve as another place to stack books rather than function as a workstation. Consequently, it was even messier than the desk in the study.

Anne felt the chilly wooden floorboards through her socks. She waited for Julia's husband to kick her out, or at least get annoyed she'd come into his room without being invited.

He sat on a narrow pencil-post bed pushed to the far end of the room. He was watching her with a profound weariness. *What now?* his gaze seemed to say. On the floor near his feet, a table had been knocked over, dumping a lamp, some books, and a picture across the bare wooden floor. He'd had to step through the broken glass from the picture frame to sit on his bed.

Without a word, he returned to the task Anne had interrupted when she opened the door, pouring whiskey into a heavy crystal tumbler he held with a trembling hand.

He poured more into his glass, mesmerized by the oily swirls of amber liquid trapped inside. When the tumbler was filled nearly to the rim, he stopped pouring. The hand that held the whiskey bottle dropped limply to the bed—so limply Anne thought the bottle would slip to the floor and join the collection of broken glass at his feet.

He didn't appear to notice her as she walked carefully around the bed to avoid the razor-sharp slivers of glass, then crawled across the bed to reach the whiskey bottle. Evan didn't say a word as she reached around him and pulled the bottle from his fingers.

"I'll just put this away for you."

Anne backed off the bed carefully, so she didn't bounce the mattress and make him spill his drink. She put the bottle on the only clear surface she could find, the floor beneath his desk.

What to do now? The fury that'd motivated her to invade his room had seeped away as she stared at this pathetic man.

Anne decided to get the tumbler away from him. The effort of holding the glass had pulled the muscles of his arm and back and neck taut. His arm was shaking.

She crawled back across the narrow bed, this time coming up on his right side to kneel on his pillow. Steadying herself with a hand on his thigh, Anne reached forward. "Why don't I take this? I know you said it can give you something else to think about, but maybe a hot bowl of soup would do you just as well."

He let her take the glass from him. Then she leaned even further forward and put the glass on the floor next to the overturned table. The lamp was within her reach, so she plucked it off the floor by the shade and put it beside the tumbler. The bulb was undamaged despite its fall; it flared to life when she switched the lamp on.

"Sorry about that," Anne said when she moved her hand off his thigh. "You've a minefield of glass . . ."

Her voice died away.

"What?" he croaked.

"Your face," she whispered.

He took in her shocked gaze. "That bad?"

"It's just bruised."

"I don't want your pity." He stood. The room filled with the sound of crunching glass. He clumsily crossed to the opposite side of the room, kicking a stack of books as he passed. The heavy leather volumes teetered and then slumped over, domino-like, narrowly missing another stack. "I'll hardly feel them in another day."

Now that she had space to move, Anne leaned over the bed and, using the edge of a book, swept the worst of the glass into a pile.

"Leave it, Anne," he commanded in a thick voice.

"If I leave it, a piece of glass will cut you when you least expect it."

Anne dropped her feet over the edge of the bed and stood in the spot she'd cleared free of glass. "I'll have to be careful, but I think I can manage to find enough clear floor to walk out." She righted the table and arranged the lamp, books, and broken picture carefully on its scratched wooden surface. The tumbler of whiskey was relegated to the windowsill, behind the lamp.

"See? Almost done." She glanced around, looking for something to dust with, and ended up pulling the tails of her cotton blouse from her jeans.

"I said leave it," Evan told her when she bent to awkwardly smear the dust off the table. She straightened at the harsh sound of his voice.

"I'm sorry," she said, then glanced at his fists, which had clenched into tight balls. His expression was ominous. "I was only wanting to help."

"What sort of help did you have in mind?"

A flush of anger went through her. Who did he think he was? "I can assure you that I don't think of you in *those* sorts of terms."

He crossed the room with a pair of lunging strides and was reaching for her neck when she backed out of reach. She was pressed against the edge of the bed, leaning away from him.

"I told you I don't want your sympathy." He dropped his hands. "You need to just go away."

"I can't," Anne said.

"Of course you can. Call a taxi. Give them an address. Leave."

"I can't leave. It's taken me too long to find Julia."

Puzzled, he said, "Julia's dead."

"I know, Evan," she whispered, though she wanted to scream to release the pent-up grief she'd hidden for so long.

His puzzlement turned to suspicion. "Who are you?"

She took a deep breath. "Evan, I'm Julia's sister."

There was dead silence.

"Get out," he hissed ferociously. She could smell the whiskey on his breath. "Get out of my sight right now."

"You can phone my solicitors if you don't believe me." When he didn't speak, she rushed on. "I didn't know I was adopted until eight weeks ago. And then when I was told I had a sister . . . I was so happy that I would be part of a family again. Then I came here, and realized I'd arrived two years too late."

"Why tell me now?" He walked back to the bed and sat down, skin pale, eyes unfocused.

"I never intended to tell you at all," she admitted. "But with what's happened, it was just a matter of time before the police told you. They know who I am."

"And who's that?"

Her expression was forlorn. "Someone very much out of her element."

The door to his room opened, and Anne turned.

Mary stood in the doorway. "I told you not to bother him," she said.

"Mary, everything's fine." Evan's voice was weary. "Anne's no bother."

"It's not fine, Evan." Mary walked into the room, ignoring the broken glass and the disarray. "How much more do they expect you to take? Police stopping here whenever they please, upsetting our routine. This one"—she pointed in Anne's direction—"running around doing God knows what."

Anne stood. "I've told you what I'm doing."

"And you think we believe that? All you've done since you've been here is run around the town asking everyone questions about our poor Julia. You're probably a reporter."

"She's Julia's sister, Mary."

Mary sucked in a breath, her gaze ping-ponging between them. "She can't be," Mary whispered. "Julia would have told us she had a sister."

"She lied to us about everything else in her past, Mary—why not a sister?"

"Why did she lie?" Anne asked.

Breaking the tense silence, Evan said, "I don't know. I suppose she was afraid I would look down on her. She should have known me better than that."

Mornay walked into Anne Knightsbridge's room without knocking.

"Does one become exempt from the rules of common courtesy when one is recruited on the force?" Anne asked. "Or are you simply assuring yourself I'm fit enough to be arrested?" Her voice was calm and cool, completely at odds with her flushed skin.

Mornay crossed his arms over his chest. "I wanted to see if you were okay. Mary came rushing down the stairs in a dither."

She turned around and stared at her reflection in the mirror above the dresser. "I think she's afraid she'll have to share her precious Evan with someone else." She yanked open one of the dresser drawers and pulled out a shirt of the Marks and Sparks variety. He was impressed with the pains she'd taken to disguise her true identity.

"What did you expect to find here, Anne? Julia's long gone."

She whirled around, the expression in her eyes so

intense, so full of pain, it felt as if she'd just slapped him.

"Have you any idea what it feels like to be alone?"

"Maybe I do," he answered carefully.

She held his gaze for a moment, as if assessing the measure of sincerity in his voice. She turned back around and stared at the picture of her adopted parents. "I can't describe the feeling I had when I was told about Julia. And then it was explained, in very careful legal terms, why I wasn't given this information before I was twenty-one." Her voice lowered to nearly a whisper. "All those years I spent alone while Julia was out in the world somewhere. And when I'd finally found her, she was dead."

"So you say."

She stared at his reflection in the mirror. "You think I'm lying?"

"You lied about the fight you had with Ina Matthews. Why did you lie?"

She lifted her chin defiantly.

"You do realize you can answer these questions during a formal interview," he pointed out.

Silence stretched between them.

Anne exhaled sharply. "Ina said she was going to tell Evan who I really was."

"How'd she know?" Mornay asked. "There's no resemblance between you and Julia save the color of your hair."

"She said she guessed."

He shook his head. "Perhaps Julia told Ina she had a sister. That would seem more logical than a blind guess."

"Ina didn't go into details."

"Have you really only known about Julia for eight weeks?"

"Why should I lie about that?"

He shrugged. "Any number of reasons. Jealousy—"

"Jealous of what?"

"Your sister's happiness, for starters. You can have anything in the world you feel like writing a check for, but I suspect you're not as happy as she was."

"If she was so happy, why would she kill herself?"

"What if she didn't kill herself?"

Anne's aura of vulnerability slipped away completely. In its place was a cold, flat, barely restrained fury. This was the real Anne Knightsbridge.

"Get out," she said. "Before I report to your superiors how thoroughly you question female witnesses."

At that precise moment, Claire opened the door to Anne's room and leaned inside. "Everything all right?" she asked.

"Yes," Anne answered. "Sergeant Mornay was just leaving."

"Listening at the door, were you?" Mornay asked quietly as he led the way downstairs.

"Thought it was the wisest thing to do, considering what happened the last time you two were alone together."

He paused on the lowest step and stared up at her. "Contrary to popular belief, Claire, I can exercise self-control when needed."

He realized after he'd spoken that this was the exact position he'd been in yesterday morning with Byrne, except Byrne had been the defensive one on the lower step.

"I'll believe that when I see it."

He nearly smiled.

Claire's expression solidified into hard planes. "You think this is a joke?" she asked. "You're a police officer. You don't have random sexual encounters with witnesses, even consensual encounters. They think that point is so important they've actually written rules about it. Remember them? The rules?"

He pointed to the scars on his face. "This is what following the rules gets you, Claire. So no lectures."

She stared at him for nearly a minute, then asked quietly, "Why'd you sleep with her?"

"Why does any man sleep with a woman he's not remotely interested in? She lets him. And I imagine she did it because she wanted leverage."

"Did she get it?"

"Haven't you ever done something just because you could?" he asked.

"I can't afford to ignore the consequences of my actions. And there are always consequences to face, sooner or later."

They went into the kitchen, which was empty.

Mornay nodded toward the ceiling as Claire filled two mugs with hot water, unwrapped two tea bags, and plopped them in the water. "Are we underestimating them?" he asked.

"It's easy to underestimate people, especially when they make a habit of lying." She gave him a pointed stare and plunked down the mug in front of him. "Ina Matthews's body is to be released tomorrow."

Mornay stopped trying to find a comfortable spot on the hard wooden stool. "And we haven't made an arrest yet. That'll be all we hear in the news flashes tonight."

"You've the mackintosh and the partial prints."

"What partial prints?"

Claire pushed a printout in front of him. "I didn't want to tell you in front of Mrs. Hodgeson, but they've pulled two partials from the belt buckle of the mackintosh and some fibers. The fibers have to be analyzed yet and compared to those pulled from her clothing."

"Any idea whose prints they are?" Mornay asked, though he had a fair bet he knew the answer.

"None. They're not showing up in SCRO."

The Scottish Criminal Records Office only kept the prints of past criminal offenders.

"Ina Matthews and Sarah Jenkins have been ruled out."

"Did everyone's prints here get taken?" he asked.

"I don't know."

Constable Dunnholland burst through the kitchen door. He immediately bent over, hands on his knees, gasping in air. "I've run all the way from Sandrington Hall."

Apparently Dunnholland didn't realize what this said about his athletic abilities, since Sandrington Hall was less than half a kilometer away and it had taken him and Byrne less than ten minutes to briskly walk the distance.

"They're going to think we've stumbled across

another body." Mornay's expression darkened. "We haven't, have we?"

Dunnholland shook his head. "I tried to reach you on the pager and mobile. I've been checking everywhere."

For appearances, Mornay did the cursory check of his waistband for his pager, and then shrugged. "Must have left it in my car. My mobile's got a dead battery," he said, knowing he'd switched it off purposely to avoid any calls from Byrne. "Inspector Byrne need me?"

"A Mrs. Robertson has been trying to find you," Dunnholland said between gasps. "She's ringing from the Royal Infirmary. . . . There's been an accident . . . her daughter."

Mornay stood abruptly as anxiety pierced through his abdomen.

Victoria.

He had to steady himself by putting a hand on the table as Dunnholland's panting voice continued, "Pamela Robertson . . ."

Mornay's relief was so profound he thought he was going to be ill. He barely heard the remainder of what Dunnholland was saying, as his gaze roamed to the window above the sink. The sky above the shivering leaves of the trees seemed an even more brilliant shade of blue than it had this morning.

When have you ever cared about the color of the sky, twit? You're just taking up time to avoid thinking about Victoria.

Mornay forced himself to listen to Dunnholland.

"The driver wouldn't pull over . . ."

Dunnholland's voice faltered at Mornay's sudden

black-eyed glare to Claire. She shrugged and asked Dunnholland to repeat more slowly what happened.

"They went off the road and into a tree after a chase. The chase started when they were signaled to pull off the road. The driver was killed instantly. Mrs. Robertson's daughter was thrown from the vehicle."

The only emotion Mornay could summon was a dull surprise that something similar, or worse, had not happened sooner. "And Byrne's pulled you from the investigation to look for me?" he asked carefully.

Dunnholland shoved a thick finger between the collar of his uniform and his neck. "Well"—he cleared his throat with a cough—"it was actually Chief Inspector McNab. Mrs. Robertson kept calling, see? Wouldn't accept that we could only take a message for you. I tried to explain about your investigation. But she insisted on speaking with the chief inspector."

"And Chief Inspector McNab, who prides himself on his rapport with the public, took the call?"

"Well . . . yes." Dunnholland fidgeted with his tie, loosening the thin black strip of material, then tightening it back again, causing his collar to cinch up ridiculously high. "He's had me looking for you."

Mornay started tapping his spoon lightly against the side of his mug. Claire was watching his movements as if each gesture were revealing some hidden secret. Mornay averted his eyes and studied the light glinting off the curved basin of the spoon and calmly asked, "What did Mrs. Robertson say to Chief Inspector McNab to warrant pulling a police constable away from his duty during a murder inquiry?"

Dunnholland glanced at Claire, seeking sympathy by giving her his best wide-eyed-innocent look, but she was too interested in his answer to rescue him from Mornay's questioning.

Dunnholland cleared his throat again, and his splotchy features turned an even more florid shade of red. "She said her daughter might lose her baby. She said you would want to know."

Mornay nodded slowly to himself as he stared at the spoon trapped between his fingers. Claire shooed Dunnholland out of the kitchen, handing him the remaining scones and telling him to share them with the constable on duty at the end of the drive.

"The mysterious pregnant girlfriend? Victoria's younger sister?" Claire said as she watched Dunnholland go down the walk. "Is that why you had me call one of my pals in Traffic?" Her voice was an octave higher than usual. "So you could win some tiff with your girlfriend? Did she go and find another boyfriend while you were on duty?"

Mornay winced, but refused to allow Claire to provoke him. "She's not my girlfriend."

Claire ignored him as she set about tidying the kitchen. "Are we going to have any other surprises or have we reached today's quota?"

He refused to answer.

"You'll have to go to hospital then," she said matter-of-factly.

"And what about this investigation?" he asked.

Claire finished stacking the dirty mugs and plates in the sink before answering. "If I make any arrests, I'll be sure to let you know."

"I need a couple of favors, Claire."

Mornay found a scrap of paper and quickly wrote down what he wanted her to do before she could object. "You'll need to find Chief Inspector McNab and ask him these questions personally."

Claire read the questions he'd written. Then she raised her head and gave him a long, hard look. She turned and, with shoulders held stiffly back, walked out of the kitchen without uttering another word.

chapter thirteen

Mornay watched a grubby boy, no more than six years old, crawl onto the end of his gran's hospital bed. His parents, distracted by the plaintive wails of their even grubbier toddler, did not see the boy settle near his gran's head and start popping colorful Smarties into her open mouth. The old woman had the grayish pallor of the terminally ill. She looked like a stroke victim; the left side of her face was considerably more drooped than the right. Colored spittle was working its way into the creases around her mouth. Though her right eye fluttered occasionally, she made no movement to stop her grandson's impulsive generosity.

She probably couldn't, and the parents of the boy were oblivious.

Mornay backed out of the ward and told the ward

nurse what the boy was doing so he could be stopped before she choked. He'd come by to see Sarah Jenkins—for no particular purpose except to delay the inevitable confrontation with Fiona Robertson. But Sarah had already been released.

Mornay walked down the hall toward the emergency entrance of the hospital wondering how one daughter had turned out so completely different from Fiona, while the other had turned out *exactly* like her mother. Fiona spent her time at the corner pub, reading gossip columns and thinking of new ways to spoil Pamela. She'd never held a job for more than a month, but then, she'd never had to. Fiona's greatest achievement, in Mornay's mind, was passing on her slight artistic bent to Victoria, where it had blossomed into a formidable talent that Fiona rarely acknowledged, unless she needed a quick loan of cash.

Though Victoria hadn't said, Mornay was sure the idea to send Pamela to a drug rehab clinic had been hers alone. Fiona had never been big on her motherly responsibilities; Victoria had always been the one to see to the family. Mornay could remember being in awe of Victoria when she was seven or eight because she was allowed to use the stove. He'd not realized at the time that if Victoria wanted a decent meal, she had to prepare it herself. And in Fiona's mind, if her oldest daughter could cook her own breakfasts and dinners, she could cook everyone else's as well. One responsibility led to another until by the age of ten Victoria was running the entire household.

Mornay passed through a wide pair of swinging

doors and walked into chaos. To reach the information desk, he had to dodge a gurney being wheeled by a male orderly whose features were hidden behind a curtain of dreadlocks.

"Fiona Robertson?" Mornay asked the nurse staffing the phones. She held up her hand without glancing at him. Mornay drummed his fingers on the antiseptic-scented counter, keeping his eyes on the nurse's fuchsia-colored nails rather than on the various patients in the orange plastic molded seats that lined one wall.

When the nurse finally gave him half a second of her attention, Mornay flipped out his CID identification for her to inspect. "Fiona Robertson?" Mornay repeated.

"Third floor. Daughter's in surgery."

The third-floor surgery's waiting room was empty except for a woman with long, dark, uniformly brown hair. It was a poor job of hair coloring; she'd probably put in the rinse herself. She stood silhouetted against the window, arms crossed, with one hand stretched up to her mouth. To anyone passing, she looked like any other frantic parent, wondering the fate of her child.

Mornay guessed Fiona was reapplying her lipstick. Her hand wasn't pushed high enough to be reapplying her mascara.

She turned, recapped her narrow tube of lipstick, and with a flick of hair over her shoulder, spat out a single word. "Bastard."

Pamela in another twenty years. Mornay shoved his hands in his pockets. "How is she?"

"Don't know, do I? I'm just the mother."

Mornay watched the mother teeter across the waiting room in stiletto heels and a tight black mini, fishing through her bag for a cigarette, though the hospital's policy was no smoking. She removed the cigarette and stuffed it between her lips without lighting it, taking small comfort in its presence alone. Fiona sat in a vinyl padded chair that squeaked when she tugged down the miniskirt, which was threatening to creep up above her crotch, then stared at him with bleary, malevolent eyes.

"Maybe they've told you something, aye? Nurses like big coppers, don't they, luv?"

"Have you called Victoria?"

"No time, too busy calling you." Her voice lowered and her bottom lip started to quiver. "Pamela was asking for you." She impatiently waved one of her heavily ringed hands back and forth in the air at his expression. "Don't look so surprised."

"When are you going to call Victoria to let her know what's happened?"

Fiona pulled the unlit cigarette from her lips and punctuated her words by stabbing the cigarette in his direction. "Victoria? My Pammy is lying God knows where—these bastards won't tell me—with sausage for a face. 'Why'd you let her go out, Fiona?' That's what bloody Victoria would say to me, not 'Are you all right, Mum? Is there anything I can do for you, Mum?' Like a normal child. Fucking criticisms, that's all she ever has to say to me." Fiona's eyes narrowed shrewdly. "Where've you been, anyway? Couldn't get enough of my Pammy last month. Now I've got to send the pigs out to find you."

Mornay could feel the tension begin at the backs

of his calves and work its way quickly up his body. It was the same feeling he used to get when he was a boy, having to listen to Fiona Robertson bemoan her life while Victoria finished whatever household drudgery her mother was too selfish and lazy to do herself. And when the job was complete, Fiona had never allowed Victoria more than an hour or two of precious freedom in the garden.

It was little wonder Victoria had moved out at sixteen, but the separation did not relieve the suffocating relationship she had with her mother and younger sister.

"I've got a job to do, Fiona. So I can get paid and keep the bill collectors from knocking on my door."

Fiona pressed her arms across her abdomen in a gesture she'd used so often it was probably unconscious now. The pressure from her arms lifted her heavy breasts, making them heave through the rounded opening of her sweater. Instead of spitting more curses at him, the shrewd look in her eyes intensified.

"But you don't have to, do you, luv? Work, I mean. You've been compensated. Don't need to lift a finger for the rest of your life, if you don't want to."

"You've been misinformed."

Fiona laughed. "Well, la-de-da. Misinformed, is it? Victoria says you were in hospital for months, getting staples and screws and rods put in to hold all your bits and pieces together. Says you were compensated for injuries you got while you were in the service. And we both know it's practically gospel if it's coming from Victoria's lips, don't we, now? What else did they rearrange in those hospitals?" Fiona ran her gaze lasciviously down the length of Mornay's body.

Mornay took a step back. "When did she tell you this?" He tried to imagine why Victoria would have confided this information to her mother.

"Two months back, when she had those four caps put in, remember?"

Mornay looked down to the worn carpet at his feet. Of course Fiona knew he remembered; he'd paid for the dental work. Victoria wouldn't have allowed him to do so under normal circumstances, but her dentist wanted to pull her bad teeth and issue her a bridge, eventually. To have the teeth pulled, she would have had to wait months to be scheduled an appointment. If not for the daily pain, Mornay had no doubt Victoria would have waited. Fortunately, he was able to talk her into letting him pay for a private dentist.

"She was groggy when I picked her up from the dentist," Fiona said.

Mornay could just imagine the scene. Fiona doing her mental accounting of every elegant item in the dentist's suite, trying to understand how Victoria could have afforded it.

"I doubt she remembers, but we had quite the chat on the way home."

"I'll call Victoria."

"Aren't you the predictable one? Always running to Tori at the first sign of trouble. But, oh, when you've the urge for a sweaty grope, the faithful cow's the first one you forget. I told her years ago, all she had to do was show you a bit of leg and the rest would sort itself out. But Victoria wasn't about to take her mum's advice—not like my Pammy. I can just imagine what went through Tori's mind after all those years of following you about only to discover you'd been at her sister behind her back."

Mornay had to forcibly unclench his jaw to speak. "What do you mean?"

"You're the detective, aye? How d'ye think Pammy got to Victoria's cottage last month? D'ye think she bloody walked?"

Constable Pratt, the duty officer tonight, looked anxious when Mornay walked through the entrance. It was half past seven, quiet for a Saturday night. "The chief inspector was wanting you."

Mornay's dour expression remained unaltered. "I heard."

There were crumbs sprinkled down the front of Pratt's black sweater. The past three evening shifts he'd worked, his wife had sent him in with a baked sweet. Pratt spent his entire shift making sure there wasn't so much as a crumb left on the plate when it was time to go home.

"Is he in?"

Pratt's head flopped from side to side. "Gone to Fyvie with Mercer. They were following up some leads on Tommy Torga."

Mornay enunciated each word, not bothering to hide his irritation. "Did they find him?"

"A friend of Torga's uncle just got back from holiday. They went to talk to him."

"Byrne in?"

The younger officer swallowed and spoke quickly:

"Inspector Byrne's having his dinner at the chip shop."

"Is Claire around?"

"She's having tea in the canteen."

"Who won the pool?"

Pratt blushed furiously. "The chief inspector. Again."

After stopping by his desk, Mornay found Claire in the minuscule canteen. There was barely space in the room for the two tables and six chairs along one wall, and the cold sandwich dispenser, small microwave, and small condiment table on the opposite wall. Mornay rarely came in the canteen, preferring the chippy, where the grease was hot and the gossip was first-rate.

Mornay stared at a tray next to the microwave loaded with cinnamon rolls, that evening's contribution from Pratt's wife. Half the rolls were already gone; oily circles had been left behind on the paper liner, each circle surrounded by a blobbed ring of white icing.

Mornay's stomach pitched against his ribs. He turned away.

"Find out anything about Gregor Sandrington?" Claire asked.

"Not as much as McNab wants to know."

"Where was he?"

"Like I said, I still have some digging to do. I'll stop and have another chat with Tidmarsh tonight."

"Did you go through Julia Whelan's autopsy report?" She didn't look up from the mug of tea she was vigorously stirring. An untouched cinnamon roll sat next to the mug.

Mornay sat at right angles to Claire. He put his elbows on the table after depositing the stack of paperwork he'd just scooped off of his desk. The stack included Julia Whelan's autopsy report and copies of lab work, as well as copies of the original interviews Byrne conducted. He cradled his head on his hands and closed his eyes but saw Fiona's glossy red lips moving so immediately opened them again. It rid him of the image but not the echo of what the conniving woman had said.

"I got through most of it this morning," he answered.

Claire's spoon clinked against the sides of her mug. "How's Pamela doing?" Her gaze remained fastened on her mug.

"She broke her shoulder going through the windshield. She shattered her cheek and jaw as well as numerous other bones in her face. And I've no doubt her mother will drill their names into my brain before she's out of hospital. She broke her right arm and right leg, and a lung collapsed when she was thrown against the tree. The surgeon was considering removing her spleen when I arrived, and when I left they were deciding how to put her face back together. Much to her mother's delight, she didn't lose the baby. But it's still early days."

Claire's gaze moved up and held his briefly. "I'm sorry."

"So am I. I know what sort of hell the poor little bugger is in for, if he survives."

Mornay rubbed his eyes with both hands. Then he scrubbed his fingers through his hair, trying to massage some of the exhaustion away. "Did you know

Julia Whelan's doctor diagnosed anemia about three months before she killed herself?"

Claire lifted her mug and sipped her tea. When she put her mug back on the table she said, "Rumor has it our CID staff will be increased. A new sergeant will be added."

"Rumor has it Byrne's retiring, but you don't see me holding my breath, do you?"

A flush spread up the ivory skin of her neck. Her coloring was as fair as Evan Whelan's, but she'd gotten good at clamping down on the emotions. "You don't think the chief inspector would consider me for the new sergeant's position?"

"I didn't say that. I'm saying don't make plans until the position is official. And when it is official, no one would deserve it more."

The flush of red had reached her cheeks and her nose. He'd never seen her so upset, even after her run-ins with Byrne.

"If that's really the way you feel. Why do you always ask favors without bothering to ask what my opinion might be on the matter? Never once have you checked to see if I might have a better idea. I work twice as hard as most men at this office and everyone else gets the credit for it."

"Claire—"

"I don't want my career to suffer because you can't keep your hands to yourself, or even bother to work on the right case."

Mornay leaned forward in his chair and poked at the stack of paperwork he'd brought. "Claire, I can see you're in the mood to fight but I need you to listen. I think these two cases are connected."

"What?"

"I think Byrne let someone get away with murder two years ago."

Claire blew out a breath of air, exasperated. "Julia Whelan committed suicide."

"Bollocks." He started sorting through the paperwork, laying things out in neat piles. "Here's Mrs. Hodgeson stating how she'd found Julia the morning after she'd committed suicide. In it Julia's slight problem with depression is mentioned as well as some pressures she'd been feeling because of her husband's position in the church. We've reports from various neighbors and friends all stating very similar things: Julia was moody, Julia wasn't particularly chatty, Julia was seen wandering the grounds of Sandrington Hall. Sometimes alone, sometimes not. We've got her husband's report stating there were no marital problems, life was great. However, we've no report from Julia's closest friend, Ina Matthews."

"If life was great, why'd she get tranquilizers?" Claire asked.

"That's another question Byrne didn't bother to ask anyone," he said.

Mornay picked up Mrs. Hodgeson's statement and summarized it for her. "Julia had been alone in the small sitting room, across from her husband's study, when Mrs. Hodgeson retired for the evening. It was around ten. It was the last time Mrs. Hodgeson saw Julia alive."

"And her doctor, what did he say about tranquilizers?"

"There's no statement," he answered.

"You didn't copy it?"

"There wasn't one to copy. We've got everyone else's opinion about Julia Whelan's mental health except the one person who really knows what he's talking about."

"How did you know about the anemia, then?"

"Sarah Jenkins."

"Who was her doctor?" Claire asked.

"Hartwick, same as for Ina Matthews. Fancy going on a trip?"

"The last time you asked me that, I ended up waist deep in dead fish."

Mornay grinned. "But we got our man, didn't we?"

"And my favorite suit got ruined."

"So did mine. But I was still right, wasn't I?"

"It doesn't mean you'll be right every time."

His grin widened. "We'll never know if we don't have a chat with Hartwick. After we talk to the doctor, I'll introduce you to Oliver Tidmarsh."

Dr. Hartwick's office was on the smallish side; the reception area furniture was worn and the plants were real. The overall appearance was slightly shabby but conveyed a sense of comfort, despite the after-hours gloom.

It was nearly eight thirty in the evening. Dr. Hartwick opened the door, dressed in worn corduroy slacks and slippers. He ushered them through the office and up a flight of stairs to his flat above the office. The furniture was newer in his flat—less crowded. The television screen flashed in the corner, but Dr. Hartwick had muted the sound. Framed photographs were displayed on the walls. Most of the pictures were landscapes, and they were very good.

"You're a photographer?" Mornay asked.

"Strictly amateur. I like to hike. Taking pictures while I hiked seemed a natural extension."

"I want to ask you a few questions about Julia Whelan," Mornay said.

Claire had her notebook out. She'd angled herself crossways from the doctor, out of Hartwick's direct line of sight, but still in a good position to see his expression.

"Julia? Why? I thought you were here about Ina."

"Not specifically, though there are a couple of points I'd like to clarify later. Do you remember when you issued Julia's tranquilizer prescription?"

Dr. Hartwick was shaking his head. "I've got over two hundred patients. I can barely remember to eat lunch during the day. Julia's records are downstairs. Give me a minute and I'll run down and bring them up."

Dr. Hartwick was gone less than five minutes. He'd pulled out a pair of reading spectacles and was flipping pages as he walked back into the room. "Here we are," he murmured. He took a seat across from Mornay. "She came to me in August complaining of fatigue and trouble sleeping. I'd pulled blood the week before during a regular visit, so I knew she wasn't anemic. Since she was healthy, we tried cutting back certain things in her diet—sugar, caffeine, and the like. To no avail." He flipped through a few more pages. "After the holidays she came back— same problems except now she's a stone lighter."

"Did you ever think stress could be the culprit?" Claire asked.

"Yes, that's exactly what I thought. This is a small village and I knew that there was some tension at the rectory—Julia wasn't fitting in quite as well as Mary had hoped. I suggested a mild tranquilizer in January, but she didn't actually stop by the office for the prescription until February. She'd been taking long walks, hoping the exercise would help. Here. I've made a note." He held the report closer to read his writing. "She only took the pills for four days. They made her too tired and dizzy. Then of course the next time she comes in, we perform the usual blood tests and discover she's got a slightly depressed red blood cell count and that she's pregnant."

"What was her reaction to the news of her pregnancy?"

"She was stunned."

"But not displeased?" Mornay asked.

"She appeared overwhelmed. I don't think she was unhappy with the news; she'd been trying to have a baby for months. But she was quite emotional, on the verge of tears. We fixed another appointment for the following day so she could get her prenatal vitamins and another supplement to work on her mild anemia."

"Were you surprised she'd killed herself?"

"I was staggered."

Mornay glanced in Claire's direction briefly. "Did you tell that to the police?" he asked Dr. Hartwick.

"Several times. The man that came to question me seemed to be merely going through the motions."

"Inspector Byrne?" Mornay asked.

"That's him."

"Do you think it's possible that Julia Whelan was being sporadically poisoned during the seven months that preceded her suicide?"

"Like Ina was being poisoned?"

"Exactly."

"Perhaps. She did have a lowered red blood cell count. But if it was ricin toxin, it was being administered in the minutest of dosages. Why would someone bother going through the trouble? Isn't the point of poisoning someone to kill them?"

"One would think," Mornay agreed. "But Ina Matthews was apparently being poisoned in very minute doses also. We know it doesn't take much of this ricin toxin to kill an adult, does it?"

"You're correct," the doctor agreed. "A milligram is lethal."

"It looks like someone worked at *not* giving Ina a lethal dose."

"So it would appear," the doctor said.

"Is there any way you can find out, through these old tests, if Julia had been exposed to ricin toxin?"

"I'm afraid not."

"Have you had any other patients complaining of fatigue or showing similar symptoms to those of Julia Whelan?" Mornay asked.

The doctor drummed his fingers on the table, taking his time answering. "There's one or two names that pop to mind," he said slowly. "It would take a day or two to find out for sure."

"Could you look into it? This is very important."

Hartwick was shaking his head in disbelief. "If

there are others, then they're probably being poisoned by someone I know."

Hartwick's phone rang. He answered. "I'll be right there," Hartwick said after listening for a moment. He disconnected and said to Mornay, "Please excuse me, one of my patients has just passed away."

"Who?" Mornay asked.

"Paul Hume. He's been ill for quite some time."

Mornay pulled out a business card and jotted his home number on the back and his extension on the front, under the office's main number. "Thank you for your time, Doctor. Give me or Constable Gillespie a call. Day or night."

"I wonder why Byrne didn't write a report detailing his interview with the doctor," Claire asked.

It was just after nine, not too late to talk to Oliver Tidmarsh.

The dark uncertainties Mornay had at the rectory while questioning Byrne returned in a flood. Ina Matthews had been calling Byrne at the time these reports were being made; he'd had ample opportunity to have an interview with her before the case was officially closed by the procurator fiscal.

"Did you ever get a chance to speak to McNab about those questions I left with you?"

"The chief inspector was told informally about his promotion on March fourteenth."

"You're sure?"

She sighed. "Detective Chief Superintendent McIntyre told him. The announcement was officially made March twentieth."

Mornay gripped the steering wheel harder. Julia Whelan's body had been discovered March 11. In the nine days before McNab's promotion was announced, Byrne discovered that Julia Whelan knew she was pregnant and had shared the news with two of her closest friends. Had Byrne sabotaged the investigation because he wasn't going to receive the promotion he'd been expecting?

Mornay eased his Escort through Sandrington Hall's gates and parked near the main entrance. "I want you to take something else to the chief inspector."

Claire blinked. "He'll still be in Fyvie."

"That's why I need *you* to take this to him."

"Why can't we just call him?"

"Byrne's wandering around somewhere. I can't risk him finding out what I'm wanting to know." He handed her the note he'd just jotted for the chief inspector.

"And that's it? More footwork without any explanation?"

Mornay didn't blame her for being angry, but he didn't have an answer for her. He was hoping to work one out soon.

"You'll know soon enough, Claire. I promise." He handed her the keys to his car.

"What about you? Do you plan on walking back to Macduff?"

"I'll manage. Don't worry—there's no dead fish involved this time."

"Can I read it?" she called out after him.

He turned and, walking backward, shouted, "Be my guest."

It took her half a second. She looked up, then cursed, the words too faint for him to hear. "I don't know why I bother with you!" she shouted.

"Because I'm usually right," he shouted back.

She loudly called him a cheeky bastard, then put his car into gear and purposely spun the tires as she pulled away.

chapter fourteen

Oliver Tidmarsh let Mornay inside his cottage without going through the ritual of inspecting identification. As during Mornay's last visit, the old man took the only chair in the cottage, leaving Mornay to stand.

Mornay got right to the question. "Gregor Sandrington was gone Wednesday night. He returned very early Thursday morning. Any idea where he might've been?"

Tidmarsh took several puffs of his pipe as he stared into the crackling flames of his fire.

"He was at his AA meeting, to start. Couldn't tell you where he went after."

"AA? As in Alcoholics Anonymous?"

"That's right," Tidmarsh said.

"How long has he been going to meetings?"

"Och, five or six months now. Told me he didn't want to end up like his father."

"What happened to his father?"

"Fell down the stairs, drunk. The poor bastard broke his neck. But then, he was always drunk—it was only a matter of time before it killed him."

"I've seen Sandrington drinking champagne," Mornay said.

"Aye, well, he was going to the meetings to shape up for Ina—she wouldn't have him if he were a drunk layabout. No sense staying on the wagon now, I suppose."

"Did she know what he was doing?"

Tidmarsh shook his head. "No one knew he was going."

"How do you know?"

Tidmarsh's gaze swept his way for a brief moment, and he smiled faintly before returning his attention to the fire. "I've been going to those meetings for years. Like I said before, not much goes on around here that I don't know about."

"Except who killed Ina."

"Aye," the old man said softly. "Except who killed Ina."

"Where are these AA meetings?"

"Turriff. Every Wednesday evening, seven on the dot."

"Thanks, Oliver," Mornay said on his way out of the cottage.

The old man lifted a hand in a slow wave.

* * *

Constable Bensen, still on duty at the rectory's gate, told Mornay that Byrne had arrived fifteen minutes before.

Mornay slowed his stride to delay his meeting with Byrne.

It was just his luck that the quick-tempered man was in the rectory's front garden, smoking one of his noxious cigars. Mornay was barely in hearing distance when Byrne shouted, "Where've you been?"

Mornay wanted to return the question; Byrne had disappeared for over six hours. "Chasing ghosts. You?"

"Become a fucking comedian, have you? With all that spare time on your hands?" Byrne drew on his cigar till his ash reached half an inch in length, and then said to no one in particular, "Fucking ghosts."

Mornay shoved his hands in his pockets and examined the front of the rectory. The lights downstairs were off, but lights were burning brightly on the second and third floors.

Still puffing on his cigar, Byrne said, "Brief me, before I die of old age."

Mornay's head ached from trying to ignore the wreckage of his personal life while he tried to salvage his professional one. He had no clue how the information he'd gathered fit together. There was no logical explanation for Byrne's behavior two years ago or for his behavior these past three days.

"Bugger off," Mornay said.

Byrne choked down a bronchial wheeze that was meant to pass as a laugh. "Keep wishing, laddie. Now get on with it."

Mornay pulled out his notebook and settled down

to the inevitable. "John Dunbar is still missing. We still don't know why he had Ina's name circled in the magazine. There's been no sign of Tommy Torga, except for the unsubstantiated sightings by overly helpful senior citizens."

"What about Sandrington—any idea where he was Wednesday night?"

"Tidmarsh said Sandrington attends AA meetings in Turriff on Wednesdays. I want to confirm this before we ask him."

"An AA meeting? Why'd he show up drunk on Thursday morning?"

"We've only the American woman's word on how he arrived. They said he couldn't walk straight. Maybe there's another explanation. Something simpler."

"Does his mother have a solid alibi?" Byrne asked.

"Not really, and I might have stumbled across a motive for her," he added, thinking of his conversation with Sarah Jenkins and her refusal to answer his questions about who Ina thought Sandrington was in love with. "It's possible her son was in love with Ina Matthews. He made several comments about her that were apparently out of character."

"Did Ina and Sandrington know each other?"

"Quite well, apparently."

Byrne whistled softly. "Ina Matthews. Mother Sandrington wouldn't have liked that at all. Mercer and Gillian have found out Sandrington Hall is the only property in Glen Ross that grows ornamental castor bean plants. Tomorrow a team of us will be searching the place, top to bottom. I want you there, six o'clock sharp."

Mornay kept his gaze on the dark panes of Whelan's study windows. Where had everyone gone? "Did you get Sandrington's prints during your investigation of Julia Whelan's suicide?"

"Didn't get that far."

"Two partial prints were found on Ina Matthews's raincoat. Unknowns. Did you hear?"

"Clues," Byrne spat the word. "Imagine that. Tomorrow we'll send Dunnholland out to collect more dabs."

"Who should he start with?"

"How about someone familiar with Ina Matthews's garden? Sound good to you?" Sarcasm dripped from every word.

"That's half the bloody village," Mornay said. "He'll be taking prints for the rest of the week."

"What do you suggest? Should we post an advert? Killer wanted, inquire within. Is that how it should go?" When Mornay refused to be led into an argument, Byrne sent the butt of his cigar sailing through the air with a flick of his thumb. "What about the umbrella? Any ideas?"

"I doubt Ina would've left it behind if she'd stopped by the rectory to see if Whelan was up—it was raining. And why leave the rectory without him? I don't think she ever made it that far. Which means it was planted in the rectory to mislead us. Or, since Ina was a regular visitor, maybe it was put there to simply hide it in a location so obvious it would be overlooked until the killer had a chance to dispose of it properly. But it makes no sense to dispose of the umbrella and raincoat in two different locations."

"Someone didn't want the body discovered immediately. Maybe you should start asking yourself why. What about the good rector? Have you asked him why he lied to us about the time he left for the Hall? Why would it take him an hour to make a ten-minute walk? We need to know where he stopped along the way."

"I haven't had the opportunity to question him."

Byrne's voice softened. "Did you expect Gillespie to do it for you? Heard she's been busy running errands for you." Whoever was supplying Byrne's information was doing a first-rate job. Byrne squinted his piggy eyes in Mornay's direction. The darkness robbed the stare of its effectiveness. "Are you building a wee empire or a wee harem?"

Mornay wondered how he'd allowed himself to overlook the degree of Byrne's hostility. Had he been blind to it because he'd been working so hard to prove his own merit at the office? Or had Byrne gradually slipped into this derisive mentality as a result of the promotion he'd failed to receive two years ago?

Mornay watched the shadows lengthen as he spoke with Byrne. He tried to wrestle something productive out of his chaotic thoughts. The breeze ruffled against his hair and his cheeks. He took a deep breath and kept to the subject at hand. "The stake was a clumsy weapon. It was barely sharp enough to penetrate Ina's clothing. The worst stake wounds entered her body beneath her arms, through the open sides of her denim jumper, where her skin was covered by a thin cotton blouse. The knife's damage seemed to be concentrated on her face. Which makes no sense—why use the stake at all?"

Byrne snorted. "How many times was she stabbed?"

"There were thirty-one separate wounds on her body."

"Thirty-one," Byrne repeated. "This was no spur-of-the-moment crime. And I'll tell you something else: I think that stake was symbolic—which is why it was left and the real murder weapon taken away."

Had Mornay made the suggestion about a symbolic murder weapon, Byrne would've laughed about it until his retirement.

"With the mist and rain," Mornay said. "Anyone could have walked by with Ina and her killer out of sight behind the headstones. I think you're right," he admitted grudgingly. "We weren't meant to find the body as soon as we did. It was pure, blind luck."

Mornay didn't mention how he'd obtained the mackintosh or that Gregor Sandrington claimed to have stumbled across it at the entrance to the cemetery. Mornay suspected Sandrington was lying, but had he gone as far as the place Ina had been killed?

"Ina Matthews was carrying roses she was sure would win her Best of Show at the flower show," Mornay said. "I only found a single petal at the scene. Why would the killer get rid of the roses?"

"Roses? Well, lads, *this* should be brilliant." Byrne spoke to the trees above him. "A bloody rose!"

"Though it doesn't explain the fire." Mornay inadvertently spoke the thought aloud. Once said, he had to continue with it. "Anyone familiar enough with Ina Matthews's garden to find her garden markers should have known about the sprinkler system she had in place to water everything in the greenhouse."

"Let's get back to the roses."

A snapping twig made them turn their heads in unison. They heard someone curse softly.

"By the back door," Byrne whispered.

They walked around the rectory. There was no one at the entrance to the mudroom. Behind them, on the path that led through the cemetery to Sandrington Hall, were Gregor Sandrington and Evan Whelan.

The sound of their raised voices caused Byrne to chuckle. "Now, this could get us somewhere." He put a hand on Mornay's arm to keep him from interrupting the argument.

". . . Walking isn't a crime," Sandrington said.

"But people notice. And they talk." Evan's voice came out in a laconic burst, compared to Gregor Sandrington's drunken drawl.

Sandrington laughed. "You married the wrong woman if you didn't want people to *talk* about her. What did you expect Julia to do—lounge in bed all day while you wrestled with your muse in the study and Mary Hodgeson lorded over the kitchen? That's the heart of your problem, Whelan—thinking all is right with the world when it's really filled with narrow-minded prudes who'd sooner make someone's life a living hell than show an iota of human compassion."

"And your idea of showing Julia compassion was seducing her?"

Gregor Sandrington laughed.

The growing dusk made the men two dim shadows. Suddenly, one rushed the other and they both fell to the ground.

One of the shadows seemed to throw punches more ill-coordinated than the other.

Mornay decided Sandrington was the one getting the worst of it. There was a hard strength coiled beneath Evan Whelan's placid, almost wimpy appearance.

Evan dodged Sandrington's fists easily and fought back with a single-minded intensity that made Mornay uneasy.

"We better jump in before one of them actually gets hurt."

"You take Sandrington home," Byrne said. "I'll see to the good rector."

Evan quickly cut through the cemetery, leaving Inspector Byrne huffing and puffing and cursing behind him. He intended to circle the rectory; he felt compelled to seek out the shadows, as if the act of hiding himself would somehow lessen what he was feeling. He'd nearly turned on Sergeant Mornay when the man started to pull him off of Sandrington, and it'd taken a tremendous effort for Evan to stop punching Sandrington's abdomen and his face.

Another surge of adrenaline rushed through Evan's body. He almost doubled over with the strength of it.

Was this what it felt like to be going mad?

Somehow, during Byrne's cruel interrogation this afternoon, he'd relinquished his desire to control his anger. Now, in the throes of another tidal surge of it, Evan wasn't sure if he was capable of suppressing it again.

Evan could only imagine what conclusion Byrne would make if he saw his face. He left the shadows of the cemetery and cut across the back garden and followed the curved walk that led to the front door of the rectory. He sought the deeper shadows in the group of alders that dominated the front lawn.

Byrne, intent on finding him, didn't think to look toward the trees, but turned and followed the path. From the depth of the alders, Evan watched Byrne lap the rectory, his curses growing louder with each successive step.

Byrne circled the rectory only once. A white Land Rover was parking on the graveled niche at the side of the rectory, near the kitchen window, when he emerged from the back garden. This was the parking spot Evan had provided for visiting parishioners who wanted to come into the rectory through the kitchen.

The Land Rover bore the distinctive broad orange stripes, bordered by narrow bands of black and white checks, of the Grampian Police. When the door opened, Evan caught a glimpse of the blue lettering that spelled Grampian in a half circle above the thistle emblem of the police force.

Constable Gillespie and another man stepped from the Rover. Byrne's curses, which were carrying across the lawn, ceased when the Rover's doors closed.

Lydia Sandrington led Mornay, who was half dragging Gregor Sandrington, up a flight of stairs to his bedroom. There she left him alone to put her son to bed.

Gregor Sandrington was snoring softly as Mornay prowled the room, looking for anything of interest.

The décor was more masculine in this room—the furniture sturdier, the colors darker. There was nothing of the man's personality in the room.

He had a look at the cluster of objects on the nightstand—nothing unusual there. There was nothing interesting in the bathroom or in the desk next to the window. A large wall mirror turned out to be the entrance to a walk-in closest as big as his kitchen. It took him all of five minutes to search. Sandrington was no more inventive where he hid his valuables than a ten-year-old; he used his sock drawer.

Mornay found a ring at the back of the narrow drawer. The ring had a square-cut emerald the size of a Smartie, set in white gold. He pulled the ring out of its black velvet nest; the stone was cold to the touch. There was an inscription etched inside the band: FOR INA. FOREVER.

The ring would be gone tomorrow, as soon as Sandrington found out about the police search. He reached his hand back inside the drawer to see if there was anything else. He found the receipt for the ring at the very back of the drawer. The jeweler was located in Aberdeen. Sandrington had picked up the ring two days before Ina Matthews had been murdered.

Poor bastard.

Mornay jotted the jeweler's name and number in his notebook before putting both items back in the drawer.

During his walk back to the rectory, Mornay tried to adjust to the idea of a grieving Gregor Sandrington.

It wasn't such a leap. What he needed to know now was if Lydia Sandrington knew about her son's intentions. Would she have stopped the marriage in her own way? He needed to find out tonight, and there was only one place he could look.

Chief Inspector McNab's Land Rover was parked near the back of the rectory when Mornay turned off of the path that bisected the cemetery. Soft sounds of a muted conversation floated to him as he approached.

Claire, who had been standing apart from Chief Inspector McNab and Inspector Byrne, met Mornay before he reached the Rover.

"Sarah Jenkins was released," he told her. "I want to go over and have a chat with her. And I want to have a look at Ina's correspondence."

Claire checked her watch. "It's after ten—a bit late, don't you think?"

"Maybe, but tomorrow we're at Sandrington Hall from six till who knows when."

"I'll ring Sarah so they'll know to expect us." Claire crossed her arms and nodded her head in Byrne's direction. "Where was he this afternoon?"

"Hasn't said. Did McNab say anything when he read my note?"

"Not a word. Made me wait in the Rover while he made some calls."

"Where's my car?"

"Parked by the gate so Bensen could sit inside."

Mornay kept his gaze on the men, looking for clues in their body language. They appeared to be having a normal conversation.

"What's this?" Byrne launched directly into his

attack when Mornay approached. "Not got enough work on your desk, Mornay? You need to dig through old inquiries?"

Byrne turned to the chief inspector. "Andy, you bloody well know that the day I was pushed off the Whelan case, you could barely breathe in the chief constable's office—there were that many lawyers propped around the walls, sucking up the oxygen. I thought the procurator fiscal was going to faint dead away."

McNab held up his hands in a placating gesture. "Walter, no one is accusing you of anything."

Byrne snorted. "No? I've just got this upstart shite running behind my back, getting copies of closed cases instead of working on the one he's had dumped in his lap."

McNab looked from inspector to sergeant. Both men had their faces set in rigid expressions. During his nearly two years working CID in Macduff, Mornay had proved to be an exemplary officer. He wasn't the sort of man prone to anything rash—particularly the accusations Byrne thought he'd made. Which was what concerned him about Byrne's behavior; no accusation *had* been made. There'd only been a message from Mornay that contained a single, puzzling question. The question had enough merit to warrant him driving all the way to Glen Ross to have a private conversation with Byrne—something they'd not attempted since he'd gotten the promotion Byrne declared was rightly his.

Because of his old friend's curious response, he felt even more compelled to allow Mornay to pursue his examination of the closed case. Mornay was searching for ties to the present one, and McNab was confident Mornay wouldn't have gone off on this tangent unless he thought he'd be discovering something relevant.

When Mornay didn't immediately offer a reason why he'd obtained copies of Julia Whelan's files, Byrne started defending himself.

McNab held up his hands, interrupting. "The press is watching our every move. We've taken major hits with the increase of drug problems and the decrease in our budget. Dissension in our ranks will not improve the general public's opinion of the force or CID. We've got to pull together and get this case solved."

Byrne kicked a stone off the drive. The stone landed with a soft plop in the grass. "Spoken like a true yes-man."

McNab, who'd followed the stone's progress, swiveled his head back to Byrne. "I think we've had enough of your antagonistic behavior. Have we had someone try to eliminate whose prints *aren't* on Ina Matthews's raincoat? Like John Dunbar's, for instance."

It was a rhetorical question. Neither Mornay nor Claire volunteered to tell him what he already knew, that Byrne hadn't been around to issue the order.

Byrne shoved his hands in his pockets and scowled. "I'm having one of the constables come around tomorrow. We'll go house to house getting prints if we have to."

"As you should," McNab said. "Make sure that everyone realizes that they aren't *required* to assist, but their cooperation would greatly benefit our inquiry. I don't want to hear in tomorrow's news that we're hounding the local populace."

From his tone, it was quite clear he thought this very basic piece of policing should have already been accomplished.

chapter fifteen

Mary Hodgeson offered no greeting when she opened Sarah Jenkins's door. She stepped aside to let Mornay and Claire into the hall without a word, then silently led them to the sitting room.

Sarah Jenkins was sitting on her couch, fire lit, blanket around her shoulders, and a soft knit cap on her head to cover the plaster on her forehead. She smiled warmly when Mornay entered the room.

"Mary said you needed to look through Ina's desk. Didn't you do that the other day?"

"Briefly. We need to have another look."

"Why not wait until tomorrow?" Mary Hodgeson asked. She stood in the doorway, radiating disapproval. "Sarah needs her rest."

"We've somewhere else we need to be tomorrow" was Mornay's brief reply. "We know the way to Ina's room, and we can see ourselves out, so we won't disturb you."

"Of course. I don't mind—and don't worry about disturbing me. I probably won't sleep much tonight anyway."

Claire closed Ina Matthews's bedroom door. Mornay took a seat at Ina's desk while she went to the bookcase at the far wall. "Did Forensics look through these?" she asked.

"They only looked for candy and the like. Something that could be laced with poison."

Claire pulled a book from the top shelf and started fanning the pages, finding nothing. She picked up the next book on the shelf.

Mornay shuffled through two drawers that contained old bills, warranty cards, the owner's manual to Ina's car—the usual paperwork that most people just throw in the back of a drawer. Ina had neatly categorized them in file folders.

"You're quiet over there," Claire said.

He'd been trying, unsuccessfully, to force Pamela and her manipulative mother from his thoughts. How could he have let his life spiral out of control like this? It would probably be easier to find Ina Matthews's killer than to answer that question. McNab had given him the go-ahead to look into Julia Whelan's inquiry, but if he didn't find something to substantiate his request, he didn't want to think how Byrne would exact his revenge.

"Ina Matthews and Gregor Sandrington knew Julia was going to have a baby," he told Claire.

Claire sighed. "What's that got to do with the job

the chief inspector asked us to do? Nothing, that's what. It's time you started paying attention to what's happening under your nose."

"No one supposedly knew about the baby," he persisted. "Why tell your friends you're pregnant and then kill yourself the very same day? If the procurator fiscal had known Julia Whelan told her friends about the baby, he'd have kept the case open."

Claire turned to see him. "It's easy to assume what someone else would've done after the fact. We've yet to find a connection between Julia Whelan's and Ina Matthews's deaths."

"Gregor Sandrington bought Ina Matthews a ring. I think it was an engagement ring."

"You saw the ring?"

"It was in his sock drawer."

"You were in his room?" She held up a hand to stop him from answering. "I don't want to know what you were doing, illegally searching Gregor Sandrington's room." She changed the subject. "What did Byrne say about Sarah Jenkins's attack?"

His gaze slid away from the stack of papers he was sorting through. "Funny, that," he said thoughtfully. "He didn't ask." His eyelids felt as if thousands of pins were poking through them. "We'd better start looking at the most likely suspect—someone close to both Julia and Ina. There's a connection. Maybe it's Anne Knightsbridge or maybe it's Evan Whelan. We've just got to look harder until we find it, because Sarah's attack proves there is one."

"How's that?"

"Sarah must know something someone else doesn't want her to tell us."

Claire made a derisive sound at the back of her throat. "Why club her?"

"Maybe someone took advantage of an unexpected opportunity." Mornay opened the largest drawer. This one contained correspondence. "Jackpot," he muttered to himself, and began pulling out folders. The first contained correspondence from her school days; he put it back in the drawer. The second and third folders contained letters from university friends; none of the letters were recent. The remainder of Ina's correspondence was categorized in folders by subject: Christmas, RNRS, Taxes, Household, and Birthdays. He pulled the RNRS folder from the stack first because he didn't know what the acronym stood for. Inside the folder were several dozen letters to and from the Royal National Rose Society. He plucked out the frontmost letter, dated two weeks ago. Most of the first page was taken up with the RNRS's logo and addresses. The letter congratulated Ina on her achievement. He flipped the page over to continue reading. The second page was missing. He searched through the folder to see if the second page had been put with the wrong letter, but it was missing.

"Someone's been through here," he said. "The second page to this letter is missing."

"Maybe Ina misplaced it."

"I doubt she misplaced anything in her life, if the state of this desk is anything to judge by. It's the newest letter in the folder."

"Who's it from?"

"The Royal National Rose Society. They're congratulating her on an achievement, but I've no idea what they're talking about unless it's the rose she's been working on. We'll have to call and see if they've got a copy on file."

"Maybe you should be careful how you handle it and the folder," she suggested.

"Right." He slipped the letter back into the folder and set them aside.

There was nothing suspicious or even curious in the remaining correspondence folders, so he put them away and looked in the last drawer of the desk. The drawer contained two plastic bins with airtight lids. One bin held photographs banded together with string. The second held notes made by Ina Matthews's father. "Here's a bin of photos. We'll have to take these back to the office—it'll take hours to sort through them."

"Looking for what?"

"A snap of John Dunbar, for starters. Find anything there?"

Claire was kneeling, pulling out books on the bottom bookshelf. "Not a thing."

A piece of paper dropped out of the last book on the shelf. Claire picked it up and was about to slip it back between the pages when she read it. "Look," she said, handing the note to Mornay.

You will pay for the demands you place on him. You don't have the right.

"That's creepy in a vaguely ominous sort of way, isn't it?"

"Who's he?" Mornay asked.

"I've no idea. Do you think we should take this seriously?" Claire asked.

"Ina's dead, isn't she?"

"Right."

She yawned, stood, and stretched. "Christ, it's been a long day. Are we through yet?"

"I just want a quick word with Sarah before we go."

Downstairs, the light in the sitting room was still on.

"Sarah, do you mind if we have a look through these?" He tapped the bin with the photos. "We'll have them back in a few days."

"Take as long as you need."

"Has anyone been through Ina's room besides Forensics?" Mornay asked.

"Is something wrong?"

"Just curious."

"Inspector Byrne was here . . . was it yesterday?"

"The day you were attacked?" Claire asked.

Sarah nodded. "That's right. He was here just after lunch. Or was it later? I'm sorry, everything's so fuzzy. It was that day, but I don't quite remember when."

Mornay exchanged a look with Claire. Yesterday Byrne had disappeared for several hours. And at the briefing, he hadn't told anyone he'd searched Ina Matthews's room. What had he been looking for? Had he been the one to take the second page of the RNRS letter?

Mornay stared out the streaky windshield of his car, still parked at the curb in front of Sarah Jenkins's cottage.

"Where's that autopsy report?" he asked Claire.

"Ina Matthews?"

"Julia."

Claire turned around, stretching over the front seat to reach the backseat and the stacks of paperwork that had slid around during their drive from the rectory.

She handed it to him, and Mornay forced himself to read slowly. He rolled every word around on his tongue, letting its echo reverberate through his thoughts.

Make the connection, he repeated to himself. He was convinced the answers to the deaths of these two women were buried in these pages. Why, he couldn't say. But when this intuitive feeling struck, Mornay obeyed.

He found himself skimming again. He cursed.

Claire opened her eyes. She'd leaned her seat back and was resting while he read. "What?"

"I need you to read this aloud."

Mornay passed along the autopsy report. He picked up the crime scene photographs as well as the photographs that the pathologist had taken when he'd performed Julia Whelan's autopsy.

"You're joking?"

"My eyes are tired. I'm skimming."

"What makes you think reading by a dome light won't tire my eyes out? It'll probably blind me."

"We don't have the time to argue. Will you just read the report?"

When she spoke next, her voice was quieter and calmer. "Why don't we just go home and get some rest, and attack this fresh in the morning?"

"We're running out of time."

As Claire snapped the autopsy report up in front

of her and started reading aloud, Mornay examined the police photographs.

Julia Whelan had died in her bedroom. The dimensions of the room were different from those of the bedroom her husband currently used. This room was larger and had a broad fireplace, which hadn't been converted over to gas. Real logs were laid in the grate, ready to light. There were windows set on either side of the large canopied bed.

In marked contrast to Evan Whelan's dreary little bedroom, generous amounts of sunlight spilled through the windows, brightening the plush, handsome furnishings and setting off the subject of the photographs to perfection. In death Julia Whelan was no less lovely than she'd been in life. She lay across her bed, above the ivory coverlet, fully clothed. Her feet were crossed at the ankles. There was dirt caked into the treads of her loafers. One hand rested on her abdomen, the other was stretched away from her body—palm up, fingers slightly curled—almost like a gesture of supplication. Her shoulder-length hair stretched across the pillow, away from her face. Thick and luxuriant, her hair glimmered beneath the wash of sunlight.

With her eyes closed, Mornay could see the delicate tracings of a smoky blue-colored eyeliner pencil along the fringe of her top eyelashes—just enough to give emphasis to her eyes. He wondered what shade of blue Julia Whelan's eyes had been. Had they been the lilac blue of her silk blouse? Or the deeper, richer color of her linen trousers?

The bed was flanked by an identical pair of cherry tables topped with identical lamps. That was where the similarities ended. The table on what was obviously Julia's side of the bed held a dog-eared murder mystery, a photograph of her husband, a glass half full of water, and a small vase of budding, apricot-colored roses. Evan Whelan's table held a haphazard stack of leather-bound volumes of what Mornay presumed to be poetry, a notebook, and a small drinking glass that held an assortment of pens and pencils.

Mornay put the photographs of the bedroom aside and picked up the photographs the pathologist had taken before making his Y incision and beginning his autopsy.

Beneath the harsh lights of the examination room Julia Whelan's hair had a lackluster, almost waxy look, and her lips were shaded a faint blue. Tiny blue veins showed on the lids of her eyes, at the base of her neck, on her breasts, and beneath the arches of her feet. Mornay preferred noting these small impersonal details rather than looking at the whole of the dead woman. But he couldn't keep himself from examining the most intimate details of her exquisite body—the flawless ivory skin of her inner thighs, her triangle of dark gold pubic hair, the curve of her breasts, her pale pink nipples.

Mornay couldn't detect a hint of the child she carried—nor was there any hint of the psychological turmoil she had to be going through to consider and carry out a plan to commit suicide.

Mornay dropped the picture, which showed Julia in her entirety, and examined another. This one was of her arm, and a curious bruise on it.

"What's this?" Mornay passed the picture to

Claire, who squinted at it beneath the dim light. There were actually two bruises, one on the inside of each arm just above the crook of the elbow. The medical examiner had photographed each separately.

"Report said she'd gotten them the day before, helping Ina shift flats of plants around."

"Which report?"

Claire flipped through the autopsy report, didn't find what she was looking for, and thumbed through the other reports. "Here it is, in Mary Hodgeson's statement. She got it from moving flats around in Ina Matthews's greenhouse."

"Did Ina Matthews corroborate?"

After flipping more pages over to find Ina Matthews's interview, Claire said, "Yes."

"Let me see."

Mornay read the interview that Sergeant Percy Wilkens, Mornay's predecessor, had taken on March 11, at four in the afternoon at Ina Matthews's cottage. It wasn't a lengthy report, comprising only a page and a half of neatly typed, double-spaced sentences. Ina Matthews attested to the fact that Julia Whelan seemed well on March 10, when she'd helped in the greenhouse.

Helped doing what? The height of one of the tables in my greenhouse needed to be raised, so all of the plants on the table needed to be moved off and cinder blocks put beneath the table legs. Then all of the plants needed to be put back on the table.

How long did that take? About two hours. There was some shifting of plants on the other table, to put like-aged plants together.

Was it difficult work? Some of the more damp flats were quite heavy, but it was more tedious than it was difficult.

What was your impression of Julia Whelan's behavior? Same as usual—she was glad to be out and about. She enjoyed getting her hands dirty.

Did Julia Whelan help you often? A couple of times a week, usually, when duties at the rectory didn't have her otherwise occupied.

Did Julia Whelan enjoy her duties? It wouldn't be a duty if it was enjoyable.

How long has Julia Whelan's husband been out of town? Going on a week now. He was to return from his conference on Thursday.

Was Julia Whelan anxious or concerned about her husband being out of town? She wasn't any more anxious or concerned than she was at any other time he was out of town. A bit lonely, perhaps, but that was natural; he was her closest friend.

Mornay dropped the report on the stack. "Was it just Wilkens's reports that were dull?" Mornay asked.

"Wilkens was always dry as toast. What do you think about those?" Claire pointed to the photographs.

Mornay picked up the photo of Julia on her bed. "Seems to me that a woman who wants to do herself in ought to look a bit more distressed. She looks as if she's about to go out to lunch or shopping. Almost looks as if she's been arranged, to me."

"Which would coincide nicely with your theory that she was murdered."

Mornay ignored her sarcasm and continued,

"Look at the glass of water on her bedside table. There are no lipstick smudges on the glass."

Claire made a noncommittal sound, but something about the picture was making his warning bells go off. "How did she take her pills? Dry?"

"I don't know," Claire said. "The way she's just lying there, it's enough to give you shivers."

"That's the most sympathetic you've sounded all day."

Anger hardened her features as she raised a finger and pointed it at him. "On any other day I might be more willing to humor you, but we've spent more than enough time examining a case that has been thoroughly examined. We've got an enormous amount of work ahead of us, we're both short on sleep, and I am *not* going to waste another moment worrying about something that might or might not have happened to Julia Whelan."

Claire closed the report folders and stacked them on her lap.

"You've never struck me as a quitter, Claire."

"This isn't the time or the place to be examining these files with a microscope."

"I can't let this go."

"Why? Because you've had a hunch? We don't make arrests on hunches. We've got to produce evidence. We've got to do lots and lots of legwork, and if we're lucky, we get a break. I've helped you get these files because I trust your judgment, but the more you dig, the more it looks as if you're trying to pin Inspector Byrne with negligence rather than get at the truth behind these deaths."

"I think Byrne was intending to use the information he'd gotten from Ina Matthews as a sort of trump card for the promotion he wanted. Then, when he discovered that he didn't get the promotion, he didn't bother to make a report. He let the case close—something that was virtually guaranteed because everyone, including the woman's own husband, accepted her death at face value."

"Are you listening to what you're saying?" she asked.

"This isn't a personal vendetta against Byrne."

"I don't think I believe that."

"Fair enough." He started his car. "We'll drop the snaps off at the office and call it a night, okay?"

"Finally," she muttered under her breath, slumping into her seat.

McNab removed a crumpled pack of cigarettes from his pocket and pinched out a bent cigarette, contemplating the best way to broach the subject of Mornay's message with Byrne. His lighter blew out twice from strong gusts of wind before he was able to get his cigarette lit.

He decided on the roundabout approach. "What's going on, Walter?"

"Fucking Mornay, that's what. Why am I the only one who doesn't think the bastard shits gold bricks? What happened to the old days, when you busted your balls for a few years to earn your promotion? He's been on the force for—what?—almost four years and he's already a sergeant? He was barely on the force two years before the ink on his transfer to CID was dry."

It was easy for McNab to recall the first day he'd

been made aware of Mornay. He'd been called to the
chief constable's office in Aberdeen, something that
never happened outside of scheduled meetings.
When he'd walked into the boardroom, dominated
by an oval-shaped conference table and a view of
Queen's Street, McNab found his immediate supervi-
sors, Detective Chief Superintendent Dugan, head of
CID, and Detective Superintendent McIntyre, head
of the force intelligence section. McNab's supervi-
sors were seated across the table from the highest
ranking officers on the force, the chief constable and
the assistant chief constable. The four men had
somber expressions and seemed to be making a point
of not looking in the direction of the last member of
their group, who had taken over the end of the table.
He wore a well-tailored dark blue wool suit and an
expression of equanimity. At the sight of the men,
McNab could feel his plans to have a quiet round of
golf that afternoon start to slowly dribble away. The
blue-suited man had an open briefcase before him
and, upon McNab's entrance, pulled out several
dark brown folders and arranged them on the table.

Emblazoned on the folders was the distinctive
insignia of the Ministry of Defense: a circlet of leaves
topped by a crown surrounding an anchor, eagle,
and crossed swords. There was the briefest of nods
from the chief constable for McNab to take a seat at
the opposite end of the table, next to Superintendent
McIntyre.

In the discussion that followed, the blue-suited
man, who had introduced himself simply as Mr.
Smith, explained how it would be in the best inter-
ests of the Grampian Police to hasten one Police

Constable Mornay's CID transfer paperwork and promotion to sergeant.

McNab heard rumors later that Mr. Smith worked for British Intelligence. But Mornay being associated with MI5 or MI6 sounded too fanciful to be true. Why would he want to become a common police officer in one of the least populated areas of the country?

McNab now turned away from the brunt of the chilling wind, shoving his hands further into his pockets. A week after the meeting with the mysterious Mr. Smith, he'd found out about his own promotion to chief inspector. He took another long drag on his cigarette. "Mornay's proven himself to be a capable officer during the last two years, and he was in the military for nearly ten years before he joined the force."

"That makes it fair for him to trounce into the department and take promotions from men who've worked twice as hard and twice as long?"

The breeze blew some of McNab's acrid cigarette smoke back into his eyes. He blinked rapidly and wondered if he would ever have the strength to quit his three-pack-a-day habit. Not as long as Walter continued his aggressive behavior.

"Mornay's case is unique. You know every facet of his career is being monitored directly by Headquarters. For us to argue it here would not only be futile, but also would waste time we can't afford to lose."

"Don't fool yourself, Andy."

McNab drew on the last bit of his cigarette, and then tossed it to the gravel, grinding it with his heel.

"I think Mornay's a good man. Dependable. Nothing in his actions indicates that he's come to Macduff to do anything but a good job."

"Nothing but the fact he's broken the fucking record for promotions."

"I think it's time we concentrated on finding some concrete evidence on this case."

"Are the defense agents circling again?"

McNab sighed. "How does every conversation we have become combative? I'm not your enemy."

Byrne turned to face him. "You're just my boss."

"Since we're being blunt, you know damn well you're the one who allowed that to happen. You've never known when to just shut up."

"But I've had to learn how to take it. Right?"

McNab almost laughed with amazement. Walter had absolutely no clue. "I've been taking it for you. Who do you think has been holding the pack back from forcing you into early retirement?"

"Don't bother doing me any favors." Byrne turned on his heel and walked away.

The crunching sounds of Byrne's strides floated back to McNab. Walter was probably going to the gate to harass the poor constable posted there.

chapter sixteen

Sunday, 5:15 A.M.
Macduff

The wind whipping off the North Sea caught Mornay fully when he left the slight protection his car offered. His tie flew up, lashing him on the chin and the corner of his right eye. The sharp sting made his eye water.

For some odd reason, the wind didn't seem to be ripping at Claire. She crossed the nearly empty car park quickly and took the concrete steps two at a time. She didn't even pause to wait for him as she pushed through the front entrance to the station.

Mornay plodded along, blotting at his eye with the end of his tie. Through the glass doors, he watched Claire exchange pleasantries with Constable Taylor. Mornay shouldered his way through the door and had to squint against the bright overhead fluorescent lights.

Constable Taylor was less enthusiastic in his greeting to Mornay than he'd been toward Claire.

"Any messages this morning?" Mornay asked.

Taylor passed a blue slip of paper across the counter. "Pratt took this for you last night." There was an oily thumbprint in the center of the note; the call must have come through while Pratt was enjoying another of his wife's cinnamon rolls. If his wife continued sending him in with food, the man wouldn't be able to fit his uniform in six months' time.

Mornay read his note: *I've got some information to share regarding other patients. Edwin Hartwick.*

Pratt didn't put a time received on the note, so Mornay asked, "What time did this come through?"

Taylor shrugged. "If he didn't put it on the note, I've no way of knowing."

Mornay cursed and walked to his desk. He hadn't bothered to look at his answering machine when he'd gotten home late last night. Hartwick had probably left a message there as well.

Claire was seated at their desk, reviewing the fiber analysis results. She'd neatly lined the clear plastic evidence bags at the back of the desk. There was the piece of garden stake they'd found in the cemetery and the piece that'd been found in Ina Matthews. There was a withered rose petal; Mornay had decided to bag it. Ina Matthews's bloody clothes were bagged, as well as the broken wooden chair leg that'd been used to attack Sarah Jenkins.

All of the reports Claire had copied were stacked on the corner of the desk.

Mornay didn't feel like pulling up the other chair

and reading over her shoulder, so he walked up to Willie's fishbowl and tapped the glass.

Willie, ever vigilant for another snack, swished his flowing gold tail slightly to propel himself to the glass to inspect Mornay's finger. Willie was partial to flavored crisps; vinegar and salt were his favorite. If those weren't available he was, oddly enough, fond of salmon-flavored crisps. He let all the other flavors float to the bottom of his bowl.

When it was obvious to Willie he wouldn't be getting a treat, he returned to his niche between a pair of smooth granite stones Claire had picked up on the beach.

"Sod," Mornay said to the uppity goldfish.

Next to the fishbowl was a small rose potted in a cheap plastic bowl. Mornay pulled out the plastic tag inserted into the soil and read: R. FERDINAND PICKARD. PLANT IN FULL SUN.

"Who sent you this?" Mornay asked.

Once, months ago, Claire had inadvertently let it slip that she was fond of flowers. So at least once a week, she received deliveries of bouquets from blokes hoping to bury their faces between her breasts. Claire took the flowers gladly, but as far as he knew, the breasts were off-limits.

She frowned, looking up from the report she'd been reading. "Ross sent that. He said I might like to have something that'd live for more than a week. I need to plant it before it dies. Have a look." Claire pushed the report at him. "They've found a match."

"To what?"

Claire pointed to the paragraph she wanted him to read. "Same fibers. See? They found several of these threads on the raincoat and on Ina Matthews's body."

"So they're the same—what does that tell us? Nothing we couldn't have already guessed. We need to know where the fibers came from. We find the source, we might find our killer."

"There are some facts I'm fully capable of comprehending on my own. Now, if you'll let me finish. These fibers are silk—dyed silk. Probably from a sweater, by the size of the fibers. We've got a reason to search closets now. The problem is, it's going to take legwork and time to canvass the area, and every spare body we have will be at Sandrington Hall this morning." She checked her watch. "Speaking of which, we'd better be going if we're going to get there on time."

"Just a minute." He picked up the phone and dialed Dr. Hartwick's number. "Hartwick left a message last night," he told her as the phone rang. "He might have something interesting to tell us."

Hartwick answered directly, his voice clear. He'd obviously been awake. "I was wondering when you might call," Hartwick said. "I've looked over patient records, as I told you I would."

"Find any similar symptoms?"

There was a pause. Hartwick cleared his throat before saying, "Yes. In fourteen patients over a three-year period. Five have died since they reported their symptoms."

"From ricin toxin?"

"Perhaps" was the guarded reply.

"And you didn't suspect poisoning?"

"It's hardly a common way to die, is it?" Hartwick asked wearily. "One of the patients, Edgar Baker, was seventy-nine; he had a heart condition. Carol Meyers was fifty-one. She was diagnosed with inoperable ovarian cancer about two months before she died. My last patient to die was Paul Hume. He, too, had heart problems."

"Did you draw a recent blood sample from Hume?" Mornay asked.

"Yes, though I haven't sent it for testing yet."

"Why not?"

Mornay wished he could have seen Hartwick's expression. "I'm preparing them now to send in."

"And the others?"

"I treated them for stomach ailments."

"Any recently?"

"The most recent was in last week. The others reported their symptoms within the last four months."

"Were any patients reporting these same symptoms around the same time Julia Whelan died?"

Edwin Hartwick didn't immediately answer the question. When he did speak, his voice sounded even wearier. "I haven't gone that far back. I'll need to bring in my staff. If I can reach them this morning, we should know sometime this afternoon."

"Will it be possible to get the patients from these more recent cases in the office first thing this morning, draw their blood, and see if they're suffering from—what's the condition, again?"

"Hemolysis. What should I tell them? It's Sunday—they'll all be at service this morning."

"Which church?"

"There's only the two, Sergeant."

"Right," Mornay said as if this weren't news. "Did Ina attend St. David's?"

"Half the village attends."

Could that be his connection? Was Byrne right all along about Evan Whelan? Or were the poisonings and the stabbing committed by two different people?

"When do church services start?" Mornay asked.

"Nine."

"Why don't you give me their names," Mornay said. "I'll send a police constable around to collect them. He'll explain, *after* he's brought them to your office, exactly why they're there. That should keep them quiet and cooperative. And hopefully we'll avoid starting a general panic."

"Perhaps your constable should suggest they don't eat or drink anything," Hartwick said. "As we still don't know how they're being poisoned."

He sounded like a man walking in a fog. "You couldn't have known," Mornay told him. "As you said, being poisoned isn't common, and the poison was so mildly administered, these symptoms could've been caused by a hundred different things."

"But they weren't, Sergeant. They were caused by one, very specific thing—and I should've discovered that before anyone died."

Paul Hume lived in a complex of flats designed for the elderly. Hume's flat was small and so devoid of clutter, it felt like a hotel room. After Mornay bullied the manager of the complex into opening the flat up, he and Claire searched the kitchen first. The cupboards were empty except for three boxes of Weetabix and half a dozen cans of evaporated milk.

"I wonder why there's no food in the cupboards," Mornay said.

"Maybe he couldn't afford food."

"If I can't afford to buy food when I'm old, I'll shoot myself."

The search of the tiny lounge took less than five minutes. They split the search of the bedroom: She took the left side; he took the right. Claire found a note on the stand next to the bed, in an envelope that had a month-old postmark.

"This is exactly like Ina Matthews's note," she said.

He nodded. "So it is."

Chief Inspector McNab took Mornay's news better than Inspector Byrne. Both men stood near the servants' entrance to Sandrington Hall, which was near the largest kitchen. The kitchen was being systematically dismantled. What couldn't be tested on site, such as the contents of the freezers, was being packed and carted to vans to be taken to the lab to be tested.

Byrne's neck was red and its veins were bulging when Mornay finished relaying what Dr. Hartwick had told him. "I don't know who you think you are," Byrne sputtered. "Issuing orders like some fucking—"

"That's enough," McNab hissed. "One more word and I'll have you suspended until this inquiry is closed. Do you understand me, Inspector?"

"Yes, sir." Byrne pulled out his half-smoked cigar, crushing it beneath his heel.

"Who did you send to pick these people up?" McNab asked Mornay.

"Constable Sahotra. He'll take the blood samples to Aberdeen to be tested."

"Is everything ready there?"

"Dr. Hall is going to run the tests personally."

"Good." McNab looked around. Mercer and Gillian joined them, and McNab filled them in.

When McNab was through, Mornay said, "All of the victims—"

"If that's what they really are," McNab said.

"All of the *possible* victims," Mornay amended, "attend St. David's, including the deceased ones. We'll contact the families and ask if they've found notes similar to the ones we found."

"And they all shop or shopped in the same grocer and use or used the same post office," Byrne said. "What's your point?"

Mornay returned Byrne's stare without flinching. "We found the umbrella in the rectory's mudroom. Someone's fairly cozy with the layout there. I think we need to concentrate on locals, not Tommy Torga. Someone is targeting parishioners at St. David's."

"What about John Dunbar?" Claire asked. "We still don't know how he fits in."

"Only in regards to the poisonings," McNab said. "Ina Matthews's attack might be a completely separate crime. Dunbar could have easily come to town, argued with Ina over whatever it was he came to town for, and then stabbed her."

Mornay was shaking his head. "There's no obvious—"

"If you want an obvious choice for the poisonings,

try the good rector," Byrne said, cutting Mornay off mid-sentence. "He's been a nervous wreck from the first moment we arrived. Maybe he's cracked since his wife killed herself, and he's been poisoning his parishioners ever since. You said one had ovarian cancer? Maybe he thought he was performing a valuable community service."

"Whelan is afraid of something," Mornay agreed. "But poisoning? People are poisoned to get rid of them. Why bother to simply make them sick?"

"Punishment," Claire supplied.

Everyone's attention swiveled her way.

McNab tugged at his earlobe. "There's a gruesome thought. Anything to share before we get started?" he asked the detectives from Peterhead.

"Guess who got lucky with the national lottery?" Mercer asked.

When no one guessed, he said, "Tommy Torga's uncle."

"Why didn't we know sooner?" McNab asked.

"Different surname, as he's not a blood relative. We're fortunate to have found out at all. One of the constables in our office recognized the name in the paper."

Mornay edged away from the group. A curtain had flicked in a second-story window earlier; he kept watching it to see if he could get a glimpse of the person behind the curtain.

"How much did he win?" Byrne asked.

"Just over two million."

Byrne cursed.

"That's not the worst of it, sir," Gillian threw in. "He won the money a month ago. Just before a flurry of phone calls to Tommy. He probably engineered the escape. They've had time to buy new identities. Move to China if they wanted."

Mercer growled something under his breath at Gillian that sounded suspiciously like "Shut up." To everyone else he said, "We're sending out photos of the entire family to the airports and railway stations. It's a long shot, but maybe someone will remember them."

McNab didn't appear hopeful. "If that's it, then I've a news briefing to attend. Mornay and Gillespie, a word, please." McNab waited until the other officers were out of hearing before saying, "I've got a meeting this afternoon with Anne Knightsbridge's solicitors. Any ideas why they might want to be speaking privately with me?" McNab directed the question at Mornay.

"No, sir," Mornay lied.

McNab turned to Claire. "Constable Gillespie?"

"I really couldn't say, sir. We've hardly spoken with her."

"Did they give you any hints what the meeting was about?" Mornay asked.

"As a matter of fact, they said they wanted to discuss the conduct of one of my officers." McNab's gaze drifted across the wide lawn. "I'll get it sorted. Make sure you let Forensics know there might be other houses to search, if these other patients of Dr. Hartwick's come up positive for the ricin toxin."

"Punishment?" Mornay whispered to Claire as they walked down the same long, carpeted hall they'd come down the previous day at Sandrington Hall.

"What's your suggestion?" Her voice was defensive. "Incompetence?"

Byrne flashed them a look when they entered the room. The Sandringtons were waiting for them; the room was chilly with tension.

"Lord Sandrington!" Byrne's voice boomed out overly loud. "Is there anything you've forgotten to tell us regarding your relationship with Ina Matthews?"

Sandrington's gaze barely moved in their direction. He stood by a window, his back to the room. He continued watching the police in the courtyard below. "I don't think so."

"There's a jeweler in Aberdeen we're going to be asking about you. Are you quite sure there's nothing you wanted to tell us?"

Sandrington turned around. His face was ashen, the skin beneath his eyes puffy from lack of sleep, or grief.

"When did you ask Ina to marry you?" Mornay asked.

Byrne bristled at Mornay's interruption but waited to hear what Sandrington was going to say.

When Sandrington spoke, he sounded like a broken man. "Wednesday was the last time. I had the ring that night. I asked her twice before without a ring."

Lydia Sandrington's shock was as understated as her son's grief. They were people who'd gotten very good at hiding their true feelings; the room thrummed with the emotions both were trying to conceal. "You were going to marry Ina?"

"I *wanted* to marry her, Mother. However, Ina didn't want to marry me."

"And the AA meeting?" Byrne asked.

"After she told me no, I went to see if I could find a reason not to buy myself a bottle. I ended up in the pub across the street, and then on the pub owner's couch. Thursday morning I was going to go back and convince Ina I was worth the trouble, but I lost my nerve—"

"Sir, we've found something," Gillian said as he entered the room. "You'll want to have a look."

"Hidden in plain sight," Mercer said.

"Too right," Mornay agreed. The dagger was oddly shaped. It didn't have a true handle, just a stub of metal that was curved to fit in the palm. It had been originally designed to fit neatly in a sporran, the pouch usually worn at the front of a kilt, so the blade was short—no more than seven or eight centimeters long. Blood had dried along the blade's length. A less sharp-eyed searcher might have mistaken the blackened blood for corrosion. The small dagger was part of an extensive display of Sandrington family weaponry. The assorted pikes and swords, knives, and other weapons he couldn't name were hung from square-headed nails that'd been mortared into the stone fireplace. Smaller knives and daggers were neatly lined up on the granite-slab mantel. All of the weaponry appeared quite old. The blade edges were worn and obviously not well maintained. A faint odor of preservative oil wafted from the display.

"How often is this room used?" Byrne asked Lydia Sandrington, who was hovering at one end of the room. Gregor Sandrington stood behind her, not even mildly curious at the blood-crusted knife that'd been found on the mantel.

"We use it in the evenings for coffee and brandy."

Mornay was examining daggers displayed at the far end of the mantel. "And the general public?" he asked. "Do they have access to this room?"

"This is one of the most popular rooms on our tours."

"And you haven't noticed that one of your knives went missing, temporarily?" Byrne asked.

In shades of her former self, Lydia Sandrington said, "Obviously not, Inspector, or I would have reported it."

Mornay could practically hear Byrne salivating from across the room. He had his hands shoved deeply in his trouser pockets and a feral gleam in his eyes.

"We're going to need you to come with us," Byrne said to Sandrington. Then lazily he remembered to add, "Sir."

Before Lydia Sandrington could recover sufficiently to speak, her son said, "Just call our attorney, Mother. He'll know what to do."

chapter seventeen

Mornay sat in the backseat with Sandrington; Mercer and Gillian were in the front seat. They took Sandrington directly to Peterhead, rather than to Macduff. Peterhead's facilities would be more intimidating.

Byrne spent three hours interviewing Sandrington, and the most significant piece of information they learned, in Mornay's opinion, was that Sandrington was surprised by the fact that Ina Matthews had been poisoned. Byrne thought he was lying, but Mornay wasn't so sure. It would've taken a good actor to feign the shock on Sandrington's face when he'd heard about the poison.

Claire had Mornay's car; she'd taken it back to Macduff to follow up on the blood work Dr. Hartwick's other patients had gotten that day. Mornay borrowed a police car to get back to Macduff since Byrne had decided to go to Aberdeen and gloat about closing the case, but he took a detour to the Royal Infirmary on his way home.

Pamela had been moved to the Critical Care Ward. It held eight beds; all had the patients' feet pointed toward the nurses' station. Designed for patients, it had scant provisions for worried families. Victoria sat in a straight-backed wooden chair next to Pamela's bed, arms crossed, staring blankly at the floor. The patients in other wards were being fed their dinners. The scent of hot meals was absent in this ward. There was no sign of Fiona. Thank heaven for small mercies.

"Tori?" he said quietly.

Victoria met his gaze. "I didn't think you could come today."

"I can only stay for a bit. We've made an arrest on the Matthews case. I'm on my way back to the office to start on the paperwork."

She nodded, too numb and weary to make polite conversation.

"What did the doctors say?" he prompted when her gaze had returned to the still form of her sister on the bed. Tubes snaked from Pamela's arms and mouth, and gauze covered most of her head. The only patch of skin not covered with a bandage was beneath her chin. The rasping sound of the respirator sent chills through his body. It took sheer willpower to keep his teeth from chattering; he'd gotten that cold since stepping through the hospital entrance.

"Her surgery went better than they expected. They did a brain scan this morning." Victoria's voice got quieter as she spoke. "They told me to prepare myself. They don't think she'll wake up."

"It's still early days." He meant it to sound encouraging, but the words came out flat and lifeless.

Her gaze returned to the floor.

He took the other chair and sat. But after ten minutes he said, "Let's go and get a cup of tea."

"You loathe tea, especially when it comes in a paper cup. They don't use proper cups here."

An icy sensation ran through his body.

"What?" she asked. She was looking up at him. He'd stood without realizing it.

He walked over, took her face between his hands—as he used to before he'd left for the Marines—and kissed the top of her head.

"You're brilliant, Tori," he whispered. "You are absolutely brilliant. I'll be back as soon as I've finished up in the office. I promise."

"What did I say?" Her voice trailed behind him as he rushed out of the ward.

Driving one-handed, Mornay punched in the number to the office on the mobile phone.

"Claire, do you have Julia Whelan's files with you?" he asked when the call had been transferred to their desk.

"Yes, why?"

"I need to take a look at the stomach contents again. Read it to me."

"Hang on." Claire shuffled through papers and barked a command at Sahotra to fetch something from the conference table. "Right, here it is." She read him the list, which included citrus oil, tannin, and the unpronounceable pharmaceutical name of the pills Julia had taken.

"Tea. She drank tea."

She sighed, "I know. There's a hand-written note on the back. The pathologist says she probably had Earl Grey. It's flavored with oil of bergamot. Citrus oil."

"You didn't read that note last night."

"I didn't see the scribble to turn the paper over last night. It was so dark I could barely read the typewritten words."

"How much liquid was in her stomach?"

There was a long pause as she searched for the information. "Almost a thousand milliliters. Nearly two cups. Sandrington's locked up, pending his charges. I'm exhausted. I want to go home and feed my cat. I want to take a bath."

"Sandrington didn't kill Ina."

There was a sound over the line. She might have covered the receiver and cursed, or it could simply have been background noise. When she came back on, she said, "The answer came to you out of the blue, did it? Until you can produce a name and some evidence to go with that name, Gregor Sandrington's our man."

"Julia Whelan loathed tea," he said.

"I loathe the rubbery egg sandwiches in the sandwich machine, but that doesn't prevent me from eating them when it doesn't look like I'll have a chance at a meal for hours."

"Why would you drink something you hated to

swallow the pills you were taking to kill yourself? Why not drink something you like?"

"You're looking for rational behavior from a woman planning her suicide?" she asked.

"Sandrington told me that Julia was caught by her housekeeper diluting her tea with whiskey, she hated drinking tea that much. He said Julia was so concerned about making a good impression with Mary Hodgeson she was afraid to tell the woman she hated tea."

"Consider your source" was her reply.

"Have a look at the crime scene photos. Take a good look at the ones with Julia's bedside table in them, then tell me what's missing."

Mornay pinched the phone between his ear and shoulder to free his hand, which made for awkward driving, but he managed. He scratched the new growth of stubble sprouting on his chin. The coarse hairs were irritating the nicks he'd given himself when he'd last shaved. His scratching only succeeded in dislodging one of the scabs; it started bleeding again. He reached in his pocket to find his handkerchief. When he pulled it out, the tag he'd plucked from Claire's potted rose fluttered into his lap.

Absently, he read the thin white piece of plastic again: R. FERDINAND PICKARD. Then he reviewed what he knew. If Gregor hadn't killed Julia Whelan and Ina Matthews, who had? And why? Byrne had fixated on Evan Whelan from the start, for no apparent reason. Did Byrne learn something about Whelan during his wife's inquiry that he neglected to put in a report? That seemed the most likely explanation for Byrne's aggression. What had Byrne learned, or guessed at?

That Whelan had heard rumors of his wife's friendship with Sandrington? Had the rector decided to rid himself of a supposedly adulterous wife and used his conference in Edinburgh as his alibi? Was he offing troublesome parishioners?

Though it sounded plausible, it was still conjecture. What Mornay had was a knife that was part of a military collection, a broken garden marker that was missing its bit of copper, and a rose petal. There was also the attack on Sarah Jenkins, but he still didn't know how that related to the other parts of the case.

Byrne's strange words suddenly came back to him. *Maybe the stake was symbolic.*

"Claire," he said, to see if she was still on the line.

"I'm here," she said. "There's no teacup or teapot," she said.

"Right." That's what had bothered him about the pictures last night, only he didn't realize it until Victoria had said the word *cup*.

"She must've had the tea downstairs and then gone back to her room."

"Let's consider this scenario: She was forced to drink the tea downstairs, or somewhere else entirely, and then was taken or led back to her room."

"You don't really want to know what I think," she said.

"What was her time of death?"

"It was estimated between 10 P.M. and midnight."

Clearly she was going to need something else before she was convinced Julia was murdered. He still held the rose tag in his hand. "Are there any other reasons someone might use a marker for a plant?"

"Besides showing what the name of the plant is?"

"Right."

"What's the point? Markers were meant to have names put on them."

"Markers were meant to have names put on them," he repeated softly as he twisted the plastic tag from Claire's rose between his fingers. R. FERDINAND PICKARD, the rose's name. "Claire, did we ever find out the name Ina gave her rose?"

"I don't think so" was her hesitant reply. "Why would it matter?"

"I don't know, but we're missing the second half of that rose society letter, as well as the roses Ina was carrying when she was attacked. None were found near her body. Why pick them up? If you wanted to get rid of the roses to hide the fact someone had been attacked on the path, why not lay them on a nearby grave? Why carry them away? What's their significance? Can you put me on hold and give Sarah a ring? Ask if she knows."

Mornay had driven nearly five kilometers before Claire came back on the line. "She's not answering. I rang the rectory to see if maybe she'd gone there with Mary, but the line's in use."

"Who's on duty right now at the rectory?"

"Bensen. Sahotra's trying to radio him, but hasn't been able to reach him yet."

"Is Byrne still in Aberdeen?"

"As far as I know. The chief inspector left after Anne Knightsbridge didn't show."

"Her solicitor canceled the appointment?"

"No—she didn't arrive and her solicitor didn't want to have the meeting without her."

"Where is she?"

"No one knows."

"Has anyone bothered to look for her?" In his sudden anger, he fumbled the phone, dropping it completely as he downshifted to get around a lorry. While he didn't want Anne pressing formal charges against him, her not showing for the meeting worried him. "I should be arriving at the office to pick you up in ten minutes," he said, when he'd gotten around the lorry and fished his mobile off the passenger seat. "Keep trying to reach Bensen."

"We're going back to Glen Ross tonight? I don't want another double shift."

"What about that promotion you want? If you reach Bensen, tell him not to let anyone out of the rectory gates. Including Inspector Byrne. Who's on duty tonight?"

"Pratt and Dunnholland."

"Radio them and tell them to get to Sarah Jenkins's house immediately."

The gates to St. David's rectory were wide open and unmanned. McNab's Land Rover was parked behind Whelan's car.

"I wonder why *he's* here," Mornay said to Claire.

"Maybe he decided to speak with Anne personally."

He cut a glance in her direction.

She held a palm up. "Maybe her solicitor told him the real reason why she'd called the meeting."

He hit the brakes a bit too hard, skidding the car into the grass. If Anne brought charges against him, he'd probably be suspended pending an investigation, then he'd probably be dismissed. "If Bensen is in the kitchen eating more scones, I'll . . ." Mornay's voice faded. He wasn't quite sure what he'd do to Bensen.

"We've got Sandrington locked away, and Byrne never told him to guard the gates at all costs."

"No one should've needed to get that literal. The man ought to have the sense to know he wasn't put there to count stars."

"Maybe if you'd been around earlier you could've given him the proper instructions personally."

Mornay ignored her baited comment. The sun had disappeared. Dusk was settling in. Soon—too soon—it'd be dark. He scanned the shadows edging the drive, wondering if Bensen had wandered off to take a piss. He didn't see any flickering lights from a torch, and Bensen didn't strike him as the sort who would admire the scenery any longer than was absolutely necessary.

A halo of light was being cast into the trees from the rear of the rectory. "Let's go round back," he said.

Someone had left the outer and inner doors to the mudroom open. The outer door was propped open with a terra cotta pot; the inner door was propped open with a kettle full of water. It was almost as if someone was issuing an invitation for someone to enter.

Mornay held his finger to his lips.

Claire made a face. "I'm not Dunnholland. I don't need to be led by the hand."

Mornay's eyes narrowed. He whispered, "I'll try to keep that in mind in the future."

"Don't make promises you don't intend to keep," Claire said, not bothering with the stage whisper.

Mornay swept his hand in a wide arc. "Now that we've thoroughly buggered any chances of a surprise entrance, why don't you go first?"

Claire walked ahead of him.

The kitchen was brightly lit. The tap at the sink had not been pushed down fully, and it was dribbling a steady stream of water. The pilot light had also been left on the cook top. It sizzled and hissed from the breeze whipping through the open doors.

Claire switched the cook top off and looked at Mornay, waiting for him to comment.

Mornay reached beneath his arm, searching for a side arm he hadn't carried in over two years. He felt Claire's gaze on him as he quickly withdrew his hand and searched for something he could use as a weapon. He ended up reaching for a rolling pin in the drying rack next to the sink.

He hefted the rolling pin and took an experimental swing. "This is ridiculous," he said.

"Tell that to Ina Matthews."

"Coming along, then?"

"Wouldn't miss it for the world," Claire said. "Should I bring the mixing spoon?"

"You're a regular—" His voice stopped mid-sentence.

Lying on the floor behind the work island was Chief Inspector McNab.

Quickly they knelt on either side of the crumpled body, Claire reaching for McNab's pulse while Mornay straightened the man out so he could lie flat on his back.

"His pulse is strong," she said.

To further attest to his well-being, the chief inspector opened his eyes. "Mornay, you're a fucking sight from this angle."

Mornay grinned broadly, relieved. He gave his boss a hand sitting up.

McNab gently touched the swelling lump over his right ear and groaned. "Bastard hit me when I was looking for the tea tin. Where's Byrne?"

"Dunno," Mornay answered. "Where's everyone else?"

"I haven't seen anyone. Though that's not to say they haven't seen me." McNab checked his watch, moving it closer to his eyes until he could read the luminous numbers. "I've been lying here at least a quarter of an hour."

"You're sure you didn't hear or see anyone?"

"Not a hint of anyone."

"Did you smell perfume or cologne?" Claire asked.

McNab was slower to answer, straining to remember. "I don't know."

Mornay met Claire's gaze over a very groggy McNab. "I'll just nip upstairs and have a look around."

"What about me?"

Mornay nodded toward the chief inspector. "He could probably use a cup of tea."

"Help me to my feet," McNab said when Mornay left the room. "We'll lend him a hand anyway."

It took less than ten minutes for the three of them to thoroughly search the rectory. It was empty.

Claire called Sandrington Hall while the chief inspector doctored himself with aspirin he'd found in a cupboard near the sink. "No one's seen any of them at Sandrington Hall," she reported. "And Sarah Jenkins's line is still engaged."

"I want to check on Sarah Jenkins," Mornay said. "I'm going to walk over—I'll get there faster than driving."

"Hang on," Claire said before he could get out the door. "Think you're the Lone Ranger, riding off with your rolling pin?" She swept past him and through the door. "I'll just tag along, right?"

Mornay glanced back to the chief inspector. The older man's skin was still pale and he had to keep a hand on the work island to keep himself steady.

"Go on," McNab said. "I'll be fine."

Mornay left the rolling pin on the counter before walking out.

Claire had a head start on him. Mornay tracked her by her bobbing torchlight; she was moving fast. The breeze was sharp and cool. It carried the scent of grass and sea air.

"Hard to believe everyone's gone off for a stroll at the same time," Claire said when he'd caught up to her.

"My thoughts exactly," he said.

"When are you going to tell McNab about the missing teacup?"

"One thing at a time, Claire."

"Funny, something like that getting overlooked," she said.

"You think it wasn't?"

"I doubt it. You'll probably find out there's a very reasonable explanation for why the teacup isn't in—"

They were suddenly plunged into darkness, and Mornay heard a soft thud. He swept his hands out in a wide arc, searching for her. "Claire, where are you?"

"Down here." Her voice came low and to his left. "I tripped." She cursed.

"Claire?"

Her voice came out even softer now. "I've tripped over someone. I think it might be Bensen."

Mornay scrabbled around in the grass until he'd found the torch Claire had dropped. Pressing the switch got him nowhere, so he gave the light a couple of good thumps against his palm and it came back to life.

He shone the light in Claire's direction.

Bensen lay facedown in the spongy loam just off the path. Claire crawled forward so she could check his pulse. "There's so much blood. Someone's hit him on the head."

Before she pressed two fingers against his neck, Mornay could've told her Bensen was dead. There were no breath movements.

Claire snatched her hand away almost as soon as she touched Bensen's skin. "He's dead." Her words echoed out quiet and hollow.

She scrubbed her fingers against the leg of her trousers, trying to clean the blood off. Then she stood and stumbled away from the body, but her gaze remained on Bensen.

"Claire?" Mornay took a step toward her.

She stumbled back a few more steps, putting more distance between them.

"He was practically a child." Her voice was cracking. She looked his way at last.

"Claire, there's nothing you . . ."

She held up her hand, palm out. "Don't you dare take a step closer. Look at him." Her voice was harsh now, the syllables coming out in raspy bursts of sound. "Look at him!" she nearly shouted as one of her hands sliced toward Bensen's body, pointing.

"I hardly knew the man, Claire. What do you expect me to say?"

Tears were running down her cheeks now. She didn't seem to notice.

"He was like a puppy whenever you were around, and you couldn't even be bothered to remember his name. You can't be bothered to remember any of their names, and they still hang on to your every word. What kind of person does that make you? None of them have realized that all the chances you take on the job have nothing to do with you getting the bad guys. You take them because you don't care one way or the other what happens to you."

"That's a hell of a deductive leap, Claire, even for you."

"But we both know it's the truth, don't we?"

Tree limbs creaked ominously overhead. A car horn honked somewhere in the distance.

"We don't have time for this, Claire. Get back to McNab. Tell him Whelan's got Anne. Tell him to get someone—anyone—to Sarah Jenkins's cottage. I think that's where he's taken her."

chapter eighteen

Mornay sprinted down the path toward Glen Ross; the weak beam the torch sent out bobbed up and down erratically, casting weird shadows, making it harder for him to see. The path came out on the north side of the square. He heard a faint pulsing of music drifting through the open door of the pub.

Sarah Jenkins's cottage was on Lavender Drive, one of the four side roads that came away from the square like spokes. Lavender Drive was the first road to his right.

Everyone in town—and from the surrounding towns, by the looks—had gathered at the pub. But the street was dead quiet.

There were no lights on in Sarah's cottage. Mornay felt a fresh surge of adrenaline go through his body. Whelan had to be here—where else would he take Anne?

But what if he'd got it wrong?

He squelched the doubts and opened the gate, latching it quietly behind him. Instead of knocking on the front door or checking to see if it was unlocked, he cut across the garden and went around to the back of the cottage.

There were no lights on at the back of the cottage.

Mornay did a slow turn, searching and listening. A light shone through the shrubbery at the back of the garden. It was coming from Ina Matthews's greenhouse.

He wished he hadn't gotten rid of the rolling pin. The ruddy thing might have come in handy. Mornay edged closer to the greenhouse, keeping to the shadows.

Condensation covered the glass walls, making it nearly impossible to see inside. He could vaguely see the tables covered with their flats of plants, the main posts that supported the roof, and four blurry figures.

He heard Evan Whelan say, "Anne, don't move . . ."

The rest of the words were too low to make out. Mornay edged closer, stepping carefully on the loose, charred rubble of the ruined potting shed until he could peer through the doorway.

He should've spent half a second to find a weapon; even a rock would've been better than his bare hands. If he had time, he'd wait for McNab.

But it might be too late by then.

He took a deep breath and slowly crept across the rubble, closer to the doorway.

Anne Knightsbridge stood with her back to one of the center posts, arms by her side. Evan Whelan was standing next to her, a length of blue cord in his hands. He looked as if he were considering tying her to the post.

Sarah Jenkins was on her knees, her shoulder leaning against one of the potting tables, eyes closed. Mary Hodgeson had a hand on her shoulder, trying to keep her propped upright.

Mornay carefully took another two steps until he was on solid and relatively quiet ground from which to launch an attack.

Before Whelan had the chance to tie Anne to the post, Mornay hurtled through the door, lunging at Whelan, neatly hooking the man with an arm around his neck.

They crashed hard on the crushed-stone path.

Mornay took the brunt of the fall on his right shoulder. He managed to keep his forearm around Whelan's neck, despite the blaze of pain that shot through his body. Whelan lay curiously limp beneath him, as if he'd given up the fight before it'd even started.

In the silence that followed Mornay's unexpected attack, Anne said, "Let him go, Seth."

Mornay glanced up. Anne's gaze was clear and forthright; the left side of her face was red. A dark bruise was forming on her left cheek. Whelan had blackened her eye.

"What?"

"Quiet," Mary Hodgeson suddenly hissed. "Not another word out of either of you."

Mary was pointing a World War II service revolver

at Mornay. The old weapon was so rusted, he doubted it would even be able to fire off a shot.

"Help Evan up," she ordered. Mornay rolled to his side and lifted his arm, freeing Whelan. The man slid to a sitting position, coughing.

Mornay stood, holding both hands up, palms out, though his shoulder was throbbing with pain. "Mrs. Hodgeson," he said calmly so he wouldn't startle her. "You should put that revolver down. If its barrel is fouled and you try to fire, it might explode in your hand."

Anne Knightsbridge started laughing, the sound a shade hysterical. "That's a treat, worrying *she'll* get hurt from a fouled barrel. You wouldn't be so concerned for her health if you'd seen her using the revolver to bash in that poor police constable's head when he tried to stop us. Ask Evan—he followed us. He's the one that untied me."

Whelan nodded wearily, his gaunt face slack.

Mary Hodgeson?

"Evan, please come here," Mary said.

Mornay's gaze shifted from Whelan to Mary Hodgeson.

Anne's words came back to haunt him. *"She's afraid she'll have to share her precious Evan with someone else."*

Mary Hodgeson, the one person no one had even considered, now looked fully prepared to kill him.

Mary was holding the revolver with both hands, the barrel steady. Her gaze was cold. "That's quite enough talking."

Sarah Jenkins cringed with each word Mary spoke.

Anne continued talking to him. "That argument I had the other day with Ina in the greenhouse, Seth, the one you were angry I lied about. Mary interrupted it. Guess what she went there to discuss with Ina?"

Mary Hodgeson raised the revolver and pointed it at Anne. "I said *enough*."

Evan stood slowly, his movements disjointed and clumsy, as if he'd suddenly aged thirty years in the past five minutes. He walked toward Anne, the length of nylon still in his hand.

Mary's gaze flicked from Whelan to Mornay and back again, alarmed.

Whelan turned. He was using his body to shield Anne.

"Evan, dear, you should go home now."

Whelan winced when Mary said "dear." "Did you kill her after I left?" The effort to speak drained the last vestiges of color from his skin.

"I tried to warn her, but she wouldn't leave you alone. Ina couldn't just stay here." Mary glanced around the greenhouse and shuddered. "And continue her hobby."

"I meant Julia. Did you kill her after I went back to the conference in Edinburgh?"

"I had to" was Mary's calm reply. "Before she told you about the baby."

Mornay didn't dare shift his gaze from Mary. Where the hell was McNab, or Sahotra? He'd even be glad to see Dunnholland right now.

"All these years you let me believe we were protecting her memory from the rumors she'd been having an affair with Sandrington." Evan could barely get the words out. "But we were protecting you."

Mary's composure was starting to crack. Her arm was trembling from holding the heavy revolver. "She wasn't good enough for you. Don't you see? When she told me about the baby, I knew you'd never leave her. Your finding her with Sandrington gave me the perfect opportunity."

"Isn't this an interesting dilemma?" Byrne's voice made everyone jump.

Mary Hodgeson's expression twisted with rage. She clearly didn't know where to point the revolver, at Mornay or at Byrne.

Evan stepped in front of Anne once again.

Byrne said, "Mary, you don't have enough bullets to shoot all of us."

Was he trying to goad her into shooting? Byrne was too far away to reach her if she did start shooting. Someone would surely be hit before he could race his barrel-shaped body across the greenhouse.

Mornay, on the other hand, was within tackling distance. If only he weren't staring down the barrel of the revolver.

The tendons in Mary's neck tightened as she shifted the revolver in Byrne's direction.

Mornay lunged, and crashed into Mary just as she fired the revolver.

Once. Twice. The shots came out fast. The first went in Byrne's direction, missing him and flying out the back of the greenhouse; the second went straight up into the glass roof.

Shards of glass rained down as Mornay dove for

cover. He fell on his back, rolling partway under the table to escape the dagger-sharp shards of glass.

Mary Hodgeson was on the ground next to him, still conscious and still holding the revolver. She struggled to raise it. He swung his arm over, knocking the weapon from her grasp before she could get off a third round.

He picked up the revolver by the barrel and shook the butt at her. "Don't move again, or I'll knock you out."

He raised himself up on one elbow to see how everyone else had fared.

Mary's first shot had harmlessly gone through the side of the greenhouse, missing Byrne by five or six paces. But the hydrostatic shock of the second shot had shattered more than half the glass panels in the roof. Whelan had covered Anne with his body and gotten several nasty cuts on his back and arms. He was wincing as Anne helped him stand, glass falling out of the folds of his clothes.

Byrne lay on the ground, his face white. A shard of glass the size of Mornay's hand had skewered him through his thigh. He was conscious. Just.

Mornay hauled himself to his feet, wincing with pain, and told Anne, "Prop Whelan against a table. We'll have an ambulance for him soon enough. Right now I need help with the inspector."

Mornay used his belt as a tourniquet; Byrne's face was white and his skin was shiny with sweat.

"I can't risk taking the glass out. It might be too close to your artery," Mornay said.

"Leave it, then. I don't fancy bleeding to death today. And mind you keep an eye on that woman,"

Byrne managed to gasp. "We don't want her getting away after all this, now, do we?"

Byrne and Whelan had been taken away in an ambulance, and Mary Hodgeson had long since been handcuffed and carted away. Mornay's adrenaline had worn off ages ago. Exhaustion made every sound grate on his worn nerves; every light burned painfully into his eyes.

"Have you seen Claire?" he asked Sahotra.

"No," Sahotra said. He stood in front of Sarah Jenkins's cottage, keeping the thinning crowd behind the flimsy tape barrier.

"When did you last see her?"

Sahotra thought for a moment. "I haven't. She told us on the radio she was going to come straightaway; she said Chief Inspector McNab was attacked."

McNab had taken aspirin for his aching head and left half an hour earlier so he could break the terrible news to Constable Bensen's parents. Their loss was far greater than his discomfort. Mornay checked to see if Claire had left with him. It took five minutes on the radio. Claire wasn't with McNab. No one had seen her.

Mornay did another circuit of the cottage before it occurred to him that Claire might have used the service lane at the back of the cottage rather than come through the front, as he had. If she had used the lane, she would have approached the cottage from the back of the greenhouse.

The exact direction Mary Hodgeson's first shot went.

He started sprinting, shouting for Dunnholland

and Sahotra to follow him. Mornay darted through flowerbeds and pushed a startled scene-of-crime officer out of the way to get to the back of the greenhouse.

The space behind it was empty.

He scanned the shadows near the hedge that blocked the lane from view. A darkish shadow extended from the bottom of the hedge. Claire.

Mornay ran over, heart pounding. He slid to his knees beside her body. She lay on her back, beneath the hedge. "Claire?"

She moaned.

"Get an ambulance!" he bellowed to Dunnholland, who was standing dumbly behind him. For once Dunnholland leapt to his task.

Gently he lifted her hand so he could have a better look at the spot she was covering. "Claire, can you hear me?"

"What took you so long?" she whispered.

She was conscious; good.

Her hand was bloody. He started shivering and forced himself to sound calm. "Claire, did you get hit?"

She started coughing again. He leaned down, lifting her head so she could breathe. That's when he realized she was laughing.

"I brought the rolling pin," she whispered when she'd caught her breath. "I've no idea why."

There were metallic clangs and curses coming behind him. The paramedics were wrestling a gurney through the flowerbeds.

Claire used her other hand to push herself into a sitting position, but she was too weak to remain upright. Mornay held her up and realized she'd been lying on the rolling pin. He lifted it. A chunk the size of an orange had been ripped out of the side.

"Claire, where did you get hit?" he asked.

But the effort to raise herself had been too much. She sagged against him, unconscious.

chapter nineteen

McNab, his forehead bandaged, paced in his office, occasionally glancing over to Mornay, who stood in the doorway staring at his empty desk. It was nearly midnight.

"We haven't got proof that Byrne withheld information during Julia Whelan's inquiry," he told Mornay. "Not the kind of proof that would be required if charges were to be issued."

Mornay still had Claire's blood on his shirt and suit jacket. His eyes were red from exhaustion. His gaze was unrelenting and furious. "So he gets away with it? He never even discovered that Evan had lied about remaining in Edinburgh for the entire conference. If he had, he might've discovered that Mary Hodgeson has been poisoning half the congregation of St. David's. Byrne could've stopped it, but he didn't, because he was angry you were promoted instead of him."

McNab stopped pacing and scratched his forehead where his bandage was itching. Once in custody, Mary had admitted to using a ricin solution as one of the ingredients in her baking, particularly her meat pies. Her victims were the parishioners she felt were taking up too much of Evan Whelan's time. The solution was too weak to kill them, but it did make them quite ill. It was more explanation than the police got in some murder cases, but still wholly inadequate to offer to the survivors and to the families of Mary's victims.

A team of thirty police constables from five separate police offices were going door-to-door in Glen Ross, seeking out anyone who'd been given meat pies made by Mary Hodgeson. Dr. Hartwick's surgery had never been busier. So far they'd found eleven additional people suffering from mild ricin poisoning.

"Walter didn't know about these poisonings during Julia's inquiry," McNab continued wearily. His headache was excruciating. "He might never have discovered them. Perhaps Walter thought he deserved the promotion," he told Mornay, "but he wouldn't have received it, whatever the outcome of Julia Whelan's investigation. He's made too many enemies over the years." McNab spent a moment searching his pockets for his pack of cigarettes. He found it, shook one out, and lit it.

"Tell that to Ina Matthews and the other victims."

McNab sighed. "All of the facts Byrne had gathered in the Whelan case pointed to a suicide."

"Will that make it easier for you to look the man

in the eye when he's back on duty? Thinking he did a fair job? Before he gets back, you might want to ask why his prints were on the spade we collected outside of Ina Matthews's burned shed."

McNab could feel the color rising in his cheeks. "What?"

"Byrne's prints are on the spade that was used to hack at the sprinkler system's piping. Must've given him a fright, the sprinklers coming on after he'd clubbed Sarah Jenkins and set the fire."

"Why would he do that?"

"He wanted to get rid of the one bit of evidence that would prove he'd buggered the Julia Whelan case: Ina Matthews's rose."

"What's a rose got to do with anything?"

"The rose isn't what's important, it's the rose's name that matters. Ina named it Joshua Whelan."

McNab let his forgotten ash grow dangerously long as he waited for Mornay to finish explaining.

"Ina named her rose after Julia and Evan's child. How would she know the name, unless Julia had told it to her the same day she shared the news that she was pregnant? Why would a woman who's going to commit suicide in a few hours even bother to share something so personal?"

"Julia could've told Ina the name she picked at any time. My daughter had her children's names picked out years before they were born."

"I'm sure that's what you'd like to believe, sir."

"It doesn't matter what I believe or think." McNab's voice was steely. "What matters is what's good for the force. And this incident with Byrne would not be good for us, understood?"

Mornay's answer was a long time in coming. "Yes, sir."

"And as for Anne Knightsbridge, she's withdrawn her complaint. Is there anything else we need to talk about? We've both had a long day."

"No, sir." Mornay turned and walked out of the office.

Sarah Jenkins was tucked in her bed when Mornay knocked on her door. She'd been given a private room this time. The hospital sounds faded as he closed the door behind him. He was carrying a cup of tea, and set it on the table next to her bed.

"We seem to have a lot of these bedside chats, don't we?"

She tried to smile, but it took too much effort. "Did she really poison Ina?"

"And several others, from what we've found so far. I guess it was her way of keeping Evan from being overburdened. Who knows though, she appears to have sent her victims threatening notes."

Sarah shuddered. "How horrible. I still can't believe it, and I saw her try to kill someone with my own eyes."

Mornay took her hand. It was still hard for him to imagine that Mary Hodgeson was responsible for the frenzied attack on Ina Matthews, and still had the wits to try and make it look like someone from Sandrington Hall had committed the crime. "Don't waste your time trying to understand why," he said. "You'll drive yourself mad."

"And has this advice ever worked for you?" she asked.

It was his turn to try to smile; his effort wasn't much better than Sarah's had been. "Not yet."

"How's Claire?"

"She's doing very well. I've just left her room. The shot hit a rolling pin she was carrying, which stopped most of its momentum. The impact broke two of her ribs and knocked her out for a bit, but she only needed six stitches. She was very lucky. They're keeping her for a few days to let her ribs heal."

"How's Evan doing?"

"He's in shock. Anne's with him; maybe having her around will help. She's Julia's sister."

Sarah leaned back against her pillows and closed her eyes. "He deserves a happy ending if he can find it."

"You know Gregor Sandrington asked Ina to marry him," Mornay stated.

"Yes."

"Why didn't you tell me?"

"Because I was afraid you'd suspect him of killing her out of anger."

"Crimes of passion happen all the time, Sarah."

"I'm sure that's true—but in this instance, I was right."

Mornay leaned back in his chair, his gaze drifting from the stack of paperwork he'd been slogging through to Willie's fish tank. The office had been too quiet since Bensen's funeral. Claire would be returning to work next week. Byrne had been reassigned temporarily to Peterhead.

Sahotra shouted at him from across the room.

Mornay swiveled around in his chair.

"Tommy Torga's been picked up in Bristol," Sahotra said. "He got into a fight with a tourist."

"Serves the bastard right," Mornay said. "When will they transfer him back here?"

"Sometime tomorrow."

Not that it mattered, Mornay thought. It'd been a week since Mary Hodgeson's arrest; Torga had already faded from the public's collective attention span. John Dunbar, an old hand at disappearing, probably would never resurface.

Constable Pratt lumbered into view.

"Pratt," Mornay called out.

The younger man froze.

"You have fish tanks at home, right?" Mornay asked.

"Yeah?" Pratt offered cautiously.

"How much would it cost to put Willie in a proper tank? One with plants and air bubbles and rocks at the bottom?"

"Shouldn't be more than fifty or sixty pounds."

It was twice the amount Mornay had expected to hear. "If I give you the money, will you buy one for Willie today?"

Pratt nodded slowly. "I could do that."

"Could we have it up and running for Claire when she gets back to work?"

Pratt's nod was more enthusiastic this time. "Sure."

"Think that would make a good welcome back?" Mornay asked.

"She'll like it," Pratt said with more confidence than Mornay had ever heard in his voice. "Right fond of that fish, she is. She's called twice to ask how he's doing."

"Has she asked after me?"

"Aye, she has. She wanted to know if you'd been working on the reports. I told her you've been slaving away."

"Good lad." Mornay paused, and then asked, "Is that all she said?"

Pratt grinned shyly. "No. She wanted me to tell you to mind and check the spelling before you turned them in."